RESURGENCE

THE REDEMPTION TRILOGY

AJ SIKES

GREAT WAVE INK
PUBLISHING

GREAT WAVE INK
P U B L I S H I N G

This book is dedicated to survivors everywhere

Keep up the fire

Foreword
by
Nicholas Sansbury Smith

Dear Reader,

Thank you for picking up a copy of Resurgence by AJ Sikes. This is the final action-packed book in the Redemption trilogy. From the beginning of this series, Jed Welch has struggled to justify his own survival in a post-apocalyptic landscape. In Resurgence, his story comes full circle as he learns to lead and help others survive.

Originally published through Amazon's Extinction Cycle Kindle World, Resurgence became a reader favourite in the Extinction Cycle series side stories, and transcended to far more than fan fiction. Unfortunately, Amazon ended the Kindle Worlds program in July of 2018 with little warning. Authors were given a chance to republish or retire their stories, and I jumped at the chance to republish Resurgence through my small press, Great Wave Ink. Today, we're proud to offer Resurgence in paperback, audio, and to readers outside of the United States for the first time ever.

For those of you that are new to the Extinction Cycle storyline, the series is the award winning, Amazon top-rated, and half a million copy best-selling seven book saga. There are over six thousand five-star reviews on Amazon alone. Critics have called it, "World War Z and The Walking Dead meets the Hot Zone." Publishers weekly added, "Smith has realized that the way to rekindle interest in zombie apocalypse fiction is to make it louder, longer, and bloodier… Smith intensifies the disaster efficiently as the pages flip by, and readers who enjoy juicy blood-and-guts action will find a lot of it here."

In creating the Extinction Cycle, my goal was to use authentic military action and real science to take the zombie and post-apocalyptic genres in an exciting new direction. Forget everything you know about zombies. In the Extinction Cycle, they aren't created by black magic or other supernatural means. The ones found in the Extinction Cycle are created by a military bio-weapon called VX-99, first used in Vietnam. The chemicals reactivate the proteins encoded by the genes that separate humans from wild animals—in other words, the experiment turned men into monsters. For the first time, zombies are explained using real science—science so real there is every possibility of something like the Extinction Cycle actually happening. But these creatures aren't the unthinking, slow-minded, shuffling monsters we've all come to know in other shows, books, and movies. These "variants" are more monster than human. Through the series, the variants become the hunters as they evolve from the epigenetic changes. Scrambling to find a cure and defeat the monsters, humanity is brought to the brink of extinction.

We hope you enjoy Resurgence and continue on with the main storyline in the Extinction Cycle. Thank you for reading!

Best wishes, Nicholas Sansbury Smith,
NYT Bestselling Author of the Extinction Cycle

— 1 —

Emily Garza clenched her teeth and waited for the militia creep to pass her hiding place. She was crouched behind a fallen tree at the edge of what used to be a suburban neighborhood. The roaming militia guard followed a trail between two houses and stepped out of sight. Emily listened for his footfalls to grow quieter, hoping he wouldn't come back.

She slid a hand into her pocket and caressed a thin metal disk, the back of a watch her parents had given her when she finished college. The last time she'd seen her parents, they were smiling, just like they had been on the day she'd graduated. She didn't want to think about what they looked like now, after the virus and the Variants had destroyed the world, leaving the ruins for people like the militia to take over.

Emily had made it as far as the fence line around the neighborhood without being seen. Now she had to wait for her partner, Danitha Rice, and time was running out. The nightly patrols would change shift soon, and that meant an extra set of eyes that might see someone running through the neighborhood after curfew. If Danitha could get out of the house, make it across the

1

neighborhood, and remembered to bring the cutters, then they could escape.

But if Dani gets caught…

A chain link fence topped with razor wire ringed the neighborhood. It had been put up by construction teams helping to rebuild in Texas. Emily and Danitha were part of that effort, and it was looking good. People started growing food. Danitha and her hacker friends even got the Internet to work again. Then the militia showed up and turned the little suburb into a prison camp. They executed the first two people who disagreed with them, and that was all it took to get everyone else in line.

For a second, Emily feared that Danitha had tried to take a weapon with her. She had argued they would need a gun, but Emily refused to risk it. The militia kept all their guns with them, or locked away in one of their houses. Taking one would be next to impossible.

Please, Dani, please get here soon, she thought.

It was just past ten at night, by her watch, a cheap plastic replacement for the silver one her parents had given her.

Emily Garza, the first in the family not only to go to college, but also to stick it out for twelve straight years to become a virology researcher.

And now the first to escape from a prison camp inside America.

Scuffling footsteps sounded nearby and Emily poked her head around the tree. Danitha ran in a low stoop, coming down the graveled path from the nearest house. She carried a pack over one shoulder and twisted her head left and right as she moved, watching for the guards who could show up any second.

With a gasping breath, Emily called to her.

"Over here."

Danitha raced forward, came around the tree, and collapsed beside Emily.

"You brought the cutters?"

Danitha nodded fast and put a hand on her chest. "Let me get my breath. Thought for sure they'd see me. I been waitin' on a bullet the whole time. Swear this is the stupidest thing I ever let you talk me into doing."

"We will make it, Dani. We have to."

Emily had hope they would escape. The militia was just a bunch of fools with bad ideas, but they weren't stupid. Somebody would notice she and Danitha were missing soon enough, and then the whole neighborhood would be searching for them.

Emily remembered how it felt when the Variants ruled the streets. Nobody who wanted to stay alive would dare going outside, and definitely not at night. Now, with the monsters gone from Texas, they had the same fear still guiding their every action. Except the monsters they hid from were other human beings.

Danitha tapped Emily on the shoulder. "I got two bottles of water. You got the food?"

"Yes, the rations the militia had," she said, patting her own pack. "But only three."

Dani nodded and motioned with a tilt of her head that they should get moving.

Together, they crept toward the fence line. Danitha pulled a pair of bolt cutters out of her pack and put the blades around the bottom links on the fence.

"Do it fast, Dani. Just cut it and we can run out of here."

Danitha hesitated, worry and fear curling her brow.

Emily reached for the cutters. With a quick squeeze of the handles, the first link popped apart and sent an echoing *snap* into the silent late evening air. Birds rustled in nearby trees, and Emily worried she'd just ended their chances of escape. She moved the cutters slowly to the next link. The neighborhood was still and silent behind them.

She cut again, then moved to the next link above. Each cut sounded louder than the last, and Emily threw herself into the task, cutting, moving, cutting again. She worked in a frenzy until she'd sliced a section of the fence big enough for them to push through.

Danitha went first, shoving the chain link aside and curling it up and out of her path. She held it for Emily, who was halfway through when the shouting started.

"*Over here! I think they're over here!*" someone yelled.

Emily scrambled out through the hole in the fence, snagging her pants on the cut wire. The fabric tore with an angry rip as she flung herself forward.

Danitha grabbed Emily by the arm and helped her up. Without a second look back, they ran into the woods.

The shouting continued, a few houses over from where they'd escaped. They had to get away from the neighborhood, get somewhere that they wouldn't be seen or heard by anyone ever again. At least not until it was someone they knew they could trust.

A narrow creek trickled up ahead. Emily reached it first and slid to her knees, dropping to all fours, wanting to catch her breath. But she had to keep moving, keep running.

Wet leaves and mud pushed back against her palms as she steadied herself to stand.

Danitha was a few yards back and gaining fast when a shot rang out, echoing into the still forest. Her face went tight with terror and she sped by Emily, leaped over the creek, and ducked around a thick tree on the other side. Emily staggered to her feet and hopped over the thin stream. She pulled up at another tree beside Danitha.

"Told you they'd see us. I told you," Danitha said between breaths.

"It could have been anything they were shooting at. Maybe it's one of them out hunting again, shooting some animal."

Danitha gasped for breath and said, "Yeah? Maybe you're right. Maybe I'm the motherfucking president." Danitha slumped to the ground, with her back against the tree.

"They gon' find us," she said.

"They are not, Dani. Not if we keep moving."

"And go *where?* Look around you. What the fuck we got to move *to?* Ain't nothing out here but more trees. Nothing to eat 'cept that nasty Army food you got. And only enough of that to get us to tomorrow. We don't have any guns because you said it was too dangerous to try and steal one from them fools."

"It was, Dani. They would have—"

"Where we gon' sleep? People saying them monsters all dead, but you want me to believe that? You really think ain't none of them things waiting for us in these woods?"

Danitha's head drooped against her chest, and she began to sob.

"Nothing left anywhere. Nothing," she said.

"We have each other, *mija.* And my brother is here. He's in Galveston. We can find him."

5

"And how we gon' do that? Galveston's fifty miles away at least. And he don't even know you're here."

"He does. I got an email from him, right before the militia came. I told him we would be coming. So we have each other, we have my brother, and we have a place to go. *Allí vamos.*"

"Galveston," Danitha said with a sour laugh. "You talk like you got a helicopter hidden out here. You really think we gon' walk ourselves to Galveston?"

"Are your legs broken?"

Danitha looked up at her. Beneath the tears and frightened eyes, Emily could still see the excited face of the young woman who had walked into her office at the university, applying for an internship. That was the day the virus came. The day Emily and Salvador Garza lost their parents to the monsters.

The day the world ended.

"Get up, Dani. Galveston won't come to us."

"We're gonna die out here, Professor."

"Maybe so. But I will not sit here and wait for the answer to come."

She helped Danitha up, and together they shuffled deeper into the growing dark of the wilderness. Whatever danger they might be heading into, at least they were free to run from it instead of getting shot in the back or stood against a wall.

— 2 —

Sergeant Jed Welch leaned over the cabin cruiser's gunwale and prodded another body with the muzzle of his weapon. It was snagged on a splintered roof beam jutting from the water in Galveston Bay. Jed rode in a salvaged civilian boat with his patchwork squad, the *Hellhounds, Plus Two*. They were formed from the survivors of a Marine Regiment that fought the Variants in New York. Three squads had made it out of that mess to be reassigned on Galveston Island. The other two had disappeared in the past week, and Jed was starting to think AWOL status was better than the shit detail they got stuck with.

Their official task was to maintain perimeter security on the island's north shore while they waited for refugee boats to arrive. With zero Variant threats inbound, that translated to graves detail.

Three hurricane seasons had come and gone since the Variants first appeared and nearly swept humanity from the face of the earth. The storms had nearly returned the Texas shoreline to a blank slate. Except for the sturdiest buildings, everything on Galveston Island had been reduced to shredded ruin. The remains were testament to the power of nature, with the tangled wrecks of cars, trucks, boats, and buildings piled against the shore and mounded in the shallowest parts of the bay.

And the bodies.

Every pile of debris hid any number of withering, half-eaten, water-logged corpses, most of them human. They'd only found one dead Variant, and it had been shot in the head before it hit the water. Jed and his people had been hauling the damn mummies out of the water for days. They had to clean the place up as much as possible before the refugees began arriving, whenever that was supposed to happen. LT said they should have been there when the platoon arrived at Galveston, but the island's only inhabitants were a bunch of Army engineers and a handful of civilian survivors. The engineers bugged out yesterday, saying they had more work to do inland.

Gunny Ewell took it all as a sign they'd been dumped here by an uncaring higher command. He was the lone survivor of a failed attempt at reclaiming Houston when the Variants were still active, so he had been on Galveston longer than all of them. Jed could swear the guy was going stir crazy because he spent most of his time playing catch with a stray dog he'd adopted or pissing and moaning about their assignment. With Sergeant Jordan's and Sergeant Kipler's squads unaccounted for, every ounce of Ewell's heat landed on Jed.

On cue, the radio crackled.

"Shorewatch 1, Hometown 1, over."

Jed lifted the mic and replied, "Shorewatch 1 Actual, over."

"You still wasting time fishing?"

"Roger on that, Hometown 1. Just got another mummy for LT's collection."

"Wish I had better news for you, but if you're still finding cadavers, I'll keep you out there for a while. Call it a day at 1200 hours. Hometown 1 out."

Jed thought about the other Marines in the platoon. Sergeant Kipler and Sergeant Jordan had been with Gunny Ewell longer, and they'd had easier zones to work, with less debris and fewer bodies. But the tedium and lack of anything to do must have been too much for them. Jed couldn't blame them. The world had ended, after all. Who the fuck cared about a page eleven or a demotion anymore?

He waved for one of his squad to do the dirty work of retrieving the body they'd just found. Private Mehta grabbed a hook pole off the deck and stabbed at the corpse under the arm, just like they'd been doing all week. Usually the hook would go right in because the corpses were mostly decayed. This time it didn't.

Watching the private struggle, Jed jokingly asked, "Something wrong, Mehta?"

"It's not going in, Sergeant."

Lance Corporal Garza jumped on that. "More lube, Mehta. What do I keep telling you? Fucking boot."

"He's young," said PFC Kelly Ann McKitrick. "Give him time. He'll figure it out."

Jed told his people to cool it. Mehta was young, and probably hadn't gotten laid before the Variants ate the world. But that didn't mean he had to be everyone's whipping boy.

"Just grab it, man. It's not gonna bite you," Jed said. He leaned over and lent his hand to the task, taking the hook pole so Mehta could haul the mummy off the wood snag.

With a tug, the body came free and surprisingly stayed intact. Mehta was about to haul it to the stern when Jed stopped him.

"Hold up," he said, as he prodded the corpse with the hook pole, inverting it in the water. When it rolled face up, Jed staggered back. The body was one of the Army Engineers who'd been rebuilding on Galveston when Jed arrived. He had traded jokes with the man over coffee just a few days ago. Back then, he still had his throat intact.

The guy's neck had been torn out.

He was dressed in a pair of cargo pants and a torn up gray tee shirt, just like he was when Jed first saw him and gave him shit for being out of uniform. The dead man's bloated and sickly pale face made Jed think of the Variants. But they'd been gone from most of Texas for two years now at least. Maybe the guy was grabbed by a gator.

The bite was big enough to be a gator's, but why would a hungry predator just kill its prey and leave it to rot in the water?

"Dude was bit?" Garza asked over Jed's shoulder. Garza had his M27 at the ready now.

Jed put a hand on the weapon, pushing it aside. "Gator could have done it."

"A sucker face did that, I'd bet my balls," Garza said.

"Nah, man. They're all gone around here. A gator did this."

PFC Gabby Keoh came over from the opposite side of the boat.

"That's a Variant bite," she said.

Jed wanted to believe her, but not because he thought she was right. Two years ago, Keoh took a nasty bite on her leg from a Variant. She had a funny step because of it, and couldn't move as easily as before.

"We'll check it out when we get back," Jed said to Keoh. "Private Parsons, get back on the radio. Let Gunny know about this."

"Rah, Sergeant," Parsons said.

Private Seth Parsons was one half of the squad's *Plus Two* component. He and Private Ahmad Mehta were just nineteen, and had basically been drafted from the refugee chow hall on Plum Island, before Jed shipped out from New York. They were fast friends, and would make good Marines someday. If Garza didn't knock their heads together every five seconds.

While Parsons relayed the message, Jed helped Mehta get the corpse to the stern where they had tied the first two bodies they fished out that morning. Mehta grabbed up a loop of 550-cord and a foam float from the deck. Together, he and Jed lassoed the corpse, added the float, and tied it onto the other mummies trailing behind the boat.

"You get Gunny?" Jed asked Parsons.

"Yes, Sergeant," Parsons said.

"And what did he say, Private? Don't make me reach down your throat for an answer."

"Nothing really. Just told me to wait one, then came back on and said not to worry about it. Said we should Charlie-Mike on fishing."

Jed shrugged and looked at the bodies trailing behind the boat, focusing on the newest addition to the chain.

The man had been chewed on, and that's what killed him. But what had done the chewing? Were they really safe out here on the water? Had the Variants evolved again to become aquatic? Or was it just a gator that didn't like the taste of Army meat?

"So we going for more catch, Sergeant?" Keoh asked.

Gunny said they should, but Jed shook his head. Keoh didn't want to stay on the water any longer than she had to. And Jed had to admit he felt the same way. He'd cook up some reason for disobeying the Gunny's order.

"I want to get back. Talk to Gunny or LT. Something stinks about this. Skip, get us home, rah?"

Murky water lapped at the side of their boat as they made a slow winding path around the debris scattered about the shoreline. Their helmsman, a civilian and a Vietnam vet, took them through the mounds of ruin, aiming for the shore. He was one of the few people who'd survived on Galveston. The others mostly kept to themselves and went fishing for actual food on the ocean side of the island.

The ship's radio hummed and crackled to life, and Jed expected Gunny again. Instead, it was the LT.

"Shorewatch 1, this is Hometown actual. Over."

Jed groaned at the sound of the LT's voice. "Was hoping to avoid this until we got back."

Garza said, "He probably just needs directions to the head."

Everyone laughed at that, except Jed. He thumbed the mic and said, "Shorewatch 1, over."

"You got that body with you?"

"Roger, Hometown. Coming back now."

"Wait one, Shorewatch."

When the LT came back, he sounded pissed off.

"Shorewatch 1, what's your ETA?"

"Five minutes, max. We're passing under the causeway now."

"Belay that. Have Skip drop you at a pier on the other side. Link up with elements from the engineers there. It's their man you've got, not one of ours."

Jed paused before replying. He thought about the face on the body they'd found.

"Are we sure on that? I swear I talked the guy last week."

"I say again, negative, Shorewatch 1. You are to deliver the cadaver across the water. Make it happen, water dogs. Hometown out."

Jed felt an ache in his gut. Something didn't add up about the body in the water, and it sounded like LT knew but he wasn't saying.

"Sergeant, did I hear the pogue-ass LT correctly?" Garza asked.

"Yeah, you did."

"If he calls us water dogs one more fucking time—"

"Secure that, Garza. We all want to dick punch the LT. Take a number."

Skip increased their speed and turned their course. In a few minutes, they'd crossed the narrow stretch of bay, following the causeway and railroad bridge that connected Galveston to the mainland. Skip pulled them up to a pier that stretched out of the marshy shore. It was nothing more than mounded rocks around a mass of debris with planking nailed on top. It looked like shit, but it served its purpose, providing stable footing to walk from the boat onto dry land.

PFC McKitrick, carrying the squad's M203, was out first, stepping onto the rocks and finding her feet. She turned and lent a hand to Keoh, her partner in crime with an M4. McKitrick helped Keoh balance on the rocks and stayed with her as they climbed to the more stable planking up top. Garza got there ahead of them and marched down the ramshackle pier. Parsons and Mehta were last out of the boat, as usual.

"C'mon, you boots," McKitrick called back to them. Parsons shrugged into his pack. He was their RTO, and staggered under the radio's weight, but Mehta caught him with a hand on his back. One by one, they dismounted, nearly stumbling on the uneven rocks, and reaching hands out for support as they climbed to the top.

Jed held in a laugh and waved to Skip as he climbed out.

"I'll send someone back to collect the body. LT didn't say where these engineers are supposed to be, so it might be a while before we find 'em. You good on chow?"

"Yeah, got an MRE or two in the cabin. You go on."

"Oorah, Skipper," Jed said as he moved out along the pier to catch up with the *plus two* brothers.

"Hey, Sergeant," Mehta said as Jed joined them. They trailed a few yards behind the others.

"'Sup, Mehta?"

"Why's everyone such a dick to us?"

Jed shook his head, remembering his brief tenure as an E1 in the Marine Corps, before he caught a Big Chicken Dinner for fighting too often and giving attitude to anyone who got close enough. The Variants may have taken the world apart, but in the same stroke they'd given Jed his life back. He was a Marine again, and even though wearing a sergeant's stripes still felt wrong, the rest of it felt right.

For him, life inside a uniform beat the hell out of life without one.

"How it is. Y'all are boots, so you get treated like boots until you see combat or they decide different."

"Even Garza?" Parsons asked. "It's like he gets off treating us like shit."

"Garza's just pissed because y'all act like brothers. He lost his folks to the monsters. Still sends his sister email whenever the Internet's working, just in case, you know? If he fucks with you, let it roll off, oorah?"

"Rah, Sergeant," they said in unison.

The two privates kept quiet after that. Parsons kept shifting under the weight of his pack, and both of them struggled not to slip off the planks and into the water. They weren't much different from how Jed used to be, even if they did look like the first thing to fall off the bus. Still, Jed trusted them, same as he trusted Garza, McKitrick, and Keoh. So long as nobody outright spit back at him, that was good enough. In this new world, where having someone's back meant more than a set of stripes, it had to be.

And especially if one of the people Jed trusted to have his back turned out to be on the wrong side. Whatever the LT was keeping hidden about the body in the water, Jed knew it couldn't be good.

— 3 —

Emily and Danitha moved through the forest for most of the night. They walked as often as they could, picking up to a jog when they had to. Night sounds and the ever present threat of pursuit kept them going until they had no choice but to rest or collapse from exhaustion. It was nearly five in the morning now. Dancing shadowy shapes flitted through the sky. Those were her bats, the ones she'd spent ten years studying and admiring. The world may have become hell for humanity, but at least other species were thriving. Maybe the world would be reborn after all, just with fewer people to make problems.

Emily eyed the line of reeds and grasses in front of her, scanning for movement of any kind on the ground. Bats were one thing, but they didn't bother people. Alligators and wild dogs, on the other hand…

They had stopped at the edge of the forest to rest, in a dry and shallow ditch beside a road that separated the forest from the flatland ahead. When they'd sat down, Danitha immediately fell asleep. Emily let her doze for another few minutes before waking her.

"We have to move, Dani. It's almost morning, and we have a long way to go."

Danitha stretched and yawned, rubbing sleep from her eyes.

"Need some water, and something to eat first."

Emily groaned, not wanting to waste more time. She needed to get to Galveston and fast. If her brother was called away for something, how would she find him again? What if he'd been sent where the monsters were still active?

"You can make it a little farther," she told Danitha.

"My belly is empty and I've been running all night long. I need to eat."

Emily loosened her pack and let Danitha dig into it for one of the ration meals. The sounds of her eating made Emily's own stomach rumble, and soon enough she had a second ration opened. That left one for the rest of their journey, and they'd only covered a handful of miles so far.

"Eat only half, Dani. We have to save some, make sure we have enough for the road ahead."

"Whatever you say, Professor."

Emily's patience ran out. "Hey, I didn't choose this. I didn't make this happen."

"But you're acting like you make all the rules, telling me we're going all the way to damn Galveston *after* I agree to go with you. I could be back inside a house right now, sleeping in a bed."

"If you want to go back there, you be my guest."

Danitha stared her down, but finally gave in. She stuck the uneaten packets of food back into the ration bag and handed it over.

"Keep it," Emily said. "In case we get separated. And take the rest of this one, too."

Danitha accepted the bag from her and stuck them both in her pack. She handed a bottle of water to Emily in return.

"Only got two left. You better have one of your own. Just in case."

Emily didn't like the tension between them, but knew it would be a good long while before she could do anything about it. The sun would be up soon, and the day would be hot. They'd need to find a place to rest before the afternoon.

Danitha stood up, shrugging into her pack. Emily rose and had her pack around one shoulder when a throaty growl erupted from the grass ahead of them. An alligator twisted its way onto the road, thrashing its tail as it moved. It reached its snout around and tried to bite at something behind it.

"Shit, shit, shit," Danitha cursed, moving back into the forest.

Emily backed up to join her, and they huddled together, watching the gator defend itself from whatever was attacking it. A hissing joined with the gator's growls, and Emily's stomach went tight with terror.

Could it be a monster, she thought. *Were they still here somewhere, hiding out in the bayou?*

The gator growled loud and angry, still snapping at whatever was on its tail. A dark shape dropped from the sky and landed on the gator's back, then another came down, and another.

A beat of heavy wings fluttered through the air and Emily looked up. The sky swarmed with them, the bats she'd seen earlier. Only these were much, much bigger than any species Emily had ever seen. One of the bats landed on the road and flapped its wings. Other than its size, the creature could have been Mexican free-tailed bat. The same rounded ear flaps crested this one's head, but its eyes were enlarged, as was the snout.

It opened its mouth, revealing a deep maw set with far more teeth than any bat should have. Emily clamped a hand over her mouth when the creature hissed and ambled over to where its companions were making a meal of the alligator.

Emily spun around at the snap of branches behind her. Danitha had taken off, fleeing into the woods, heading parallel to the road. With a last glance at the bat monsters eating the alligator, Emily followed Danitha, hoping their footfalls wouldn't alert any predators lurking among the trees. At the same time, she was grateful for the amount of noise they made as they ran. They were well concealed against the bat monsters. Their echolocation would be disrupted by all the crunching and crashing.

Branches whipped at Emily's face and arms as she ran. She did her best to keep in line with Danitha's path through the trees, but the other woman had a head start and the sky was still dark under the forest canopy.

Should she risk calling for her to wait up? What if she'd been wrong and the militia had followed them?

They'd know where we are by now anyway, she thought as she opened her mouth to yell Danitha's name.

Danitha's scream came first, and Emily raced forward to catch up to her. She stood beside a tree, at the edge of the wood. The roadside ahead was lit up by the dawn light. More bat monsters gathered in the area, swooping through the sky and coming down to the ground to attack another alligator.

"We're gonna die," Danitha said. "No way we make it to Galveston now. No way in hell."

Emily wanted to comfort her, tell her she was wrong. But watching the bat monsters, she had to admit maybe Danitha was right. Maybe they should have stayed with the militia.

Confirming her worries, a heavy swarm of the monsters flocked into the marshy area beyond the road. Groups of four or five dropped into the water, coming back up with small fish clamped in their jaws.

They've evolved again, Emily thought. *Or the virus affected their morphology. Have other species been affected?*

She and Danitha stayed hidden behind a mound of deadfall that had been swept into the wood by a hurricane. The air was thick with the flying monsters now, but their pattern of flight shifted. Instead of whirling in a frenzy, they joined together into a snaking ribbon heading out and away from the marsh and woods.

"They're going back to their nest," Emily said. "They're leaving."

Danitha stayed huddled against her, not willing to look at the monsters. "They're supposed to be gone. What happens tonight, when we don't have a forest to hide in? What happens to us then?"

"We find someplace to hide," Emily said. "We find it, and then we find another, and another. Now let's go, Dani."

With half her attention always on the sky, and Danitha reluctantly following, Emily led them into the dawn, praying they would find her brother before the monsters found them.

— 4 —

Jed, Mehta, and Parsons marched off the pier and onto the semi-solid ground beyond. Garza, McKitrick, and Keoh were already several yards ahead. Jed and the two privates followed them. They passed an old sports bar nestled between the causeway and the road coming off the railway bridge. Its rooftop sign hung from one end, with the other jammed into the marshy soil around the building. A sandy patch in front of the bar gave way to a paved lane that led to the causeway ramps. Jed kept on, marching inland, toward a group of men who stood in a huddle around an overturned car. Two functioning SUVs sat a few paces away, on the onramp. The bulldozer Gunny Ewell had used to clear the causeway was still here, too. He'd left it on the bridge with the last car he'd shoved aside still stuck on the dozer's blade.

As Jed got nearer, the group around the car came into focus. Each of them had on the same gray tee-shirt, just like the body he'd fished from the bay earlier. They also wore tool belts and CamelBaks, and some had sidearms with them. Garza and the others had just reached the group and were trading fist bumps.

"C'mon, boots," Jed said, turning his step into a jog.

Parsons and Mehta managed to keep up without tripping until the last few feet, when Mehta snagged his toe on a rock and went down on his stomach. Jed was quick to give Garza and the others a look that said *cool it*. Parsons helped Mehta up, and the two of them held back from joining the rest of the group. Jed told them to post a few yards away, near the road that extended from the railroad bridge.

"Keep an eye out. And hydrate, rah?"

They nodded and dropped their packs. Jed joined the others, pushing between Garza and McKitrick.

"Make a hole, y'all," he said.

"You're Sergeant Welch?" one of the engineers asked. He was a stocky white guy with a can of Rip-It in one hand and a hard hat under his arm.

"That's right," Jed said. "And you?"

"Greg Radout, with Six Team."

"Six Team? What's that?"

"That's us. We come in after the storm and put things right. We got your six. Been doing it since before the virus hit. Decided to pick up the game once Texas was confirmed clear."

"Huh. And you're the same bunch was on Galveston?"

"Yeah, us and another group. They were on Tiki Island until yesterday," Greg said, pointing to the west, across the causeway. "They headed to the FOB with a few of our guys, up the road near South Houston. We'd be there with 'em, but I got a call over the blue net to wait for you. The refugee ship here already? I thought it wasn't due until next week."

"You're asking the wrong guy about that," Jed said.

"We ain't been doing much but pull bodies from the water. That's why we're here."

"What do you mean?" Greg asked.

"We found a guy this morning. Wasn't dead long, like the others we've been fishing up."

Jed paused, not knowing how to describe the bite marks. He didn't want to cause a panic, but at the same time he had to tell the man something. "We're thinking a gator got him. LT said he's one of your people."

Greg's eyes went wide with shock. "Who?"

"I don't know his name, but I could swear it was a guy who was on Galveston before y'all left. He's wearing your uniform. Gray shirt and cargo pants."

"Where is he?"

"Got him on the boat," Jed said, aiming a thumb behind him.

"Let's go," Greg said, already pushing past Garza and heading toward the pier. Jed and his people followed, with the other Six Team members behind them.

They made it as far as the trucks on the off ramp when an engine whined nearby. Jed swiveled his head to spot the vehicle. It was racing their way, straight down the causeway. Greg and his people held up at the end of the lane leading to the sports bar. Jed directed his squad to move forward and lift their weapons. They took up positions alongside the road, kneeling behind rubble and vehicles pushed to the shoulder. The car kept coming, barreling down the road. Jed thought about firing a warning burst, but he had no idea who was driving. It could have been one of the civilians on Galveston, but why were they going so fast?

The car came into focus as it got closer. It was a dark

green Subaru wagon with a surfboard rack on top. Jed had seen it around the island, going from pier to pier. The driver was usually a young guy with long brown hair, one of the civilians that had managed to survive the apocalypse. He had taken to surfing, fishing, and snapping pictures with a camera rig with one of those long lenses on it. Sometimes he would stop by the platoon's TOC and trade fish or pretty pictures for cigarettes.

"What's up with him?" Jed wondered aloud.

The car sped by them, leaving a gust of warm air in its wake. Jed couldn't be sure who was driving, but there was only one person in the vehicle. He called the squad to their feet and rejoined Greg and the others.

"Someone you know?" Greg asked.

"Not sure. Probably just this hippie dude who managed to stay alive somehow."

Greg chuckled, then turned serious. "You said you had one of our people down there. I'd like to see him. ID the body at least. Not that it'll do much good, but…"

"Yeah, be good to know who it was," Jed said as he led them down the lane toward the sports bar.

They were a few yards from the sports bar when a shockwave of heat and pressure sent everyone stumbling backward. An explosion ripped through the calm morning. Everyone fell to the ground clutching their headgear as debris rained down and more explosions came in succession, rocking the air and echoing into the distance. When the last of them sounded, Jed risked a look.

The others raised their heads. Greg confirmed none of his people were injured, and Jed did the same. Mehta and

Parsons were behind their rucks, still up by the vehicles. They poked their faces out from either side like a pair of scared cats. Jed waved for them to stay put. Dust and smoke filled the air, and the ringing in Jed's ears slowly gave way to the heavy slap of water against concrete.

The railroad bridge and the causeway had been blown up where they met the shore, leaving a gap of at least five yards. More holes and breaks showed down the length of the causeway.

"*What the hell was that?*" Greg demanded. "We've been working day and night putting this place back together! What the absolute—"

He flung his hard hat to the ground. His people gradually got to their feet, some of them slower than others. Jed was relieved to see his Marines helping out, lending a hand to the ones who seemed the most shook up by the blasts.

They've seen this before, Jed thought. *Probably not much different from what they did in the sandbox, dodging mortars while they try to build a bridge.*

Greg dropped into a deep squat and held his face in his hands. Jed turned in a circle and scanned the area for incoming threats. All he saw was marshland and the ravaged roadway that used to connect them to the only home they had.

Greg groaned in anger. "We've been rebuilding for months. For nothing."

Jed knew what he meant. The railroad and causeway would have been the path to repopulating Texas. Hospital ships would bring survivors into Galveston for quarantine and processing, like a modern day Ellis Island. Jed's platoon would monitor and provide security for the incoming survivors.

But the ships hadn't shown up. They hadn't even confirmed they would be coming, and Jed's platoon was down to his squad, Gunny, and the LT.

"Why would somebody do this? And how?" Greg asked, looking at Jed. "You know anything about this?"

Jed shook his head and said, "Not a damn thing." A nagging worry found its way into Jed's thoughts, but he pushed it aside. Jordan and Kipler were good men. They might have bailed from a sinking ship, but who could blame them?

"Oh shit, Sergeant," Keoh said. "Skip's gone."

Jed followed Keoh's pointed finger and saw the mess below the bridges. Blocks of concrete filled the water, along with splintered railroad ties and the rails themselves. Somewhere under all of that was their cabin cruiser along with their helmsman. Jed took a few steps toward the shore and stopped.

"We can't get him out of that, Sergeant," Keoh said.

Jed didn't want to believe it, but she was right. There was no way they'd find Skip under the wreckage from the bridges. Not safely anyway. And what would they do with his body even if they could find it?

"You had someone on the boat?" Greg asked, coming to join him.

"Skip. Old 'Nam vet. He made it through everything on his own. The virus, the Variants, all the hurricanes. Hung out on Galveston in a church."

"I'm sorry," Greg said. "And whoever we lost is down there, too. Look, I'm taking my people back to our FOB. Your hippie dude was heading in that direction, and if he did this, who knows what else he has planned?"

"If it's that hippie from Galveston, the only thing he's got planned is catching a wave. I have a hard time believing he did this."

"Who then? You got anybody on the island with enough motive and know-how to daisy chain bombs across a mile of highway?"

Jed thought about who on Galveston might have wanted to sabotage their operation. One of the civilians might have done it, but why? He'd already written off Sergeant Jordan and Sergeant Kipler. He hardly spoke with them before they took off, but he didn't think they had any beef with the rebuilding effort. Gunny was always pissed off, but that was just Gunny. And as much as Jed disliked the LT, there was no way that man could have rigged up bombs to take out both bridges. He spent too much time flipping papers and calling around the commo net.

Thinking about the LT again sent a wave of anxiety through Jed's chest. He was never far from the two-story home that served as their TOC, and that building was at the Galveston end of the causeway. "Hey, Parsons!"

"Yes, Sergeant!"

"You got that radio up?"

"Oorah, Sergeant."

"Get LT on. Or Gunny. Anyone."

Jed turned back to Greg and the others. "Our TOC might have been hit. It's close to the bridge at that end. If we're cut off... Shit, there's no other way to the island is there?"

"Not unless you have a boat, and there's nothing this side of the water worth using. Anything that still floats was salvaged a long time ago."

Greg dug in his pocket and pulled out a set of keys.

"We need to move out. You can take the Hyundai. We'll fit into the Suburban fine."

"Where's your FOB again? In case we need to shelter tonight."

"Hope your people are okay and it doesn't come to that. But… We're about six klicks up the road, past the refinery at Texas City. There's a garrison there you could try and link up with, too."

"They Marines or Army?" Jed asked.

"I don't know," Greg said as he moved to rejoin his people by their vehicles. "They got here before we did, and we haven't had much contact. If you get with them, I'll send a runner to pick up our vehicle. Good luck, Sergeant."

"Yeah, same to you. And thanks."

Parsons called to Jed. "LT's not answering, Sergeant. Same with Gunny."

Jed walked over and took the mic from him.

"Hometown, Shorewatch 1. Over."

He tried Gunny, then tried both of them twice more before giving up.

"You think they got taken out?" McKitrick asked, motioning to the ruined bridges.

"Blasts kept coming," Garza said. "Could be they went all the way back to Galveston and hit the TOC."

Jed scanned the horizon, looking for movement anywhere across the water. Greg and his people wheeled onto the causeway and moved out as a breeze swept the last of the dust from the area.

"We're ass out in the wind here," Jed said.

The squad shifted where they stood, uneasy and on

edge. Jed thought about their options again, then said, "Guess we go to that garrison up the road. McKitrick, you're driving. Parsons, you get in back with the radio. The rest of y'all squeeze in."

— 5 —

Emily and Danitha spent most of the day moving at a fast trot, sometimes running, then jogging, and finally half stumbling through the wilderness outside of Houston. They stopped to catch some sleep at the edge of a small wood, building a lean-to from more deadfall and covering it with as much leaf matter and brush as they could find before the sun dropped dangerously low. They were concealed before sundown, and ate a few more bites from their rations.

Emily encouraged Danitha to go sleep as soon as they were done eating, and thankfully she didn't raise any objections. Emily couldn't rest knowing that Danitha was still awake and might decide to run off again. Even though they'd talked about it during the day, Emily still worried that the woman's only real loyalty was to herself. And her ideas of survival did not match with what Emily had learned from her parents on the road from Jalisco.

Finally, after Danitha's breathing grew deeper, Emily laid herself down on the bed of brush they'd prepared. When the sun began to warm her face through gaps in their roof, she wiped her eyes, and shook Danitha awake.

After stretching out the cramps in her legs and back, Emily grabbed a fallen branch to use as a walking stick, or weapon if it came to that. She led the way along the edge of the wood, always aiming them to the south.

The fringes of Houston took shape amidst the fields and clustered trees ahead of them. Small neighborhoods and refinery towns jutted into a mix of marshy, overgrown fields. A hazy dense fog rose from pools of water amid the ruins. The hurricanes had almost turned the whole area into a bayou. Some farm roads still wove between the wet areas. Emily worried they would run into alligators and snakes if they went through there. She was about to propose they take the longer route heading around Houston when Danitha stumbled forward and nearly collapsed beside her.

"So tired. I am so damn tired…"

"I know, Dani. I know. We're almost out of it. The militia didn't make it this far, remember? I heard them say they stopped coming this way because the Army's out here. We just have to find them before the militia creeps find us."

"And hope they ain't friends," Danitha added. "You want to trust people wearing the same clothes as the ones talking about starting up the plantations again. I didn't know better, I'd say you crazy."

"Maybe I am. But my brother's a Marine, and he isn't about any plantations."

Emily moved up to the very edge of the field. A refinery town sat at the other side. Emily used her walking stick to push aside the rangy grass and test the ground. It was firm, which meant they might make it without any gators coming after them. Providing the field didn't turn to a marsh halfway across. She turned back to Danitha and waved her up. "We can go through that neighborhood up ahead, then we're about halfway to Houston. Chava's email said the Army has people there."

"Chava? Who's that?"

"My brother, Salvador. Chava is his name from when he was a little boy."

"He's Army? I thought you said he was a Marine. Ain't they different things?"

"Yes, they are. But we just need to find somebody in uniform. If we see somebody who looks legit, I'll ask how to find my brother. They will know where everyone is. They have to. Come on."

"I hope you're right, Professor," Danitha said as they took a few steps forward into the field.

"Stop calling me that. We're not in my office or a classroom, and there's no university left anyway. Call me Emily. Please."

"Okay. I hope you're right, *Emily*. And if you're not, you better hope they shoot you first. 'Cause I sure as hell will if this goes bad for us."

"We are not going down like that, *mija*. Trust me."

"Like I got a choice?" Danitha asked.

The woman's anger was growing worse, and Emily knew it was because they were both near the end of their will. They'd been going for so long, and with so little to keep them going at all. But her brother was out there, and close enough that she had to believe they would survive to find him.

I'm coming, hermano. Say a prayer for me. Because I'm saying one for you. Be safe and be there when I find you.

"How far to Houston now, you think?" Danitha asked.

"Maybe thirty miles. I don't know. But it gets farther the longer we wait."

Danitha nodded at that. "We going through these fields? Ain't the gators living in here?"

"The ground is solid. Not wet. There shouldn't be any alligators."

"What about them other things? The bats."

"Bats are nocturnal. They fly out when the sun sets. The longer we stand here, the closer that time gets."

Danitha didn't have anything to say to that, so Emily pushed into the field, spreading the grass ahead of her with her walking stick. The ground stayed firm all the way across, and soon enough, they were in the refinery neighborhoods east of Houston. Emily and Danitha entered the town that ringed the first refinery, and walked down the ruined streets. The place was nothing but a mess of shattered homes now. Hurricanes had come up and ripped everything apart. Cars lay strewn about, upside down and crumpled against each other, or wrapped around the few remaining trees. Torn rooftops, splintered walls and broken glass covered every inch of ground in all directions.

"Place needs a little cleaning up," Danitha said. "But I could live here. You know, make a little home for myself. Plant a garden, get some food growing."

"I'm glad you still have your sense of humor, Dani. It's what I've always liked about you."

"Keep 'em laughing. That's what my dad used to tell me. Make 'em laugh, keep 'em laughing. Wish it worked the way he said it would."

"What did he say?"

"Said people can't take time to hurt you if they too busy laughing."

"Reminds me of my grandmother," Emily said. "She was always quick with a joke when me and Chava would fight."

They continued that way, trading stories of childhood and trudging toward Houston. They came to a nicer suburb, a long stretch of wealthy homes on either side of a single street. Overgrown farmland stretched out behind the houses, dotted with clusters of trees. The houses here were spaced apart, among what used to be wide lawns and small trees. Now the whole place looked more like the trail of a tornado's passing, with garbage and ruin covering all the open ground in a path that followed the street into the distance.

"I'd rather rebuild here," Emily said. "These homes are nicer than anything I've lived in."

Danitha didn't reply and Emily turned to see her stooping down and moving toward an overturned car at the edge of the street. Emily followed her, crouching low and scanning the area, trying to identify what Danitha was focused on. They got to the car and huddled behind it.

"What is it, Dani?"

"They found us. Go look," Danitha said.

Emily risked a glance around the front of the car. A group of armed men wandered in between the ruined homes on the other side of the street. They didn't move like they'd seen anything, but just roamed around, eyeing the rooftops.

Emily dropped back to a crouch beside Danitha and whispered to her. "They didn't see us."

"Yet. What are they doin' here?"

Emily craned her neck to see around the car. "They're looking at the ground now."

"I bet they're tracking, like they're following somebody."

Emily's stomach clenched at the thought that they'd been followed. But if that were the case, they'd have heard these men behind them. And none of them looked familiar, other than being white, wearing military clothing, and carrying too many guns.

"They're militia creeps," Emily said.

"Let's get gone then. Back the way we came. Any which way."

Danitha drew in a sharp breath. Emily spun around to see what had startled her. Danitha was a few steps away from the car and turned, so she faced the houses behind them. She'd frozen, half crouched, and Emily saw why.

At the house two doors down from their position, a small figure perched on the shredded roof. It took Emily a moment to realize it wasn't a child or even a small man or woman. It was a monster, like the ones the virus made. It tasted the air with its tongue and flicked its head side to side, like a cat sniffing after prey.

Neither Emily nor Danitha moved, not even to breathe. Finally the monster crawled to one side, facing away from them. It dragged something behind it, something heavy that was tied to its neck.

A whistle echoed along the street and Emily's breath caught on a cry of fear that she only just held in. The monster's head snapped up and it sniffed the air, then leaped down from the roof to land on all fours. Its joints did that clicking thing that always made Emily want to run and hide. Nothing alive should sound like that when it moved. Nothing but a demon straight from hell itself.

Emily cowered behind the car, grabbing onto Danitha's arm and pulling her closer. As she moved, Danitha's foot scraped across chips of glass on the pavement.

The monster stopped and twitched its head back and forth again. A whistle echoed once more, and the demon thing crawled forward, across the sidewalk and into the street. A metallic scraping sound followed it. When it passed across Emily's field of vision, she saw what the monster was dragging: a chain attached to a metal collar.

Oh no. Oh no no no no no no, Emily thought.

The monster paused in the street again. Emily got a closer look at it, and her heart thudded heavily in her chest as she took in its changed appearance.

It had a longer face than the first monsters she saw after the virus. Unlike those, this one had a short snout instead of the nearly flat nose and bulging lips. And while this one's hips moved in a way that made Emily think it could walk upright if it needed to, it was clearly more comfortable on all fours. It held its head above the ground, swiveling left and right as if searching the air for a scent or a sound.

Another whistle split the air, sharp and angry. The monster's chain scraped across the pavement as it ran to join its master. The scraping stopped and was replaced by a low whining. It sounded like a begging animal.

"They made them into pets. Militia dudes made them things into their dogs," Danitha said.

Emily shivered next to her and whispered, "They have those things on their side now, *mija*. If they see us, we have no chance. Stay perfectly still. Don't move a muscle."

A motor echoed from somewhere nearby. Soon enough, the rumble of a heavy truck came down the street, passing right by their hiding place. Brakes squeaked, and the truck idled in the street. A door opened, and feet hit the pavement. A latch was undone, or maybe the truck's tailgate. Something creaked, and Emily winced at the scraping of the chain again. She had to clamp a hand over her mouth when a man's voice said, "Here ya' go, boy. Fresh meat."

Steady growling mixed with the sound of chewing and slobbering. Danitha curled up tight against the car and put her hands over her ears. Emily wanted to do the same, but she had to listen to the men. She had to find out what they were doing here.

Other voices joined in a quiet conversation. Emily strained to hear them.

"He wants more bats, man. We got plenty of doggies," one of them said.

"I know. But I like this one. Go on, boy."

Emily heard the man throw something, and the monster raced after it with its chain scraping and rattling across the pavement. The men laughed, and it was the sound of evil relishing in delight at what had happened to the world.

A door in the truck groaned open, and a new voice said, "Mount up. Wolfpack is heading home. We'll get the bats another time."

"Thought he said he wanted more by tonight," one of others said.

"He changed his mind. Mount up."

The truck doors slammed shut and the engine started with a deep rumble. Emily risked a look around the car she hid behind. The men were in a military vehicle, a Humvee, but she couldn't see any of them now. The Hummer drove down the street slowly. She heard them pick up the dog with its chain, and then the engine revved and they roared away.

Emily and Danitha looked at each other, both too scared to dare utter a sound after what they had just heard.

— 6 —

The Six Team vehicle was still in view, but quickly moving to the limit of Jed's vision. McKitrick had them moving at a good pace down the highway. It was mostly free of debris and vehicles, but now and then she had to slow down and swerve around a wreck, or a damaged part of the road. They stuck to the tracks left by Greg's people and whoever was driving the station wagon that sped off before the bridges went up.

Jed sat in the front, scanning their surroundings out to the horizon; Garza and Keoh were in back, doing the same. Mehta was squashed between them his pack on his knees. Parsons was crammed into the rear area with the radio. He kept making checks to see if Gunny or LT were still out there. He'd even tried Jordan's and Kipler's squads. So far, he'd got a whole lot of nothing in reply.

Jed dragged his eyes from the marshland and focused on the roadside, watching for anything that might spell a threat. After the first mile or so, he relaxed and let the emptiness scroll by. If the TOC was gone, and the LT and Gunny with it, then he and his squad were on their own. He had a mission to follow at least: find whoever was driving the station wagon. But beyond that his job was to make sure he and his people survived. If they got lucky, maybe they'd run into Jordan or Kipler out here. AWOL or not, numbers meant safety.

The terrain around them gradually gave way from swampy fields to firmer soil. Birds flew to and from nests among the still standing electric towers. The air buzzed with insects, whole swarms of them filled the area, wafting up from the bayou terrain.

"Sergeant, got contact," Garza said from the back seat.

Jed turned to look and spotted the figure, a lone person walking through the marshes about twenty yards from the road. He told McKitrick to slow them down to a crawl.

"Somebody get some binos on that dude," he said.

Mehta dug his pair out and handed them to Garza.

"Maybe a hunter, Sergeant. He's got a dog with him," Garza said.

"Weapons?"

"Not that I can see, but he could be hiding it. He's got one arm down, like maybe he's carrying something."

"Fuck it. Nobody we care about. Let's go."

This is some next level bullshit, Jed thought to himself as they got back to rolling down the highway. He had faced bad odds in New York City, but at least then he knew who the bad guys were and how to find them. Or avoid them finding you.

Up ahead, Greg's truck disappeared into the haze rising off the bayou.

McKitrick put on a little more speed. They reached the fork in the highway and veered east, aiming toward Texas City, where Greg had said they might find a military unit. Jed had McKitrick slow down a bit while he sighted through his ACOG, scanning the refinery up ahead. He caught the outline of watchtowers beyond the oil tanks.

"Keep going," he said. "Saw some watchtowers that way. Gotta be the garrison Greg was talking about."

McKitrick drove ahead for about a hundred yards until they reached another fork. The highway going north was in better shape than the one they were on, but Jed had her continue ahead, aiming at the refinery town and the watchtowers he'd seen. The road took them into the refinery field. McKitrick slowed them down as they passed between oil tanks and the pipelines connecting everything in a maze of metal and sand. Some of the tanks had holes in them, like they'd blown up or been hit with some kind of explosive round.

"You think that was on purpose?" McKitrick asked.

"Maybe," Jed said. "People here might have tried to start a fire to keep the sucker faces away."

"Think it worked?" Garza asked.

"Doubt it. The whole place still looks like shit. Sucker faces went through this place for damn sure."

As the town came into view, Jed put up a hand.

"Hold up," he said.

The scenery changed up ahead, and in a big way. The nearest neighborhood sat behind a wide perimeter of open ground, and was hardened with twin chain link fences topped with coils of razor wire. Suburban houses behind the wire looked more like camp structures than homes. Obstacles extended across major access points. Watchtowers stood along the fence line, and Jed spotted roving patrols inside the perimeter.

The neighborhood was definitely rebuilt in places, and hardened. But something felt off about it.

McKitrick asked, "Anybody know the password—"

Jed put up a hand for silence. "Take us into some cover, McKitrick. Over there, behind that oil tank."

She wheeled them off the road and into the refinery area, bringing the vehicle out of the watchtowers' direct line of sight. The trade off was that Jed couldn't see much of the neighborhood either.

"Give me the binos, Mehta. I'm sure they've seen us already, but they aren't shooting. I just want to know what we're walking into."

Mehta handed them over. Jed got out and moved up to the oil tank. He crouched and peered around it. The guards in the towers faced his way, but weren't aiming weapons at his position. Two of them had binos up and were watching him. The ones on the ground walked the perimeter in pairs, casually strolling like Lance Corporals on a fire watch.

They all wore dark blue fatigues, Navy work uniforms.

Jed got back in the SUV. "Bunch of dudes in aquaflage," he said.

"Navy?" McKitrick asked. "What're they doing here?"

"No idea, but they look legit."

He hoped he was right.

Anybody could have salvaged gear from fallen service members or ripped it off from an abandoned supply point. Jed had seen as much happen in New York. But he wanted to trust these people. He needed to if his squad was going to get any kind of shelter or support. At the very least, maybe he could get directions to the Six Team FOB.

"Parsons, try the LT again. Hell, see if you can raise anybody."

After two attempts and no reply, Jed told Parsons to try a frequency they'd used a week ago.

"Still nothing, Sergeant."

"Shit. Okay, y'all. I'm gonna walk us in. McKitrick, keep it slow, about three yards behind me. Anything happens, break for cover. If you have to dismount, stick to overwatch teams. But let's not expect it to go down. They have eyes on us, too, so keep your weapons loose, fingers off the bang switch, hands in the clear. That goes double for you, Garza."

The Lance Corporal smirked, but nodded his agreement. "Roger that, Sergeant."

Jed got out and led them around the oil tank. McKitrick coasted behind him. He walked with one hand on the butt of his M4, and the other held out to his side, palm open. As he neared the gate, about ten yards out, he was hailed from a guard tower.

"Halt and state your business," the guard said, while aiming his rifle at Jed's chest. Jed released the butt of his weapon and walked forward, with his hand up and palms out. He was less sure that he'd come to the right place, but figured he'd try the only play he had.

"I'm Sergeant Welch, USMC from Galveston. We're cut off. Greg Radout said we should link up with y'all here."

The guard relaxed and let his weapon hang as he said something into a shoulder mounted mic. A moment later he called down to Jed.

"Keep your hands away from your weapons. Tell you squad to dismount and move up closer. Anyone touches a weapon, they'll be painted hostile."

"What the fuck, man? We're on your side."

"Nobody named Greg Radout lives here, and nobody told me anything about the Marines from Galveston paying us a visit again. So you're lying, lost, or you're here to cause trouble. We aren't taking chances."

Jed cursed again, then turned slowly back to his squad. McKitrick had the SUV idling in place, about five yards behind him. Garza was leaning out the window, and he had his weapon in his hands. Jed hollered for him to let it go just as the ground between him and the SUV was peppered with small arms fire from the guard towers.

— 7 —

Emily and Danitha waited until the truck motor faded into the distance, and then quickly ran to the nearest house, pushing the rotted door aside and stumbling into the ruins of a family's home. Trash and filth covered the floors, and the acrid reek of death wafted up from somewhere inside. Danitha retched once and whirled around, fleeing the house. Emily followed close behind, not wanting to lose sight of her again. Not here, and not now.

Not with those men and their monsters near us, she thought.

"Behind the house, *mija*," Emily said, guiding Danitha past wrecked cars and overturned patio furniture. They cut around the neighborhood, avoiding the street and following a shallow drainage ditch behind the houses. Every footfall, every snap of a branch or rustled bunch of grass threatened to freeze Emily in her tracks. She couldn't shake the feeling they were being chased by a dog monster. The image of the one they had seen burned in her mind like a scene of torment. She wanted so desperately to forget she ever saw it.

And yet as much as she hated the idea, she had to accept they were a result of the virus that had been released upon the world. Just like the bats, the dog monsters had evolved after the virus affected their DNA.

Before Emily had evacuated her university with everyone else, she'd used the last precious minutes of Internet access to read a little of what had been discovered by scientists studying the Variants. CDC researchers on Plum Island had learned a lot about the creatures, and had distributed what they could to other scientists around the world, before the entire information infrastructure collapsed.

Emily counted herself lucky, having a chance to learn about the monsters at a distance. The first ones to appear were mutated humans, affected by a virus that triggered hyper-rapid epigenetic changes to their DNA. The Variants that followed had been an evolved species, growing from the initial anthro-morphs into something far more dangerous to humanity. Other species had been identified as offspring of the Variants, including some ghastly varieties found in Europe. But the bat and dog morphs Emily had seen were clearly evolved from those species themselves, not derivates or offspring from their human-like ancestors.

Bats and dogs have a common ancestor, she thought. *And are more closely related than either is to humans. If the virus evolved to affect either of them, it could, conceivably, have adapted to other species as well. What other horrors are out there?*

With those frightening thoughts racing through her mind, Emily led Danitha closer to the refinery that waited ahead. A wide road divided the overgrown farmland around the neighborhood from a maze of pipes and oil tanks. Garbage and storm debris covered the ground in places, but Emily could see a path into the refinery area.

The neighborhood ended where the street took a short jog to one side, leading away from the homes and to a gas station that sat against the main road in front of them. They'd have no cover if they crossed from there, and would have to run over open ground just to reach the gas station.

"What do we do?" Danitha asked. She sounded so exhausted, and that made Emily feel her own aching fatigue weighing her down even harder.

"The gas station. We go there. Hide for now. Rest."

"And then? You still think we gonna make it to Galveston."

Emily had a reply on her tongue, but the whine of an engine snapped her mouth shut. She dropped down and slunk back behind the last house in the neighborhood, looking everywhere for the vehicle. Finally she spotted a small pick up truck, coming out of the refinery. The driver turned south, leaving a trail of dust in their wake.

"This is our chance, Dani," Emily said. Without giving fear a chance to stop her, she raced forward across the open ground for the gas station. Danitha's footfalls sounded in the earth behind her and soon they were collapsing together against the wall of the building, where a single gray door stood half open. Debris was mounded up around it. After examining it for a moment, Emily had to accept that someone had purposefully made a path to the door.

She stayed in a crouch and leaned over to push on the door. It swung a few inches before stopping. A loud twang echoed from inside the building and something flew past Emily's head. She crouched against the wall and searched the ground for what had nearly hit her.

Something thin and dark had bounced off the pavement. Emily went to retrieve the object. It was a short arrow.

Danitha shook her head and said, "Uh-uh. Somebody putting traps on that door. I am not going in there."

Emily was inclined to agree with her, but the familiar whine of a surging motor came down the road.

"We're in the open here," she said, before shoving on the door and rushing inside with her head down. Nothing else came flying at her. She turned and called to Danitha, but the woman was already inside.

"It's the militia men. They coming back, and now you got us inside their hideout."

Emily shushed her and moved deeper into the building. They'd come into what used to be the back room of a convenience store. Empty shelves lined the walls, along with a cage of empty water cooler bottles lying on their sides. A small puddle formed beneath one of the bottles, but the others were all long since dry. A small crossbow hung on the wall opposite the door they'd come in. A string connected it to a pulley hung above the door.

Outside, the motor's noise swelled in volume, then slowly faded as the vehicle passed the gas station and continued down the road.

"See," Emily said. "We're safe. Only for now, maybe, but nobody is coming in here after us."

"And what do we do now we in here? Wait for them to come back?"

"Maybe there's something we can use for a weapon inside."

"And now you talking about weapons, when we could've had some—"

Emily stopped her with a look. Now was not the time for *I told you so*. Danitha got the hint.

"So we go hunting around in here. What about traps like that one?" she asked, pointing to the crossbow.

"Be careful. We have to get somewhere we can hide, and this is the best we have now."

Danitha wore a heavy frown on her face, and it took her a moment before she nodded her agreement.

They moved through the space cautiously, and didn't find any more traps, or set any off. But they didn't find much of use either. Someone had used the building as a hideout. The shelves inside the store were jammed up against the front windows like barricades. Bullet holes pockmarked the walls, and blood stains marked the floor in places.

Only a single cooler remained standing. It didn't work, of course, but it was in decent shape. Everything else was either smashed or pushed to the front of the store.

Danitha walked over to the cooler. "Hey, Professor," she said. "There's some food in here."

Emily joined her and they checked around the door for wires or anything that could be a trap.

"Looks okay," Dani said.

"I'll open—"

The sound of wheels on gravel cut her off. The truck had come back, and it was outside, behind the store.

The store counter was overturned against a wall, near the front of the space. Danitha ran to it, and slid onto the ground where she balled up with her hands over her ears. Emily followed her and tucked herself behind the counter, shivering with fright.

She felt around on the floor for anything she might

use as a weapon, and now regretted denying Danitha's suggestion that they arm themselves before fleeing the militia neighborhood. Her hand brushed against something metallic and boxy. Whatever it was, it filled her hand and felt heavy. She could strike out with it if she had to.

As they waited, Emily dreaded the eventual sound of footfalls entering the store. A glint of light caught on the object in her hand, and she held it out enough to examine what she had found.

It was a magazine, like for the weapon Salvador carried. He'd shown her one when she visited him at Camp Pendleton. This one was full of bullets though, shiny brass and copper reflected bits of light filtering in through gaps in the barricade.

Footsteps finally broke into the silence of the space, slowly coming closer.

Danitha clutched at Emily's arm, but she held a finger to her lips. She held up the magazine and mimed striking with it. Danitha nodded, even as she shivered with terror. Emily was only just holding herself back from screaming and racing out to meet their fate head on. That's what Chava would have done. He'd told her always to throw the first punch if she had to, and now here she was hiding.

Emily was about to rise up and confront whoever had come into the space when a young female voice said, "Well. I guess I have company. So who wants to die first?"

— 8 —

Jed threw his hands out to either side, waving and shouting. "Cease fire! Friendly! Friendly!"

"You were warned!" the guard shouted down to him. "Keeps your hands off your weapons or you will be painted hostile!"

Garza was half out the window and had his M27 at the ready.

"Put it down, Garza!" Jed shouted at him, then whirled around to face the gate guards. "We're fucking friendly!"

They'd stopped firing, but still had their weapons trained on Jed and his squad.

"You can say that all day," one of the guards yelled back. "We'll believe you when we're ready."

"And when does that happen? After you shoot us so I have to prove I can call in a nine line?"

The guards all passed a few words between them. Some of them shrugged, as if they accepted Jed was legit. But the one who first hailed him still refused to let them in.

"You're not expected, so we have to treat you as

potential enemy. Sorry. That's how it is now. Wait one," he said and leaned down to his shoulder mic again.

"You got commo to Galveston?" Jed asked.

The guard carried on his commo before answering Jed's question with one of his own.

"Who wants to know? You still haven't given us all your names. Anybody can put on a scavenged set of digi-cams and call themselves a Marine. How do we know you didn't steal all that gear?"

"You motherfuckers want to come down and inspect us in formation?" Garza yelled. He'd let his weapon hang slack again, and had his hands out to his sides.

"Stand down, Garza," Jed said. "Y'all dismount. Weapons down. C'mon."

"Sergeant…" Keoh said. None of them had gotten out, and not even Garza looked ready to move any closer to the gate.

"These guys are jumpy, that's all," Jed said, waving his people forward. "I trust them. Now c'mon."

McKitrick turned off the engine and got out. Garza followed, then Keoh. The *plus two* brothers were last, again. As the squad got closer, Jed waved them forward, hoping they would cool down. Garza was ready to go off. McKitrick, Mehta, and Keoh were only a little less on edge, and Parsons looked about ready to shit himself.

Jed turned back to the gate. The guards above stayed as they were: weapons up and aimed at his face.

A door opened in the house nearest the gate, and a lanky older man stepped out. He closed the door and made his way down the front walk, keeping an eye on Jed and his people. He wore the same Navy fatigues as the guards and carried a sidearm. At the gate, he stopped with his hands on his hips and yelled out to Jed, "You want to explain yourselves to me?" he demanded.

Jed couldn't see the man's rank, but he held himself like an officer, and sounded like one.

If it walks like a dick and talks like a dick, Jed thought.

"Sir, we're US Marines, from Galveston—"

"Then you're the only US Marines in Texas. How'd you make it off the island before the bridges went up?"

"I—Sir, we were this side of the bay when it happened."

How does he know about it? Jed wondered. *Does he have commo we don't?*

"Care to explain *that* to me? How come you knew to be on this side of the water? Maybe you're the bombers and you're here to finish what you started."

"Bombers? Sir, we're with the—"

"You want me to believe you're really with the Marines, then you'll have to show me some proof."

Jed wanted to holler at the guy or, better yet, beat him into accepting the truth. But whoever he was, he had four men with weapons trained on Jed and his people. Bringing a fight to the situation wouldn't help Jed's chances and might just end him and his squad where they stood.

"Sir, if we could prove ourselves to you, we would. All we have is our word right now. Our TOC isn't replying, and it sounds like you know more about what happened to them than we do."

The man blew out his breath then called over to one of the guards on the ground.

"Let 'em in. I'll handle this."

The guard paused just long enough for the guy to

build up steam and let it out.

"I said open the damn gate!"

"Yessir!"

Two guards on the ground moved forward, one with his weapon up, the other with a key ring. He unlocked the gate and swung it wide, bringing his own weapon up to cover Jed's entry. He waited at the gate until his people came up.

"Keep cool, y'all," he told them before turning to enter the neighborhood.

Now that he was closer to the guards, Jed confirmed them as sailors. Their uniforms were in bad shape, but these guys were Navy all the way. Most of them were close to Parsons and Mehta in age. The guard with the key ring gave McKitrick and Keoh a once over as they passed through the gate.

Jed spotted the guy's E4 rank insignia. He was too busy checking out McKitrick to notice Jed stepping into his face and glaring. Through clenched teeth, Jed said, "I think you might be concentrating on the wrong AO there, Petty."

The guy stepped back a pace and sent a pleading glance to the other guards. They chuckled and ignored him.

"Fix yourself, Early," one of the guards said to the guy with the keys. Jed moved past the man and led his squad forward. The gate was quickly closed and relocked behind them, and the guards went back to walking the perimeter.

The old guy with the pistol on his hip waved them forward.

"Welcome to COP Gray. I'm Commander Mercer," he said and quickly lifted his eyebrows, like he expected

Jed to do something.

Jed straightened his posture and lifted a salute. "Sergeant Welch, sir. 25th Marines, Galveston."

Mercer snapped a salute and walked back to the house he'd come from, waving a hand for Jed to follow. "Come with me, Sergeant. Your people can stay here and help watch my gate."

Turning to his squad, Jed said, "Keep it extra cool. No bullshitting, rah? I bet this guy eats UCMJ, shits it out, and eats it twice."

"I heard that, Sergeant," Mercer called over his shoulder. "And you're not wrong. That's why I'm in charge here."

Jed could have kicked himself for getting caught out like a boot. But Mercer didn't sound pissed off, at least not yet.

"You have a garrison here, sir?" Jed asked as he moved to follow the commander up the walk to the house.

"Sort of," he said, turning around at the door to the house. "I have my men, enough to keep us safe for now, plus a headquarters element handling commo and staff crap. And about a hundred and fifty civilians trying to rebuild their lives with nothing but hope and the scraps we've managed to salvage. We'll talk more in my office."

Mercer's guards cast sideways looks in their direction. Jed could hear the men in the guard towers making commo checks, confirming all clear outside the wire. His squad milled around just inside the gate. Garza had a hand on his weapon again, and so did McKitrick and Keoh. The *plus two* team of Parsons and Mehta hung back from the others, but kept a ready posture, with their weapons held close.

Jed took in the hazy air hanging above the refinery they'd walked through. It looked a lot like industrial areas of New York where he'd fought against the Variants. He felt a nagging worry about them for second, but it passed as quickly as it came.

They entered the house. Mercer took a seat behind a desk to the left of the front door. Armchairs and couches lined the walls of the front room. A darkened hall stretched back into the house. None of the lights were on in the front room either, and it took a bit for Jed's eyes to adjust to the dimness. It didn't feel much different from offices on Parris Island. Mercer even sat in the same posture as Jed's squad leader would on the many days Jed had received an NJP. Oddly, the whole scene felt like home. So he played along.

He came to attention in front of Mercer's desk.

Mercer's lips curled into a grim smile. "Who told you to come here, Sergeant?"

"Nobody, sir. We'd linked up with Radout and his people, down by the causeway, then we separated after the bridges went up. Radout mentioned you—"

"Separated. Dirty work done, they went their way, you went yours. That it?"

"Yes—No. Sir, it was…we didn't—"

"Who blew the bridges? You or them?"

Jed's assessment of Mercer switched in a heartbeat from showboat to asshole. He couldn't decide whether to just shoot the man and get it over with, or stick to answering his questions honestly. The guy obviously trusted Jed enough to bring him and his people into his perimeter and leave them armed.

But Jed's patience with being labeled a terrorist had reached a limit. He relaxed his posture, put his fists on the edge of the desk, and stared the commander in the eye.

"Sir, we didn't bomb anything. We're lucky to be alive. There's a sapper on the loose around here, and we're on the same fucking side as you."

Mercer stared back at him, then let out a short laugh and said, "Spoken like a Marine. Okay, Sergeant, secure the attitude, but you and your people are in my good books. Now how about telling me how you got here? You mentioned Radout. You mean that Six Team bunch?"

Jed straightened a bit and brought his hands back to his sides before he replied.

"That's right, sir. We'd found a body in the bay and our LT said it was someone from Six Team."

"I know Greg Radout. Good man, even if he is on the wrong side of things. Who's your LT?"

"First Lieutenant Staples."

"And he's the one not answering at your TOC."

"Yes, sir. The body we found was chewed on, like a Variant attack. We couldn't confirm, but—"

Mercer waved a hand at the air.

"Bodies are a dime a dozen in this state. And if you're telling me the monsters are back, you can walk that story back up the ass you pulled it from. If they were back, I think we'd have seen them already. They're attracted to noise and movement. We've been making plenty of both in the past two months rebuilding this neighborhood, no thanks to Radout's bunch. Have you seen any of the things? What evidence do you have?"

"Only the body we found, sir. It had bite marks on it that looked like a Variant."

"Looked like. Who confirmed this for you? You have CDC people with you? Which one of you is the scientist?"

Jed felt the conversation slipping out of his hands, and he didn't have anything he could use to get hold of it again.

"What did you think you'd find here, Sergeant Welch? I'm genuinely curious. You think we're here because CENTCOM wants us here? You think that's why you were on Galveston?"

"Yes, sir," Jed said, surprised at the direction Mercer was going. "We're supposed to receive refugees there, process them, and move them inland to the rebuilt neighborhoods. Like this one here, I guess."

"Yes, and you guess wrong, Sergeant. CENTCOM is a joke. Whatever's out there pretending it controls things is a farce. There is no central control anymore. The president was always a figurehead, and now he doesn't even exist. We're in the same boat as you here, cut off from real support and flapping in the wind. But we're surviving, because of people like me taking charge of the situation. And now I have to figure out what to do with you."

"Sir?"

"You can stay here, but not for long. We barely have the resources to house or feed the people we have, let alone a squad of hungry Marines. And even though I'm smiling as I look at you, on the inside I'm not entirely convinced you're friendly. The last Marines who came through here were none too pleasant to my people. So I can't fully trust you. I can't afford to take that risk."

Jed's mind spun back to what the gate guard had said about Marines being here *'again'*.

"Sir, which Marines? Was it Sergeant Kipler? Jordan?"

"I didn't get their names, but it was a squad of men who had been on Galveston. They came, they saw, they made me uncomfortable. So I sent them packing, same as I'm going to do with you. When I know I can trust you."

"Sir, we're—"

"Save it, Sergeant," Mercer said, standing up. "I don't think you're a threat. If I did, I'd have taken your weapons off you when you walked through my gate. But, I need to know I can trust you before I let you leave."

"Sir?"

"I can't just let you walk out of here. What if you go running back to your master? The *sapper*," Mercer said with a devil's smirk twisting his lips.

Jed had no answer for the man. His throat was dry. If they were on their own, and Mercer's crowd was the closest thing they'd find for a command structure, then Jed had managed to land his people deep in the suck without even trying. But if Kipler or Jordan had been here, maybe some of the sailors talked with them. They might have some idea of where they went after Mercer kicked them out.

"Sir, we'd be happy to get out of your hair and—"

"Negative, Sergeant. You're inside my wire, so you're mine to command. You'll be part of my security apparatus for the time being."

"And how long is that, *sir*?" Jed asked, with a growing dislike of the officer standing in front of him.

"As long as I require, *Sergeant*. You're on the north

perimeter. I saw six people in your squad, that makes three teams. Two roving, one in the tower. Monitor the area for activity."

"With respect, sir, we just needed to get somewhere secure and try to establish commo with Galveston."

"Good luck with that, son. They're not answering. I've been trying to raise them ever since the *sapper* pulled his move. No, you're working my perimeter, Sergeant. If you can prove you're friendly, you'll be free to head off into the wilderness later. Your first shift starts now until 1800 hours. You'll be off duty from 1800 to 0200, then on again. Wash, rinse, repeat until I know you can be trusted."

Jed didn't want to ask what would happen if Mercer decided they couldn't be trusted. He brought his feet together and straightened his back, lifting his right arm in a salute as he met Mercer's eyes. The man returned his salute and told Jed he was dismissed.

"You'll want to stop by our supply to get radios for your people. I expect hourly updates."

"We have a radio, sir," Jed said. "Our RTO—"

"Will use our gear," Mercer said, coming around his desk to open the front door.

Jed nodded, pivoted on his heel, and left the house.

His squad was where he'd left them, alive, armed, and looking just as uncomfortable with the situation as Jed felt himself.

What the hell did I get us into? he wondered.

Mercer stepped out of the house behind him to say, "Supply is two houses along on the right." He pointed down a street that went into the neighborhood.

Jed nodded at the man and motioned for his squad to

follow as he moved off to get the radios for their first guard shift in Mercer's compound.

This ain't no neighborhood, he thought. *This is a warlord's domain, and we just got ourselves stuck in it up to our eyeballs.*

— 9 —

Emily stared into the shaken, bloodshot eyes of a girl who probably hadn't taken a bath in weeks. Her face was darkened with dirt and grime, some of it looking purposefully applied. Her hair stuck out from under a dark gray knit cap. Some of it caught flecks of light leaking into the space, reflecting hints of bright red. She wore a combination of military uniforms, too, with a too-big black and green patterned shirt on top. Her pants were the gray, black, and white style Emily's brother always called *cosplay camo*.

The weapon she held was just like Chava's, only longer.

And it was empty.

Emily held up the magazine she'd found. "You need this, *chica*?"

The girl's eyes went wide with anger. "I ain't no *chica*. Now gimme that!"

"Uh-uh," Emily said. "If I give you this, you'll kill us, or take us prisoner and take us back to the militia people. You're with them, aren't you?"

"No I ain't."

Emily wasn't ready to hear that, but at the mention of

the militia, the girl shrank into herself, pulling her rifle up close and tight.

"You're afraid of them," Emily said. "Why?"

"If you know about them, then you don't need to be asking me that."

"Okay, so you're on the run from them, too—"

"Didn't say I was running. Just said I wasn't with them assholes. Now gimme my ammo and let me get out of here."

"This isn't your hideout?"

"Hell no. What kind of stupid person hides out next door to the men trying to kill her?"

Emily looked between the girl and Danitha. A handful of years separated them, maybe more. The new girl could have been of age, but Emily doubted she'd seen a day past sixteen.

"*Mija*, you are safe with us. We're not going to hurt you or let the militia find you."

"Longer you take to give me my ammo, the less chance I have of getting away before they do find me. Now—"

"You have a truck. Outside. Let's leave together. All of us."

"No way. I ain't taking on no baggage, and 'specially not tainted goods like y'all are."

Danitha's lip curled at the comment. "Girl, you need to look all the way into a mirror before you come with that noise."

"It ain't like that. I mean y'all are wanted, and they're paying a bounty for you. Last thing I need is to get mixed up in that. Now for the last time. Give. Me. My. Ammo."

As she spoke, the girl reached one hand to a knife on

her hip. She unclipped it and drew it out slowly. The blade glimmered in the streams of light filtering into the space. Danitha grabbed the magazine out of Emily's hands and stood up, holding it above her shoulder like a brick.

Emily put her hands out, stepping between them. "No, no, no. Just cool down. Please. We can help each other," she said, looking quickly from Danitha to the new girl.

"Just give me my ammo," she said.

"Come take it," Danitha spat back.

"We're not going to survive like this," Emily said to both of them. "Put them down. All the weapons. Please."

"Why should I trust either of you?" the new girl asked. "Y'all could just hand me over to the militia if I'm not careful. Use me to get out of your own mess."

"They want you too?" Danitha asked. "What the hell for?"

"None of your damn business."

"Please, Dani," Emily said. "And you, what is your name?"

The girl answered by holding her knife out, pointing it at Danitha.

Emily knew she had seconds to stop something terrible from happening. With a deep breath, she stepped in front of Danitha and held her hands up, hoping to convince the new girl to relax.

"My name is Professor Emiliana Garza. I'm a virologist. Dani was a graduate student in my classes. We escaped a neighborhood the militia took over. They killed people who didn't agree with them, and who weren't—"

"Weren't white like them. I know. I seen it done

around here. That's why I left them fools. I won't be part of that. But that don't mean I'm fixing to run with y'all. I just want my ammo so I can get back to surviving on my own like I been doing."

"How long?"

"What?"

"How long have you been out here? Living like this."

"Few weeks? A month? I don't know. Time's not important anymore."

"Have you seen the monsters? The bats and dogs?"

The girl's eyes flashed wide but narrowed just as fast. "You trying to trick me? Everybody knows the monsters are gone. They been gone for years."

"No, *chica*. No, no, no. They are back. Not the same ones as before, but they are here. We've seen them. Please, we need to get to Galveston. My brother is a Marine there. We'll be safe. Please, take us there in your truck."

The girl hesitated, but lowered her knife and finally put it back in its sheath. She held her rifle in the other hand for a moment, then let it hang on a sling that she'd made out of an old belt. "Still would like to have my ammo back," she said.

"Not until I know for sure you ain't gonna shoot us with it," Danitha said.

Emily turned to face her. She was still holding the magazine like a club. Emily put out a hand for it, and Danitha shook her head.

"We have to show her we can be trusted. I trust her. Please, Dani."

Finally, after several tense breaths, Danitha relaxed and passed the magazine to Emily. She turned around and held it out to the girl, who snatched it from her and slotted it into her weapon. She pulled back on a handle and Emily got a brief glimpse of the brass and copper of a bullet before the girl released the handle.

For a second, Emily thought she had doomed her and Danitha to die, but the girl let the gun hang on its sling again, then looked Emily in the eye.

"You said y'all are going to Galveston?"

"Yes, my brother is there. With the—"

"With the Marines. Yeah, I heard. But how come I ain't heard about any Marines being in Texas? I know we had some Army around Houston, but they either got themselves killed or joined the militia."

"I told you, Professor," Danitha said with a sneer. "Didn't I say the Army was just as bad as the militia?"

"Maybe so," Emily said. Then, to the other girl, "But if we can go in your truck…"

"No chance," she said as she stepped back from them. "I'll tell you this though. If y'all are heading south, you want to stay away from Baytown. That's a militia stronghold, and that's gonna make your trip kinda hard, since only one bridge makes it over the bay between here and Galveston, and it's the one goes from Baytown to La Porte. You could try heading into Houston and turning south around Channelview, but I wouldn't if I were you. Army and militia had a big fight up there last year. Wasn't the good guys who won."

Emily choked on her fear. They were right back where they'd started, only now it was worse because the militia knew they were in the area, and they'd placed a bounty on their heads. Danitha was right. They should have taken guns, if only to make sure *they* decided their *own* fate.

The girl stepped back a few more paces, slowly, and then with more purpose. She was at the door before Emily managed to speak.

"*Please*," she begged. "Help us get out of here."

"Where to? I ain't driving all the way to Galveston. Won't be able to trade for enough fuel to get that far anyway. Truck only has another couple miles in it before I have to go scrounging up another one."

Emily could see the cage of empty water bottles behind the girl. "You're running low on water, right? They have food and water in Galveston. Places to sleep that aren't filled with garbage and broken glass. How long can you survive hunting for food? What happens when you run out of bullets?"

The girl stayed with her back to them, standing at the threshold. After a deep breath, she turned back to them. Her face went slack and she sucked in a breath as tears spilled down her cheeks.

"Y'all really got food and shelter waiting on Galveston? People you can really trust?"

Emily nodded sharply, hoping Danitha wouldn't say anything to ruin their chances. After another shaking breath, the new girl shook her head and said, "Shouldn't be doing this. But come on. Quick before I change my mind."

Emily put a hand on Danitha's arm and guided her forward.

"I don't like this, Professor. We should keep going on our own."

"You won't get very far," the girl said.

When they reached her, at the back of the space, she held out a dirt covered hand. "My name's Angie."

Emily took her hand.

"Thank you… Angie."

"Truck should get us through Mont Belvieu. Militia ain't around here much. Only reason they been here is probably looking for you two."

Angie led them outside. Her truck was parked behind the store, tight against the wall so it would be concealed from the road in both directions. It was a small pickup, missing both bumpers and bits of trim, and was probably blue or green underneath all the mud.

"Dirt makes it harder to see at a distance," Angie said. "Took all the chrome off it so they wouldn't spot me so easy if I had to be out in daylight. You don't like it, you can walk."

They climbed in, with Danitha going first to sit against the passenger door. Emily went next, and Angie got in to drive. She slid her rifle down between her seat and the door, and drew out a pistol from underneath her seat. She held it out to Emily.

"Here. Y'all need to be able to shoot back if we get spotted. You know how to work a gun?"

"No," Emily said, shaking her head.

"Ain't got time for shooting lessons right now. When we get somewhere safe, that's the first thing we do."

Angie tucked the pistol back under her seat, started the engine and drove them away from the gas station.

"Easier to hide by staying off the roads," she explained as she pulled onto the shoulder. They bounced across the rough ground, and swerved to avoid wreckage the storms had swept into the area. After a few hundred feet, Angie peeled to the right and took them into the maze of pipes and oil tanks in the refinery fields.

The whole area was a mess of shadows and hiding places for the monsters, and Emily was sure that any second now they would be swarmed by hideous bats or snarling, rabid dogs. She held her fear close around her, making sure to watch in every direction she could in case something came for them. Danitha was doing the same, but also kept looking in Angie's direction until the girl spoke up about it.

"I ain't gonna kill y'all. Would've done it back at the station if I was."

"Then what are you gonna do?" Danitha asked.

"Get you as far as this truck will take us. After that, or if it comes to it sooner, we part ways. Need y'all to know there's only one head of hair I care about, and that's mine. Expect y'all to be thinking the same thing about yourselves if you want to survive out here."

Emily nodded at that, but didn't know what to say in response. Her safety felt secure not too long ago, when she and Danitha were living in a community of people rebuilding the world one neighborhood block at a time. Now she was on the run from bounty hunters and murderers, and her only company were two people who had yet to say a kind word to each other.

She tried to find words that would smooth things out, but nothing came to her. She was still thinking about how to make things better for them when a dark shape separated from an oil tank up ahead. It sprang to the ground, landing behind a pile of debris. Emily tried to find it, and screamed as a dog monster jumped from another debris mound, shrieking as it flew toward the windshield with outstretched clawed hands.

— 10 —

Jed and his people rallied at a corner, just down from the house that served as Mercer's office. He needed to fill them in, and he needed to know they were still his people. Without any command structure other than Mercer to point at, Jed would be the source of all the squad's direction. And that meant he'd be the source of all their troubles as well.

Shit don't roll on flat ground, he thought.

"All right, y'all, two things. First, either Kipler or Jordan was here before us. The guy who runs this place said he had a squad of Marines show up recently."

"Where are they now?" Garza asked.

"He doesn't know or didn't say. They pissed him off and he gave 'em the shove."

"Nice guy," McKitrick said. "So we're back to square one. No help and no idea where to look for help. I could get used to this if it didn't remind me of the Corps so much."

Jed had to laugh at that, but got back to business quick. "I know this is some serious green weenie bullshit. Mercer's got himself strapped like a Taliban warlord, and even if his people look like they're on our side, I don't doubt they'd put us down if he ordered it. So we gotta play along, play nice, and get gone the minute we can."

"Why can't we leave now?" Keoh asked, sending a look over her shoulder at the gate guards.

"He wants us to pull fire watch until 1800—"

"The *fuck?*" Garza yelled. "I ain't—"

"You're gonna stand post like the rest of us, Garza!"

In a quieter voice, Jed said, "Mercer says he needs to know we're cool. It's like he thinks we're part of some OPFOR shit. He took what I told him about the sapper and turned it around like it was us that bombed the bridges. He knows that Radout guy and his people, but didn't seem too happy with them. And him sending Kip's or Jordan's squad for a walk makes me think he's afraid of anybody with authority around them."

"They were here?" Garza asked.

"Can't confirm. He didn't have names for me. Just said some Marines showed up, made him unhappy, so he told them to get fucked. What really spun me was him saying CENTCOM is dust. Gone."

"What?" McKitrick asked. "Then who the fuck's calling the shots?"

"He is," Jed said. "That was his whole story. There is no *higher* anymore."

"Did you tell him about the sucker faces being back?" Keoh asked. "You know that body wasn't just chewed on by a gator, Sergeant. That was—"

"I know what I think it was, Keoh. But I only saw as much as you did, and we haven't spotted any of the things since we got here, or any real sign that they're back. Shit, I hardly got a word in about the sucker faces anyway. Mercer either didn't want to hear it, or wouldn't believe me no matter how much I told him. He's got something working on him, like he's afraid but doesn't want to show it. He used the same breath to say we were in his good books and that he doesn't trust us."

McKitrick cleared her throat. "So we're standing guard for him while he does a background check?"

"Yeah, something like that I guess. We're on the north perimeter and tower. We get radios from his supply at that house up the street. Then we're on until 1800. Back on at 0200."

"How long does this shit detail last?" Garza asked.

"He didn't really say. Just until he's ready to trust us."

"Motherfucker," Garza said. "I get a chance, I'ma—"

"Stand post," Jed said. "Stay with me, Garza. This is grade-A horseshit, and I know it same as you, but it's the best thing we got for now. There's nothing out there for us to fall back on. No TOC to call for extraction or close air support. Nothing. Kip or Jordan might have been here before us, but who knows where they are now. Parsons, you tried to get them again?"

"No, Sergeant."

"Well start doing that. Once we're at our guard posts, make checks with them on our freq. If we hear from them, we'll link up as soon as we can. If not, we can link up with Radout once we're out of here."

He let that settle in, and was relieved to see his people coming around, standing straighter, more alert and engaged with their surroundings. But Garza still needed some convincing.

"Look, I don't trust these Navy guys to have our back unless the shit really starts to go down. But they're in a jam just like us. Nobody they can call for support or direction. Mercer's decided he's the be all, end all, and these sailors are marking time to his beat because they don't have anyone else to follow. That means I need all y'all to be on point while we're here. Eyes out, on the ball. No dick-dancing. Parsons, Mehta, y'all ain't boots after this. This is y'all's first deployment."

Jed was glad to see the others nod their approval. He needed his squad at their best for whatever would come. With a final nod, he moved out to the supply point. It turned out to be a bunch of shelving crammed into a suburban double-car garage. The space was stacked full of wet weather gear, work lights, boxes of nails, hand tools, and bags of concrete. Cases of MREs and jugs of water lined the back wall, with some medical supplies tucked in here and there. A corpsman's bag hung from a coat rack by the door leading into the house.

A lone sailor in fatigues, and wearing his cap backwards, stood in the middle of it all, pushing a stack of blankets onto a shelf above his head.

"Yeah?" he asked as Jed approached.

It was the same guy who had unlocked the gate and made eyes at Keoh.

"You wanna fix that cover, Petty?" Jed asked. He waited while the guy rotated his cap around to face front. His attitude stuck out from under it, but Jed wasn't going to waste any more breath on the idiot.

"Commander Mercer said we'd get radios here. We're on the north perimeter."

"Didn't hear anything about this, but you're inside the wire and still strapped, so I guess that's good enough."

Garza spit on the ground, then said, "Sure as fuck hope it's good enough. We're not part of your shitshow, but that old man seems to think he owns us for now, so here we are."

Mercer may have been the sailor's chain of command, but he wasn't in the room. Jed was happy to let Garza blow off a little steam at the dirtbag supply clerk.

When the sailor didn't budge to help them, Jed reminded him.

"Petty Officer Early, my name is *Sergeant* Welch. We need three radios. Green gear if you got it."

The sailor turned and moved to a shelf. He gave Garza a hard look as he dug around and came up with three radios. They were older than anything Jed had ever seen.

"Old Gulf War gear," he said, handing them over. "They still work, but aren't good for much. Batteries haven't been made since before 9-11. I have a few around here, so if you run out of juice, send a runner back."

"Can't give us spares to take with us? Save us the hump?" Jed asked.

The guy shook his head and looked at his feet.

Jed didn't bother arguing. He took the radios and gave them to Parsons, Keoh, and McKitrick. The supply clerk raised his eyes to stare at Keoh again, and Jed had to step between them to break his concentration.

"What's the freq?"

"Huh?"

"The freq, dipshit. For radio checks."

"Oh, yeah. Gate and perimeter are on channel three. Towers use four."

Without a second glance at the guy, Jed turned and led the squad to their duty for the day, hoping the next eight hours would pass without incident.

"Never thought I'd feel homesick for Galveston, but

this shit is ridiculous," Keoh said. "We really gonna do this, Sergeant? Eight hours standing post with nothing but some squid's word this is legit?"

"We play it straight and get gone as soon as we can. Just another stop on the trail."

"Kinda makes me miss going fishing," Parsons said as they trudged down the empty suburban street toward the fence line at the end.

"Fishing for the dead," McKitrick said. "I never thought I'd be happy to hear those words."

Two of Mercer's guards walked across the street up ahead, pausing to look at Jed and his squad. One of the guards said something into his shoulder mic. They continued on their path a moment later, disappearing into the neighborhood.

Jed turned at the next street, heading north. They passed between more houses lining narrow streets. The yards were clean, mostly, with only a few piles of debris or trash visible. These were all heaped at the curb, like they'd be collected by a trash truck. As they passed one, the stench of rotten food hit Jed's nose.

"Guess the garbage man ain't coming," Keoh said.

Curtains flicked aside in every home they passed, and Jed caught a few stares before the curtains fell back in place.

The longer he spent in the neighborhood, the less it felt like a bunch of homes and the more it looked like a prison camp. They passed a small park that had been replanted with new trees recently. Saplings stood out amidst patches of reedy grass and mud. Playground equipment rusted and leaned over like it might fall any minute.

The north fence line was straight ahead now, one block along their path.

"If this place is legit, they've really got their work cut out for them," McKitrick said.

They were almost at the fence when Jed paused in front of a half burned house.

"Let's check this out," he said, waving his squad up behind him.

The front door swung on broken hinges. The deadbolt had been kicked in, too. Jed slowly pushed the door open with the muzzle of his weapon. He went inside, checked his corner and took a position along the front wall. Garza and the others filed in behind him with weapons up, but they all relaxed soon enough.

The house was like every other Jed had been into since the virus hit, only something worse had happened here. Blood splatter decorated the walls and ceiling. Tracks through the debris and gore marked where the bodies had been dragged. They led to the back rooms, which had suffered the most damage from the fire.

People had been killed in this house, and whoever did it tried to burn the place down, hoping to cover their crime.

Jed walked through the rooms that hadn't been destroyed. Each was a tangle of overturned furniture, clothing, family photos, and personal possessions. Scratches and claw marks stood out on the walls like angry scars. But if monsters did it, why was the door kicked in? And why burn the place? The Variants were intelligent predators, but they didn't care about covering their tracks.

The squad made a thorough search of the place, and

Jed had to continually choke back his rage. Pieces of the family's life lay everywhere like the aftermath of a tornado.

The bodies were in the back bedroom, or what was left of it. That's where the fire had done the most damage. Jed felt like he should check them out, see if he could tell how they'd been killed, but looking at the remains he gave it up as a hopeless effort.

Like he'd been forced to do in New York, Jed clamped down on the urge to yell at the sky, curse God, curse anyone and everything responsible for what had happened to the world. He never got the full story about where the virus came from, who started it. But the result was undeniable. Humanity's days were numbered.

We did this to ourselves, Jed thought.

He led his squad out of the house and to the fence line for their day of guard duty. As they were preparing to separate into teams, a skinny, shaggy looking white man wearing aviator shades came down the street. He waved to Jed.

"Hey, you're the other Marines. Right?"

The guy smiled, and the skin of his face pulled tight against his bones. His teeth were stained and cracked. The tee-shirt he wore was ripped under both arms, and was really more of a rag than a shirt.

Jed nodded. "What do you mean '*other Marines*'? And who's asking?"

"I ain't giving my name."

"Why the fuck not?"

"Just… Look, it's cool here. Like, things are okay. Nothing bad's happening. Like the other guys said. Semper Fi, right?" He backed away, waving his hands as if denying everything he'd just said.

"You know what happened in there?" Jed asked, nodding his head at the burned house.

"Aw, that? Nah. Just an accident. People shouldn't smoke in bed I guess."

"The fuck do you know about it?" Garza asked.

The guy flipped a finger at Garza, then spun around and stalked back to a house at the end of the block.

"Go on smoke some more, fucking crackhead," Garza called after him. "Let me light him up, Sergeant."

"We got bigger problems than crackheads yanking our chain, Garza. Let's just play Mercer's game so he lets us go without any trouble. Sooner we can forget about this place, the better."

But Jed knew he wouldn't be forgetting anything he'd seen today. Not for a long time.

From what he'd seen in the burned house, Jed could no longer deny that the monsters were back. Which meant Mercer was full of shit.

It was only a matter of time before they would spend every second of every day fighting for their lives again. But where were the monsters, and how had they stayed hidden for so long?

— 11 —

Emily felt against Danitha as Angie swerved their course hard to the left. The thing that had leaped at them crashed against the front fender with a screech of claws raking down metal. It hung on, scrambling to get a grip and climb onto the hood. Danitha pushed upright and nearly climbed onto Emily's lap once Angie had them straightened out. She had to shove them both over to maintain control of the truck.

"Y'all stay off!" she hollered at them as they raced in between oil tanks and piping.

The monster tumbled away with a final rake of its claws down the side of the truck, and a shriek that pierced Emily's ears. Mounds of storm debris covered the ground ahead, and she worried more of the things would come out of the shadows at any seconds.

"The hell *was* that?" Angie yelled as she tore a path through the refinery, bumping them over ruts and divots in the dirt.

"One of them monsters," Danitha said. "That's what it was. One of them monsters. Dog one. I saw it. You believe us now, Little Miss Attitude?"

Angie didn't answer. She just kept driving them

around the wreckages of the oil refinery, and Emily was glad to see the girl avoiding areas with lots of high structures. She wove them back and forth across the rough ground, around piles of split tree trunks and broken cars, trash, and the ruins of buildings. They were surrounded by all the debris that a super storm leaves in its wake. And Emily knew the monsters were lurking inside or behind it.

Danitha slapped a hand on Emily's arm and tugged. Emily turned to see Danitha pointing off to their right, at the towering structures of the refinery. Small shadowy shapes hopped from tower to tower, and crawled along pipes.

"Angie, get us away from here. Fast!" Emily shouted.

"I'm trying!" she yelled back. "Ain't been into this place yet and I don't know the paths like I do at the one up the road. What are those things?"

"They the damn monsters, girl!" Danitha said. "We told you they back, but here you come with your gun knowing everything about everything."

"Dani!" Emily shouted as she pulled her away from the passenger door. A dog monster leaped at the truck from a mound of debris and smashed into the glass, snarling and scrambling as Angie sped them along.

The monster had one clawed foreleg grabbing around the windshield, and Emily got a close look at the creature's body. It was shaped very like a dog, with a hollowed abdomen and tight ribcage. Its claws even looked more canine than the monsters she had seen when the virus first came.

"Will one of you shoot that fucking thing!" Angie yelled, slapping the pistol into Emily's lap.

Danitha was still pressed up tight against her, but Emily managed to get the gun up and around her.

"Cover your ears, Dani," she said, and Dani reached one hand up to shield her left ear. She kept her head pressed tight against the seat.

"Just fucking shoot it!" Angie screamed again, and swerved them around another pile of splintered tree limbs. More snarling and whining sounds echoed throughout the refinery area and Emily stared in horror as the shadowy figures on the piping and towers all dropped out of sight, heading down, toward ground level.

She looked at the one on the truck. Its face was hidden from view, but it was climbing onto the top of the cab. Emily pulled the trigger and felt an intense pressure in her ears, then a violent ringing. Angie's muffled voice only just cut through the noise.

"You hit it; it's gone! Now let me drive!" she said, pushing her shoulder against Emily's back.

Emily stared at the hole in the window beside Danitha. Bits of glass fell into the truck until they hit a bump and the whole window collapsed in little chips. Emily helped Danitha sit up straight, but kept one arm around her, holding her away from the wind blowing into the cab. The monster's claws had left deep gouges in the dry mud caked around the windshield.

"Told you they was back," Danitha said. "We told you."

"Yeah, and I don't know what you shot, but I know it wasn't no monster. Not like the ones the virus made."

"It was," Emily said. "A new animal type."

"How the hell you know that?"

"I'm a field biologist. I used to study viruses that

affected bats and their ecology. We've seen bat Variants already, and a domesticated canine variety, too. That one looked like a wild canine. The monsters are back."

Angie sniffed and shook her head, like she didn't believe a word Emily had just spoken.

"I am not lying to you, Angie."

"Never said you were, but I'm not sure you ain't lying to yourself about what you saw."

"Dammit girl," Danitha said. "We know what we saw."

"Maybe you do, maybe you don't. Whatever it was, I ain't sticking around to do a meet and greet. They still chasing us?" Angie asked.

Emily checked the truck's mirrors as best she could as they bounced and rattled through the refinery. Small shapes flitted in and around the structures behind them, but nothing was outright chasing them. At least not that she could see.

"I think we got away," she said. "They don't look like they're following us."

"I'm getting back on the road," Angie said, yanking the wheel hard to the right. They swerved around another debris pile, then went over a berm and were on pavement again. Grass stuck up on either side of the roadway, and in the middle. Cars and trucks sat skewed along the shoulder, most of them smashed up like they'd been pushed off the road by something bigger. Some appeared to be drivable, assuming they had fuel in the tank.

Their path was clear enough for Angie to put her foot down, and she did. Soon enough they were racing away from the refinery, heading south, with the fading afternoon sun lighting their way.

Shadows slanted across the road as they passed telephone poles that had survived the storms. Emily stared at each one as they approached, fighting against the urge to see every shadow, and every dark object, as a monster lying in wait. She kept worrying they'd be swarmed by a pack of them, even as Angie relaxed her grip and tapped out a rhythm on the steering wheel with her fingertips.

Emily realized she still held Angie's gun. She wanted to put it down, but worried about it going off.

"Please, take it back," she said to Angie, but the girl would hear none of it.

"No way. You got a kill with it, and your first time, too. That means it's yours. How it works now."

"How what works?" Emily asked, placing the gun in her lap.

"Rules of the Aftermath," Angie said. She continued, explaining how the survivors in this part of Texas had started out as a collective. Everyone doing their share to put things right. Rebuilding, reclaiming, salvaging, and scavenging.

"Somebody called it that, the Aftermath, and pretty soon everyone was saying it. I learned a lot from those folks. How to hunt game, clean it and cook it, and how to stay alive."

"Why are you alone then? What happened?"

"Militia happened."

"You were there, when they came?"

"They didn't come. They were there from the beginning. It was just a bunch of yahoos when it started. Guys who had stockpiled. You know the ones. Always talking about the *End Times* like it would be a good thing.

IKES

Then it happened and they weren't so sure. Didn't want other people taking their stuff. So they set out to be the big fish, so they could say who got what and when."

"Sound a lot like gangbangers," Danitha said. "You know, the ones they was always saying we should be afraid of?"

"Pretty much like that, yeah," Angie said. "They just took over small neighborhoods at first, then bigger ones until they were the only show in town. Army came in finally. A lot of us thought that'd be the end of it. But nope, not for the Lone Star Militia. They didn't even bother asking what the Army was doing here. Just started shooting."

Angie looked off to the left as she spoke, then turned her eyes back to the road ahead. The air blowing in the shattered window chilled the hand Emily had wrapped around Danitha's shoulder. She pulled her closer, away from the chill.

"Y'all lost anybody in this?" Angie asked.

"My parents," Emily said.

"And you?" Angie asked, motioning with her chin toward Danitha.

"Whole damn family. Brothers, sister, my mom. They all got sick with that virus. I didn't have to see it though, and I thank God every night for that mercy."

"What about your father?" Emily asked.

"He was a cop, so he went out to help when it all started. I never saw him again."

Emily turned to Angie. "And you? Did you lose someone?"

She took her time to reply, and when she did it was through tears she struggled to hold in.

"My sister. When—when this all started. She dated a guy. He said he used to be a SEAL, and we believed him. He was big enough for it. When the monsters came, he came for us. Said he'd protect us."

"And?"

"And he didn't. First time a monster showed up, he went all rabbit on us and my sister got killed. Right in front of me."

"How'd you live?" Danitha asked.

"I shot the fucking thing," Angie said. "And then I had to—"

Emily put a hand on Danitha's arm, and motioned with her eyes to drop the subject. Angie didn't need to be put through the misery of reliving horrors.

They drove on for what felt like miles. Overgrown pasture land gave way to more ruined neighborhoods that framed the roadway cutting around Houston. When they passed a road sign, Emily's breath caught in her throat.

"That said Baytown. You told us you weren't taking us to them!" She grabbed at the pistol in her lap, but Angie was faster and knocked it to the floor.

"I'm taking us around the militia camp. Don't worry."

"How can we trust you?" Danitha asked, anger again cutting through her voice.

"Because the Baytown Militia have a price on my head same as the Mont Belvieu one has a price on yours."

"Baytown, Mont Belvieu—How many are there?" Emily asked. "You said Lone Star first."

"That's the big group, the ones in Houston. They mostly control the city and let the other guys run their games in the suburbs and out here."

"What's Baytown want you for?" Danitha asked.

"For that POS who got my sister killed. He brought me there after it happened, and I thought we'd make it okay. They're mostly good folk there. They were happy to have more hands to do the work. That man was big and strong, and said he used to be a SEAL. They believed him, too."

"What happened, *mija?*" Emily asked.

"He told me I reminded him of my sister. Kept telling me until one night I figured out what he meant."

Her hand went to the knife on her hip. Danitha made a sound like she approved. Emily tried to read her face, but Danitha turned to look out the window. They rode the next few minutes in silence except for the whine of the engine and the crunch of the tires over bits of debris in the roadway.

Finally, Angie pulled down an offramp to a frontage road that went between two stands of trees. To the south, it was just a single row of dying and overgrown trees. A forest shrouded the landscape on the other side of the road.

"We can hole up at a house down here," Angie said. "Ain't much of it left, but it'll be shelter for the night."

They traveled a little ways and then Angie turned them onto a lane that took them south, alongside a pasture, and ended in a wide drive in front of a long ranch house shrouded by tall trees. The windows were all broken and the walls were covered with graffiti.

"This place is safe?" Emily asked.

"Safe as can be," Angie said. "Used to be my uncle's place. We get inside, you'll want to stay with me. Don't go wandering off. I got traps all through it."

She drove them around the house, and parked the

truck under trees that hung over a backyard lawn. Most of it was overgrown and rangy, but Emily could see the manicured landscape that once lived beneath. The trees had provided good shelter against the hurricanes coming up from the coast. Storm debris mounded against the trunks, and hung in the branches. But the yard and house were fairly untouched. At least by natural events.

The windows were shattered, and the walls marked up with painted symbols, abbreviated Bible verses, and declarations about the end of the world.

"Folks around here didn't like Uncle Floyd," Angie said. "Thought he was weird because he was a rich man who liked to cook and wasn't married. They didn't even wait for the virus to do it. They just came here one night and killed him. I found him the next day and buried him over there, by his favorite tree."

She pointed to the far side of the yard where Emily could just see a wooden cross made of two broken boards, planted beside a thick tree.

"I better go see if I can get us something to eat. Y'all can wait here in the truck."

Emily and Danitha both nodded.

"I'll try to be back quick. Keep the gun ready," Angie said, reaching down to collect the pistol from the floor. She handed it to Emily, who took it and held it in her lap. Angie opened the door, lifted her rifle, and got out. She closed the door, waved at them and vanished into the growing darkness.

— 12 —

Jed and his squad stood together on Mercer's northern perimeter. The Navy man had hardened things up front, but back here he'd only set in a single line of fence and with no razor wire on top. A thick tree line, full of shadows and debris, marked the end of the neighborhood, just outside the fence. Jed got a chill watching the trees sway in the slight breeze blowing up from the coast. He wanted to believe they were safe, that the monsters were really gone. But it never failed that a flicking leaf or jostled branch would make him do a double take. It was the wind, and he knew it. But after three years of worrying when the next shadow he saw would be the monster that killed him, Jed had to fight the urge to see danger in everything.

"Not much cover around here, Sergeant," Garza said.

Lance Corporals. Always got something to say, Jed thought.

"I see that, Garza," he said, staring into the trees beyond the fence. "Ain't like there's anyone shooting at us either. At least not yet."

He put Garza and Parsons up in the tower with binos. The *tower* was just a platform set back about five yards from the fence. It had been made of old pallets mounted in a grid and supported by posts sunk into the ground. A partially extended aluminum ladder leaned against the platform.

Parsons coughed in disgust. "The towers up front had proper cover, and roofs. The fuck is this hillbilly shit?"

"Mercer put his resources where they'd do the most good for him," Jed said. "He wants people showing up at his front door to think he's hardened the whole place. He's not expecting any threats from this side. Typical warlord mentality. Or maybe he just ran out of fence."

McKitrick and Mehta walked the line from the tower, heading around the neighborhood to the east. Jed and Keoh walked in the other direction, following the fence around the suburban homes. Some were occupied, but most sat empty, half ruined, or completely destroyed. Jed spotted at least two more that had been burned, but without going into them, he couldn't tell if the fires had been deliberate or just one more result of the world ending.

At the corner of the neighborhood, another pair of guards sat on a platform just like the one Garza and Parsons occupied. Jed waved to them, but they didn't return the greeting. One of them spoke into a mic, then went back to watching the trees. Jed could play that game, too, but it wasn't worth the effort.

All they had to do was suffer Mercer's command for a day or so, and then they'd be free to look for Kipler or Jordan's squads. Or, more likely, catch up with Radout. Maybe they could find that hippie, find out what had happened on Galveston, and get back there to help.

If there's anything or anyone left who needs help, Jed thought.

They passed the afternoon in relative silence, with only

radio checks and updates to Mercer breaking the monotony. Parsons tried to raise Kipler and Jordan every hour, but got nothing. If Jed had known the apocalypse was going to be so much like the war in Iraq, he might have stuck it out instead of forcing his leaders to chapter him for bad conduct.

Keoh's radio stopped working around 1730, and her leg started bothering her around the same time.

"Haven't been on my feet this long since Crucible," she said.

"I can get the battery. You stay here with Garza and them."

Keoh wasn't having it. She'd never been one to let her injury result in special treatment, and she wasn't about to start now.

"I'll race you, Sergeant," she said, moving out at a slow jog.

Jed joined her, enjoying the momentary challenge after the shit day they'd had. They got the battery and were back on the fence line just as daylight faded into dusk. The forest now had extra shadows, and Jed had to force himself to stare into the growing dark, to convince himself nothing would happen.

"Almost done, y'all," Jed called to his people as all three teams met near the tower. They had maybe five minutes before their shift ended, and he'd already seen Mercer's relief teams coming up the street. They'd just past the burned house with the Jamaican flag.

A gunshot split the air behind him and Jed whirled around to see Garza slapping Parsons's shoulder, then grabbing his body armor and hauling him around.

"Fucking boot! What're you shooting at? There's

nothing out there!"

"Garza!" Jed hollered. "Chill out. Parsons, what the fuck? Did you see something? Unless it's about to kill you, get confirmation before you shoot."

"Oorah, Sergeant. Thought it was a sucker face. In that tree there."

He pointed at a thick tree with gnarled limbs sprawling and twisting in every direction, like some wild tentacle beast standing in the middle of the woods.

Jed climbed onto the platform and got between Garza and Parsons. "Let me see," he said, lifting the binos they'd been using. He scanned the woods, checking every shadow, every shape, until he was certain nothing was out there. He gave the binos to Parsons and was about to remind the kid to maintain better weapon discipline when the forest erupted with birds taking flight. Hundreds of them, small and large, burst from the trees and scattered, cawing and chirping like mad.

A low growling came from the tree line. Jed checked his people. They'd all heard it.

"Back to the street. Move back," he ordered, pushing Parsons toward the ladder. He let the private get down first, then followed, jumping down the last few feet to the ground.

Jed thought about calling in to Mercer, but he didn't have a visual to report. If it turned out to be an animal, he'd be killing their chances at getting released from duty in the neighborhood. Even with just a few minutes in the guy's presence, Jed knew that Mercer was the kind of officer who'd pile on the work for even the smallest fuck up. Still, if Jed was right about the threat…

"Somebody, let Mercer know what's up. Tell him we

got possible contacts out here."

"On it," Mehta said. He relayed the message, then said, "Relief team's coming up the street, Sergeant."

Jed forced himself to look away from the fence line and glanced over his shoulder. Mercer's teams were at the end of the street now, watching Jed's squad and talking together. One of them stepped forward and called out to Jed.

"Does your guy need some remedial? What's up with the ND we heard?"

The other guards laughed and Jed was about to flip them the finger when Keoh's startled voice stopped him dead.

"*Sergeant Welch!*"

He spun to see her taking aim at something. She hadn't fired yet. McKitrick and Mehta had their weapons up a few paces away and were scanning the forest for movement. Even Parsons was squared away this time. Garza stepped forward, to be in line with Keoh. Jed joined them and they each covered a zone of fire beyond the wire. They all stood about ten yards from the fence, but in the gathering dark, the forest kept its secrets wrapped up tight.

"Anybody got movement?" Jed asked. Nobody confirmed, so he ordered them all to fall back and make room for their relief.

"False alarm?" one of Mercer's guards said as the teams approached.

Jed didn't answer, just gave the guy an eye full of attitude for his trouble.

Something slammed into the fence and rebounded into the tree line. Parsons was jittery as fuck, shaking where he stood. Jed put a hand on the kid's shoulder.

"Easy, Parsons. Eyes on your zone, and wait for contact before you fire."

"R—rah, Sergeant."

Keoh shouted again, and fired. Garza opened up with a burst, too.

"*You got contact?*" Jed yelled at them. "*What're you shooting at?*"

He could hear Mercer's guards readying their weapons behind him. Soon enough they were in line with Jed's squad, moving out to either side in two-man teams. Altogether they had a dozen weapons aimed at the tree line.

One of Mercer's men stepped forward, closer to the ladder for the guard tower.

"I see something moving out there," he said.

Another of Mercer's people moved up to join the first man.

The forest exploded with movement. Dark shapes flung themselves forward, crashing into the fence. Others launched from the lower branches of trees, and came streaking into the safety of the wire. Everyone fired, sending rounds into the onrushing horde, but Jed saw the futility of trying to hold their ground.

"Fall back! Back! Everyone move!" he yelled as he fired at the forms emerging from the woods in a steady flood. Small crumpled bodies mounded on the soil beside the guard tower and at the base of the fence. But even more got through, and Mercer's men near the tower disappeared under a swarm of snarling, spitting beasts.

Jed's squad backpedaled fast, firing as they moved. Garza and Mehta had joined two of Mercer's men and moved in tandem, running and covering as they went.

They reached the street, and Jed counted his people as the bullets flew downrange.

Keoh and McKitrick had teamed up. Jed had Parsons with him; Garza and Mehta were still with Mercer's guys. He couldn't see the other sailors, but he heard their screams from near the fence line.

As one, Jed's squad and the remains of Mercer's watch teams made a retreat into the neighborhood, passing the burned house, then the house with the crackhead standing out front still wearing his sunglasses and leaning against the wall like he was watching a parade.

"I told you. It's cool here," he said. Jed couldn't believe it. The guy lifted a hand to his mouth and popped something in, like a piece of candy.

"Get inside! Shelter in place!" Jed yelled. If the junkie heard him, he didn't show it. He just stood there grinning like an idiot. A small dark shape separated from the entrance to the house and moved toward him. Jed pivoted to shoot, but the shape turned out to be a dog that sat behind the guy in the shadows. He leaned down and said something to the animal, then they both went back into the house. Jed watched them go, trying to get a better look at the dog. It moved with a weird hop, like it was missing a leg.

Gunfire erupted from behind them and off to both sides, and Jed gave up on the crackhead to lay down covering fire with Garza. Keoh led the other members of the squad, bounding from cover to cover and putting more distance between them and the skittering monsters that darted around the street.

Shouting mixed with the rattle and pop of small arms

in every direction. Screams filled the air, and the two men from Mercer's guard turned and ran.

Jed yelled for his people as he turned to follow. "Hellhounds, rally at the supply point!"

Dark shapes sprang up on rooftops to his left. They crawled forward in groups of four or five.

"Rooftops! Take 'em down!" he yelled.

They fired in teams, focusing on their zones to cover their retreat. One by one, the small creatures slid off the roofs in lifeless heaps. But more shadowy figures appeared right behind them, only to spring down to the ground and stalk forward like a pack of hunting wolves.

The things weren't any bigger than dogs, but Jed couldn't get a good look at them to tell exactly what they were. The screams that echoed around the neighborhood told him enough, though.

Keoh had been right. The Variants had returned, and they'd evolved again.

Jed and his squad ran in two-person teams, shooting down clusters of the small monsters as they leaped from rooftops or sprang around the side of houses. The squad leapfrogged to trash and debris piles, moving fast and only pausing to provide covering fire. They reached the corner and saw Mercer's guards up ahead, firing at shadowy figures that had climbed on top of a house. They kept shooting even as a small swarm of the monsters crawled onto a roof across the street. Jed yelled for the men to turn around.

He fired at the monsters, but the dim light and their speed made it impossible to hit them at this distance. By the time the sailors noticed them, the monsters were already on their backs and bringing them to the ground.

The men screamed and thrashed, and then went still as the beasts fed on them.

"*The fuck are those things?*" Mehta shrieked as he shot at them.

"Variants!" Keoh said. She fired at a cluster of them charging across a lawn in her direction. "I knew it! They're back!"

Jed ordered them all to keep moving. The supply point was at the end of the next block. He had no idea what kind of munitions Mercer had there, but the house and garage were intact. They would provide shelter and equipment.

He and Parsons directed their fire at groups of the monsters coming at them. Garza and McKitrick took out another bunch when they were still a few yards away. Jed couldn't see any other movement after that, but screams and gunfire continued to echo around them. In just a few minutes, the whole neighborhood had gone hot. The things had to be coming in from every direction.

We may not have a way out of this, Jed thought.

The sun lowered to the bottom of the sky, and darkness crept in around them.

A vicious howl and guttural snarl froze them all in their tracks. The rooftops around them sprouted more dark shapes, crouched and stalking toward the eaves.

A larger shape emerged from the shadows behind them, at the corner they'd just turned. It separated from a pack of the smaller monsters and pushed its way through the growing ranks of the beasts on the street. Jed didn't want to believe what he was seeing. It was a Variant, a human one with a sucker face, claws, and clicking joints. The monster wore the tattered shreds of a tee-shirt. Jed couldn't see much more in the near darkness around them.

The sucker face snarled and gave a sharp bark, then reared up and howled. The smaller ones around it all joined in, braying to the sky.

"McKitrick," Jed said. "You got the 203 loaded, right?"

"Rah, our only HE round," she said.

"Do it; then we run."

McKitrick fired into the mass of monsters. As the squad ran with all they had, the round erupted behind them, sending a gust of heat over their backs, followed by the shrill barks and growls of the monstrous horde that chased them down the street.

— 13 —

Emily and Danitha waited in the silence. Night sounds filtered into the cab through the broken window. Danitha snugged herself closer to Emily as the last slivers of light faded from the sky.

"She left us here," Danitha said. "Run off with that gun of hers and left us here."

"She'll be back."

"You think? And what if she ain't? What if that gun she left you ain't got any bullets left in it? Let me see it."

Danitha had the pistol out of Emily's hand before she could blink. Fatigue had come for its due; Emily's hands were lead spoons in her lap.

"Dani, please," she said, hoping the woman would settle down. But Danitha's anxiety was equal to Emily's exhaustion. She aimed the pistol out the window and pulled the trigger. The gunshot cracked loud in the confined truck cab, and both of them jumped with fright. Danitha put the gun on the dashboard and leaned back against the seat.

Another gunshot sounded in the night, followed by two more. Emily clenched her fists, digging her nails into her palms.

A shape emerged from the trees at the edge of the yard. It moved slowly, and at first Emily couldn't think to do anything but stare at it. Then Danitha had the pistol in her hands again, and was pointing it toward the figure in the darkness.

"Dani, no!" Emily shouted, pushing the gun aside.

Angie appeared at the driver's door, lugging something behind her. She opened the door and leaned halfway into the cab.

"Y'all get spooked at something? What'd you shoot for?"

Neither of them answered, and Angie shook her head at Danitha. "Be careful with that thing. Should be the professor holding it anyway. It's her gun, remember?"

Danitha took a shuddering breath and lowered the gun into Emily's lap. She took it, making sure to swivel the safety catch down. Chava had shown her how to do that on the same day he'd shown her the magazine for his rifle. She found it odd the things she remembered now, with so much of her life gone and so much of his around her every second. Danger, fear, worry, and threat.

"Can we go inside?" she asked Angie.

The girl nodded.

"Got us a gator for dinner. Just a little one, but the tail's got at least two pounds of meat on it."

They got out of the truck and followed Angie into the house. She led them through a maze of debris, occasionally lifting aside a tree branch or a chunk of broken roof that lay up against the house.

Inside, she brought them to the fireplace, which stood in the middle of the house, against a rotting kitchen wall. Parts of the upstairs floor were missing, and metal ducting had been rigged up to exhaust the fumes through an upstairs window.

"Chimney's blocked up by birds. Took me a while to figure out how to vent the smoke," Angie said, as she dragged the dead alligator across the floor. "But this place is safe, so long as you stay with me and don't go wandering around the rooms."

Emily met Angie's eyes and did her best to communicate she understood, but the words faded from her thoughts before she could utter them.

"Y'all look about ready to fall over, so why don't you do that?" Angie said.

She pointed at two mattresses that stood out amidst all the filth and wreckage. They weren't clean, but they looked like actual beds with sheets and pillows piled on them.

"Got those from upstairs. Go on and catch a few winks. I'll wake you up when food's ready."

Emily was already on the mattress, sitting. She felt Danitha sit down beside her. Seconds after her head sank into the comfort of a real pillow, she let sleep carry her away from everything she had suffered over the past two days.

When Emily awoke, it was to the smell of roasting meat. The room was lit by a warm glow, and a mild tangy scent wove through the odor of charcoal and crackling fat. Emily put a hand out to push herself up when a familiar chittering filled the night air outside. She froze and searched the room for movement.

Angie sat beside the hearth, where a small fire burned, sending smoke pluming into the metal ducting.

"Did you hear that?" Emily asked. "The bats are outside."

"Yeah, I know. They're always out there eatin' bugs. Between them and being covered in mud, I haven't been bit by a mosquito in months."

Emily wanted to believe her, but she couldn't shake the fear that the bat monsters would swarm into the room any second.

"They never come inside?" she asked.

"Nah. Not enough for them to hunt in here. Bugs get in, sure, but there's plenty more outside."

Emily wondered if that was the reason, or if it was because the bats simply hadn't found Angie hiding in here yet.

"You hungry?" Angie asked as she stirred the fire beside her.

A chunk of meat sat above the flames on a spit. Angie turned it once, then shaved some off with her knife. She put it on a cloth napkin she lifted from her lap and handed it over to Emily.

"Regular picnic, ain't it?" Angie said, with enough of a smile that Emily let herself feel relieved they had found the girl. Or that she had found them. Maybe the bats outside were just bats. Maybe they'd found safety after all.

"Thank you," she said, taking the food from Angie. Danitha sat up next to her and leaned forward to inspect the meal Angie had made.

They ate in silence at first, until Emily felt ready to speak.

"You've survived this way for months now?"

"Yeah," Angie said. "Actually glad I ran into y'all. Didn't realize how lonely I was after—"

Emily waited, letting Angie find the strength to continue.

"Was only supposed to be at that gas station for one night. Sat down to clean my rifle when them guys in the Humvee showed up. I had to bug out fast and forgot to grab my magazine. Guess that was fate playing with us."

"Maybe God had a plan for us," Danitha said.

Angie sniffed at that. "Hope it's better than the one he had making that virus."

Emily said, "Where did you go? When those men came?"

"Refinery. Not the one we went through. Farther up the road. I had a hide up there, under the pipes. Got the truck wedged in so good, nobody could spot it. I was worried they'd find me because they had a dog with them. It was making all manner of noise and racket, and one of them yelled about it not *obeying* proper. He shot it and then they left in their Hummer."

"It wasn't a dog," Danitha said.

"How do you know?"

"It was the ones after us. Same as we saw in that last town. They had a Humvee, too…"

Danitha paused and looked to Emily for support. Angie looked between them.

"Go on and do your telling," she said.

"They are using them as dogs," Emily said. "But they're not dogs anymore. They're like the monsters from the refinery. The virus has changed them."

Angie stared at her, chewing on a chunk of alligator meat. She shook her head.

"No way. I been out here long enough, I'd have seen one. Hell, I'd be dead by now probably. I don't know what y'all saw or what came chasing us in the refinery, but it wasn't the monsters."

Emily couldn't tell if Angie simply didn't want to accept it, or if she really thought Emily was lying. But it wasn't worth fighting about. Not now. They'd had some sleep, and they were filling their bellies for the road ahead. Their water wouldn't last for long, but with luck they'd find more.

"We should get to Galveston as fast as possible," Emily said. "I don't know how long my brother will be there. But it's only been a week since I heard from him. I have to trust that he is still there."

"Trust'll get you far in the Aftermath," Angie said. "Unless you trust wrong. Then it'll get you dead. Or worse."

"How about we forget the *worse* talk," Danitha said, "and get on with how we gon' get to Galveston. We ain't even halfway there yet."

"Truck only has another few miles in it. We use it up, then we walk until we find another ride. Shouldn't be long, but we'll want to get an early start. Leave before sun-up, and that ain't too far off."

"What time is it?" Danitha asked.

"Almost five now. I let y'all sleep a good six, seven hours. You needed it."

"Thank you," Emily said.

"Don't mention it."

They ate some more, quietly passing the napkin back and forth until the alligator tail was gone.

After they'd finished, Danitha asked again about their plans to reach Galveston. "How do you know we'll find another truck after that one outside runs dry?"

"I don't. Might be a car, or a van. Or a damn tractor trailer. Only thing that matters is the gas ain't rotted yet. We're spoiled for choice in case you ain't noticed. Cars up and down the roads all around—"

She stopped and put her food down. Angie moved so fast Emily could hardly tell what she was doing. She reached up into the chimney and pulled something. A large metal mixing bowl dropped down, and Angie caught it, placing it over the spit and glowing coals. Wisps of smoke curled around the edges of the bowl.

Angie turned to them as she grabbed her rifle. She put a finger over her lips, then pointed toward the front of the house. Emily and Danitha sat still and watched as Angie left the room, stalking forward with her rifle up.

A shrill whistle sliced into the room from outside, and was followed by a snarling and screeching, then a shout.

Danitha flew backwards, away from Emily, and plastered herself against the wall beside the mattresses.

"They found us, and they brought them things. They brought the dog things."

"Maybe they brought dogs, but that don't mean they're gonna get us," Angie said. She was at the windows in the next room, looking outside. She lifted her rifle and fired two quick shots, then dropped to her knees and crawled out of view. Gunfire exploded outside, crackling and sending bits of wood and chips of glass flying into the room that Angie was in. Emily grabbed for the pistol on the floor, and pointed it toward the windows, but the trigger wouldn't move.

More gunfire peppered the night. Every time the house was struck, Emily jolted, fearing the eventual pain of being hit herself.

A snarl sounded outside, and then a bark that mixed with a screech.

Angie shouted something, then fired again. A man's voice cried out in pain, but was quickly drowned out by more gunfire.

Bullets sprayed into the front room, and some came through the doorway into the room where Emily and Danitha hid. Angie came crawling in from the other side of the room, from a doorway that led to the kitchen.

"Y'all want to get killed? Get down!" she yelled at them.

Emily nodded, and pushed Danitha to a prone position, then moved to lie down beside her. Angie was shooting again, as more bullets ripped into the wood around the windows. Splinters and dust rained into the room, mixing with the trails of smoke still curling from under the metal bowl covering their cooking fire.

A fiery hot pain shocked Emily's arm and she rolled away from it, fearing that somehow the fire had been spread and they would all burn alive. Then she felt the wet heat of blood soaking into her clothing.

She screamed and clutched at the hole in her coat where a dark stain rapidly spread, and the pain threatened to consume her.

"Put pressure on it!" Angie shouted from where she crouched by the windows. "Keep it covered and put pressure on it! Stop the bleeding!"

Angie lifted up and fired again, then twice more. She was by Emily's side a second later, pulling some fabric out of her pocket and slicing it with her knife. She wadded up a piece and pressed it over the wound in Emily's arm, then used the other piece to tie the bandage on. Emily cried out, but forced herself to breathe as steady as she could. Danitha sat beside her, holding the pistol aimed into the next room.

"You can relax," Angie said. "I got 'em all."

Danitha lowered the gun and met Emily's eyes. "You okay, Professor?"

Emily tried to answer, but the pain in her arm turned her words into a strangled groan.

Angie put a hand on her forehead, like a mother comforting a child. "We'll get you stitched up later. Right now, we gotta go. Only three of them out there. Like I said; I got 'em all. But they had to get here somehow, and that means they brought us our next ride. So let's go."

Emily nodded, and turned to Danitha. She'd sat back against the wall and was staring up at the ceiling. Emily followed her gaze to a hole in the floor above and her breath caught.

A dog monster perched at the lip of the hole, staring down at them with its teeth bared and a sickly growl coming from its throat. Angie screamed a curse as the monster leaped forward with a hideous shriek.

— 14 —

Jed's squad tore down the street, heading straight for the supply point. Gunfire rattled around them, mixed with howling, screeching, and screams. Somewhere out there, Jed knew civilians were being attacked by the monsters, but he had no hope of surviving unless he got his people to shelter, and fast. Garza was down to his last magazine, and the rest of the squad was burning through their ammo as well. They only had gas or smoke rounds left for McKitrick's 203, plus a few frags between the rest of them. Jed felt the fear of failure creeping in. His squad was counting on him, and he'd ordered them to retreat. To run away.

Can't let doubt get in the way, he thought. *Gotta return fire, find shelter.*

Mercer's supply was just ahead on the left. Jed risked a look over his shoulder as he ran. The monsters were still after them, but the horde had shrunk. He counted maybe a dozen or so on their tail. Smaller groups peeled off to the side, bounding over lawns, and into the remains of ruined houses. Some leaped onto rooftops and let out howls while others raced forward, swarming the neighborhood with their screeches and growls.

Jed fired at two of the monsters that had mounted a car parked in a driveway. He hit the car first, and the things jumped off, joining the group that chased the squad.

They reached the supply point, but the garage door was closed.

"Front door!" Jed shouted. "Stack on me! Garza, keep 'em off our six!"

Jed raced up the front walk, and slammed his boot into the door above the handle. It flew open with a splintered crash and rebounded off of something as Jed pushed his way into the house. He checked his near corner and ran his wall, pacing forward to post by a hall leading off the entryway. McKitrick and Parsons had come in after him and posted to his left, by an overturned couch. She ran the wall to the far corner before flashing a quick thumbs up. Parsons stayed just inside the door, with his muzzle covering the space behind the couch.

Garza and Mehta rushed inside, with Garza still firing in bursts. Mehta's rifle cracked as he covered a zone to their right. Together, they picked off the last of the monsters that had been after them.

Jed scanned the room they'd entered.

The couch was against the front wall, beneath a large window. It had been pushed closer to the entrance, and had blocked the door from opening all the way when Jed kicked it in.

"Get that couch. Block the door," he said. Garza and Mehta came fully into the house, and closed the door. McKitrick and Parsons slid the couch across it, holding it shut.

"It's a poor man's barricade, but it'll slow them down. Keep back from the windows, y'all. Don't let 'em see us in here."

The squad shrank into the corner between the entry and the hall that led deeper into the house.

Straight ahead from the door was a larger room with the remains of a TV hanging off the wall. The back wall of that room faced onto the yard behind the house. Sheets of plywood had been used to partially cover the sliding glass door, but one pane was still intact. Jed could see muzzle bursts outside, in the yards between the houses. He was about to order the squad to move that way to help when screaming replaced the gunfire. The only sounds after that were snarling and growling.

"Sergeant," Parsons said. "I got blood here."

Jed turned to where Parsons was standing, beside the hallway. Thick splatters followed a trail into the darkness. A smeared handprint marked the wall as well.

"Eyes up, everyone. Garza, Mehta; y'all got our six. Parsons, with me. Let's go."

The hall grew dark as pitch the farther they moved into it, until Jed could only just make out the corner where the floor met the wall. Before the monsters were confirmed, he would have chanced using his flashlight. But now, it was better not to see than to risk being seen.

As they moved ahead, Jed caught more sounds from outside. A door had to be open somewhere, because he could hear the crack of nearby gunfire mixed with screeching. Then, as before, screams replaced the shooting, and were followed by an ugly silence. Underneath it though, and closer, Jed caught a moaning of someone in pain.

"Might have contact here, might have wounded. Keep sharp."

The squad continued, stepping slow, until Parsons gave a startled cry.

Jed swiveled to this right, and found himself looking into the garage, at Mercer's supply shelves. Weak light sliced into the garage through the narrow windows in the main door. Jed couldn't see the person, but someone was in there, and they were injured. A weak groan came across the space, followed by a sound Jed hadn't heard in over a year, a sort of sucking and snarling. It was a sound he had hoped never to hear again.

He moved into the garage, going down a short step to stand on the concrete floor. Remembering their visit earlier, he knew that the shelves in front of him were stuffed with wet weather gear. The next set of shelves to his left had the radios on them, with MREs on the other side. The construction equipment was on the last two sets of shelves, by a door that led outside. That was where the noises came from.

Jed tapped Parsons on the shoulder, signaling him to follow. He whispered over his shoulder for McKitrick and Keoh to stay at the door, and to tell Garza and Mehta to keep watch in the hall.

The sucking sounds grew louder, and the moaning stopped. Parsons waited behind him, and Jed could feel the fear radiating off the kid. He put his hand back, pressing on Parsons's chest.

"Hang back," he whispered.

Jed paced forward one step, then two. He waited. The noises continued, so he moved again, slow and sure. One step, then two. He pivoted to his right, aiming down the last aisle between the shelves and the garage wall. A shadowy form, like a lump, sat beside the door, hunched over something else.

Jed took aim, fired once, then twice. He sent one more round in to be sure the thing was dead. Then he called his squad forward.

"Close the door into the house. Barricade it and then we'll get lights on so we can see what we're dealing with."

Keoh was behind him and flicked her red lens on. "Glad it was him," she said.

Jed turned his light on and looked at the body. It was the Petty Officer who couldn't keep his eyes off Keoh and McKitrick. The monster had chewed a hole in his chest.

"Where's the sucker face?" he asked, roving the floor with his light. A trail of blood marked a path toward the front of the garage.

"Shit, it's still alive!"

Screams erupted from one aisle over, then a rattle of gunfire that impacted on the garage ceiling. Jed raced around the shelves. "It's on Parsons!" he yelled as he rounded the shelving and his light showed him the monster wrapped around Parsons's neck, with its face buried into his collar. The private's body slumped against the shelving, then slid down to the floor. Jed followed the monster's movement down, firing as he tracked it. He saw it jerk with the shots until it fell away from Parsons and lay still in the growing pool of blood.

Jed roared his anger. The others were there now. Someone was checking Parsons, but Jed knew he'd fucked up. He'd failed Parsons, letting him hang behind as he stalked forward on his own. He'd forgotten his training and his battle sense, and Parsons was dead because of it.

"He's gone," Garza said.

Keoh or McKitrick said something then, and everyone had their lights on, scanning the shelves, top to bottom, checking for more of the things.

Jed was too angry to focus. He stalked back to the sailor's body. He wanted to kick him in the teeth, to let out his rage at having been led into this place by the man's dying moans. He'd been a useless pogue, just an idiot in a uniform, and now Jed had lost a man because he thought the idiot was worth saving from the monsters.

"Sergeant?" Keoh said. "I'm sorry."

Jed turned to see her standing behind him, a look of shame on her face.

"What for?"

"I should've checked on Parsons, made sure he was good. I pushed by him after I heard you shoot. I wanted to see if this dude was dead, and—"

Jed was in her face in a flash. "Listen up. I'm the reason he's dead. Me. Not you. Not even him. I fucked up."

She nodded, and Jed let that be enough. Maybe she didn't believe it yet, and maybe she never would. But the monsters were still attacking the neighborhood out there, and Jed still had four people counting on him.

"Mehta, can you get Parsons's tags and ammo?" he asked.

"Rah, Sergeant. And his grenade."

"Grab the radio, too. Just swap packs. Move whatever you need from yours. Make it quick."

Mehta mumbled *Errr*, and set to work.

"Rest of y'all, grab whatever chow and water you can. See what Mercer was hoarding in here."

"I'ma ratfuck his whole MRE stash," Garza said.

"Just get what you can carry. We're safe inside for now, but we can't stay in here. Gear up, then we move out. There's people outside who need help."

"Sergeant," McKitrick said. "I think Mercer's people lost. Can't you hear them?"

"Who?" Jed asked. He gave his attention to the world outside the garage for the first time since he let Parsons die. The gunfire had slowed down. A few cracks and short bursts came across the night before going silent. The snarling and screeching remained, and sounded like it came from every house in the area. The only thing Jed didn't hear anymore was human screaming.

"They're all dead, Sergeant," McKitrick said. "We go out there, it'll be the same for us."

Jed went back to where Parsons was lying. The sucker face was there, curled up in death. He kicked it to turn it over and slapped a hand over his mouth. The thing looked almost exactly like a pitbull until you got to its head. The face was longer than a pit's, and the mouth had needle teeth all along the jaw line, and sticking out around the muzzle. Its tongue lolled out of its mouth like a dead snake.

A loud thump on the roof snapped everyone's attention upward. Jed aimed and was about to fire when a second thump sounded. A third followed, and then a swarm of them came, bumping and scrabbling across the rooftop.

A shrill whistle echoed across the night and Jed felt his stomach turn.

"What the hell was that?" Garza asked.

The whistling continued, and Jed could swear he heard men's voices calling in the night.

"C'mon now! Time to go!"

"Good dog!"

"C'mon now, boys! C'mon!"

The thumping on the roof became a din of skittering and scraping claws. Soon, the entire neighborhood echoed with the cries and braying of predators on the hunt.

Jed looked at his people, one at a time, meeting their eyes. He saw in their faces everything he felt in his own chest: the resolve he'd come to expect, but not without a measure of fear.

Mehta wiped a tear from his cheek. "Sergeant, what the fuck did we just hear?"

"Something that shouldn't be real. Something crazy," Jed said.

"There's people working with those things," Keoh said. *"People!"*

"I know!" Jed hollered. "I seen it in New York. Makes sense that's not the only place that had collaborators. But this is different. In New York, the Variants were the masters. Shoe's on the other foot in Texas, I guess."

"We're so fucked," Garza said.

"We are not," Jed shot back. "We shelter in place. Use the gear in here to harden things up. If they find us, we give 'em hell until there's nothing left to give. If they don't, we leave in the morning. Let's move Parsons and the other ones inside if we can."

With nods and quiet grunts of agreement, his people went to work. Jed breached the door going into the house and confirmed the hall was clear. Then he went carefully inside and barricaded the front door with more furniture from the room with the television. He could still hear the monsters howling and snarling in the dark outside, but they were moving away.

Jed went back to the garage and grabbed the dead sucker face by the hind legs. He flung it into the front room of the house. When he got back to the others, he helped Mehta move Parsons's body inside. A door down the hall led to a master bedroom with an actual bed in it. They put Parsons there with his arms crossed over his rifle on his chest. On their way back to the garage, they ran into Keoh. She was hauling the dead sailor into the house by herself.

Jed sent Mehta to the garage, to fortify their shelter. Then he helped Keoh carry the sailor into the bathtub.

They joined the others and worked as fast as they could to barricade the main garage door, side door, and the door back to the house. They left that one the easiest to breach, in case they needed to retreat inside.

By the time they'd finished, they had stacked bags of concrete around the smaller doors. The shelves were moved to prevent access through the side door and main door.

"Two on watch at a time. Two hours," Jed said. "McKitrick, Garza; you're first. Wake up Keoh and me next."

His Marines acknowledged the order with muffled *Errs.*

The center of the floor was empty except for the puddle of Parsons's blood. Jed opened a sack of concrete and spread it over the mess. Then he lay down beside it, and did his best to let sleep take him from this place and its horrors.

— 15 —

As the monster came down at them, Emily pushed herself backwards with her legs, still holding her wounded arm. Angie's arm moved upward, and Emily saw the monster wrap its claws around Angie's hand as it bit at her face. The girl fell onto her back, and the monster followed her to the floor. They landed with a crash in front of the fireplace, then both figures lay motionless.

Danitha was behind Emily, but came forward now. "Is it dead? Is she dead?"

"No," Angie's shaking voice answered. "But I'm hurt. Get it off me. Please."

Emily moved off the mattress and shuffled on her knees to where Angie lay beneath the dead monster.

"Help me, Dani," she said, slowly reaching with her good arm to grab the creature. Touching its skin made her recoil, but she steeled herself and got a grip around its neck.

"Just pull it off," Angie said. "Fast. Please."

With a jerk, Emily yanked the thing away from Angie, and the girl's scream pierced her heart. Her knife was stuck in the monster's chest up to the hilt. She'd killed it, but two thick cuts marked her shoulder where its claws had sunk in. Blood jetted and poured from the wound. Her hand and wrist were cut up, too, but her shoulder got the worst of it. Emily put her good hand over the wounds, but the blood kept coming, and she knew they couldn't help Angie.

"Make a sling," Angie said, her voice growing weaker and shaking. "For your arm—use the curtains. Front room by the…"

Danitha came over and took the girl's hand in her own. Emily pressed harder with her hand, even though she knew it was futile. "*Mija*, no, you stay with us. Stay here. You helped us. We will help you."

"Look for traps," Angie said. "Next to cars. Usually on the driver side."

"What traps, Angela? What do you mean?"

"Militia…traps cars that have gas in 'em. Catch people outside their wire. Find a trapped car…find a ride. Get on…Galveston."

Angie's eyes rolled up and she shook for a moment before she stopped breathing.

After some time spent sitting in the dark, over Angie's body, Emily stood in a daze. She went to the dead monster and pulled Angie's knife from its chest. She wiped the blade on its side, then walked into the front room and tried to slice enough fabric from the curtains to make a sling for her arm. Danitha came to help.

"I ain't hurt yet. Let me do it," she said.

Emily gave her the knife and went back to the mattresses to wait. She stared at Angie's face, so peaceful and quiet in death. The girl had scared her when they'd met. Emily cursed herself for doubting Angie's sincerity, for thinking that she would betray them.

She had saved their lives, and ultimately gave her own life to do it.

Danitha brought a strip of the curtains in and fashioned a sling to hold Emily's arm against her chest. Moving her arm caused more pain than she thought possible. She felt her eyes close, and snapped awake to find herself lying on the mattress with her arm in agony.

"Dani, I can't do this. My arm is broken."

"My turn to push us, I guess," Danitha said. "Ain't a question of can or can't, Professor. Just a question of do or don't. C'mon and let's get going."

Emily opened her mouth to speak, but held back. She had words she wanted to say. And none of them felt good. Nothing that found its way to her tongue would be helpful now, so she simply nodded her agreement.

"Okay, Professor. Let's see about what she was saying. How the militia guys who came here must've had a car. And if they don't, then we go looking for cars with traps, just like she said."

Emily hesitated, wanting to do nothing but scream at the world.

"C'mon now. Don't be wasting Angela's sacrifice. She gave herself, and we need to respect that."

"You—you're right," Emily finally said. Choking back tears and anger, she let her arm rest in the sling Dani had made. There would be time to grieve and mourn. Time to cry, and time to scream at God.

Danitha picked up both of Angie's guns. She held the pistol out to Emily, who took it and slid it into her coat pocket. Danitha held the rifle in both hands, just like Angie had done. She led the way out of the house, going into the rooms Angie had been in when the shooting happened. They moved slowly and carefully, with Danitha looked at every piece of floor she stepped on in case one of Angie's traps was there.

Outside, the sky hung above them like a shroud. Emily could make out the boxy shapes of abandoned vehicles along the frontage road they'd taken to get here. Somewhere in the tangle of cars and trucks might be the militia vehicle. Or maybe the attackers had walked here, just like Emily and Danitha had done.

All they had to do was get through Baytown and across the water to LaPorte. From there, they would follow the highway south to Texas City. Driving or walking, they would get there. She would see her brother again, and they would be safe.

They stood in front of the house until the sun crawled high enough to illuminate the ground better. Three dark shapes lay in the pasture. Two near the edge closest to the house, and a third farther back, near the road. A black truck was parked beside the fence there.

"See, that girl wasn't lyin'," Danitha said. "Militia brought our ride to us."

Emily had to fight to keep from falling to her knees. Her fatigue, and the pain of her injury threatened to overwhelm her with every step. But she kept on, trailing only a few feet behind Danitha as she went to each of the men Angie had killed. She stripped them of their ammunition first, then searched their pockets. She found the keys on the body closest to the road.

"Bingo. Now we got a ride out of here," she said.

Emily looked at the dead man by her feet. His unshaven face was sprayed with blood from a wound high in his chest. Some of the blood had gotten into his eyes.

She looked closer and nearly stumbled backwards as she reeled away from the dead Variant.

"Dani—Dani, his eyes!"

They were yellow, veined with blood. His lips bulged out just enough to remind Emily of the monsters that had eaten the world, but his teeth were still normal. Emily drew the gun from her coat and pointed it at the dead man's face. She crouched and moved closer, so she could see his mouth better.

Tiny needle-like teeth protruded from his gums, above his human teeth.

Dani shivered and stepped away from the body. "Professor, what are they? Tell me they just dead men. Please."

"They are monsters, Dani. New ones."

She looked at the man's body, examining it for more signs that he had been infected with the virus. His hands were still human, and his joints all seemed to be normal as well. She prodded his knee with the pistol, to see if it would click. The leg moved like a human leg. Emily stood up and staggered away from the corpse, still holding the gun aimed at its face. She noticed the man's uniform then. He was dressed like Chava, in the same camouflage and boots. It could have been a militia creep who had stolen the uniform from a real Marine, but Emily couldn't shake the feeling that she was looking at one of Chava's brothers.

"We gotta go, Professor," Dani said. She'd moved away and was looking into the truck.

Emily joined her and they climbed in. The engine was

still warm. It fired right up when Danitha turned the key. She had them back on the main highway quickly, traveling south at a good speed, and only slowed down to avoid debris or vehicles that hadn't been pushed off the road.

"Tank is half full," Danitha said. "That should get us to Galveston."

For the first time since they had escaped, Emily felt a dread that their plan was going to be all for nothing. If the dead men had all been Marines, and they were all infected, would her brother be also? Would she see him again, and would they be safe with him on Galveston? Or would they be going into a trap where her own brother would try to kill her?

She was still thinking this when Danitha muttered a curse.

"Headlights on the road behind us," she said.

"Dani, step on it. Get us out of here."

Danitha stomped down on the gas and the truck surged forward. Emily gripped the dashboard and braced herself with her feet against the floor. They flew past cars and trucks smashed together along the shoulder. Emily kept looking over her shoulder then back to the road ahead. The lights behind them were getting closer.

Then Danitha shrieked and the truck swerved. Emily spun back to face the windshield in time to see a van burst from a tangle of wrecked cars on the shoulder. A truck with a push bar on the grill shot out from the other side of the road. Danitha slammed on the brakes and Emily only had time to scream before they were struck and she rocked forward. She slammed back into the seat by a third impact from behind.

Men climbed out of the vehicles with guns aimed at them.

One shouted, "Get your hands where we can see 'em! You do anything else, you're dead!"

— 16 —

Jed let Keoh rack out after their guard shift. He thought about waking up Mehta and pulling the last shift with him, but he couldn't bring himself to do it. Instead, he sat up by himself staring at the garage door and daring any of the monsters or the men outside to try getting in. They were still out there, calling their dogs and whistling. The snarls and barks had turned to whines.

After a while, the monsters and their masters were gone. Everything was silent except for Keoh's and Mehta's soft snoring, and Jed's groaning stomach. He should eat, but couldn't imagine doing it. His mind and body only had the energy to sit in the cold stillness.

Occasionally he would glance at the pile of concrete dust in the middle of the floor.

Jed let the others sleep until dawn began to creep in around the cracks in the doors. He woke Garza and Keoh first and had them watch the door back into the house. McKitrick roused herself and went to wake Mehta. When everyone was up, they had a quiet meal, then restocked their packs with as many MREs as they could carry.

"What's our plan, Sergeant," McKitrick asked.

"We check outside, see what's up. If it's clear, we head for Radout's FOB. If it's not, we fight our way out."

With Garza in the lead, they breached the door leading inside and quickly moved down the hall to the entryway. The stink of death filled the house.

Jed took point at the front door after the pushed the couch out of the way. He stepped into the cool morning air with his rifle at the ready. Birds fluttered in the trees nearby. Some smaller ones picked at the ground around the houses. Buzzards would circle then drop down to the street. Jed forced himself to ignore them. He didn't need to see what they were eating.

Every house had been attacked as far as Jed could see. After a few steps down to the sidewalk, he let his weapon hang against his chest. There was nothing to shoot. No threat to respond to.

Bodies littered the ground. Jed thought about scavenging the ammo from the sailors' weapons. The streets looked empty of any threats, but he needed to confirm that before he set his people to doing anything with their heads down.

"Anybody got movement?" he asked.

"Nothing," McKitrick said from Jed's right. The others came back with the same from their positions behind him.

"Let's check Mercer's place," Garza said. "I bet he stayed hid while his people got chewed up."

"I hate to say it, Garza," Jed answered, "but you're probably right."

The gate to the neighborhood had been left open. Their SUV was turned around on the road, and on its side.

He led the squad to Mercer's front door. It was open a few inches. Jed knew what they would find, but he still let himself hope that Mercer was inside, alive and unharmed. It was all about numbers. As long as he wasn't completely crazy, Mercer could help them survive.

But Mercer wasn't alive. He was lying on the floor inside his house, right where Jed had been standing when they'd had their chat. The monsters had their way with him. Streaks and smears of blood trailed away from the body and toward the windows in the next room. They were all broken from the outside. Large rocks sat here and there on the floor.

A file folder and notebook spilled some papers across Mercer's desk. A set of keys lay amidst the shattered glass near Mercer's hand. Jed picked them up, then checked the papers on the desk.

"Sonofabitch," Jed said as he read the pages. "Y'all, I think we found our bomber, or maybe one of them."

The squad whirled to face him. Garza was next to him first. The others slowly stepped closer, keeping their eyes on the access points around them.

"I got diagrams of the daisy chain here," Jed said. "And y'all aren't gonna like this. He was working with Kip."

"*What?*" Garza was looking over Jed's shoulder and reached a hand for the page. Jed let him take it. He'd seen enough to settle his fears. Kipler's name was scrawled under the diagrams beside a note about how much ANFO it would take to destroy the causeway.

"They used fucking IEDs," Garza said. "Kip always talked about hunting bomb makers in Fallujah. Motherfucker was probably taking lessons. You think that was him last night, Sergeant? With the dogs?"

"I don't know. Didn't hear his voice, but I only had a few days around him before he went AWOL. Could have been his squad out there. I'm more worried about where those guys were headed last night. Sounded like they had a destination."

"You thinking they're going back to Galveston?" Keoh asked.

"Maybe. If Kip has it in for all of us, could be he's bringing the horde home to roost. If that was him last night, I mean. Shit, we need to be moving, y'all. Police up some ammo on the way out—"

A heavy diesel motor rumbled outside, snapping Jed's attention to the windows.

"Watch the windows. McKitrick, at our six. Watch the hall in case anyone tries to come behind us. Mehta, you and me on the front door."

A convoy of three vehicles pulled up to the open gate. The first vehicle was a pick up with more primer than paint on it. It was followed by an SUV with the same coloring. The final vehicle was a desert color five-ton truck.

The driver of the SUV got out and shook his head and the overturned vehicle beside the road. He came around the front of his SUV and Jed recognized his walk.

It was Greg Radout.

Jed rushed outside and called to him, waving as he headed for the gate.

"We're over here!"

Radout startled and went for his sidearm, but relaxed when Jed got closer. The squad came out to join them.

"Looks like they hit you here after they were done

with us," Radout said. "They stormed our camp. I lost more people last night than the entire time I was in Iraq."

"Shit man, I'm sorry. How'd you know to come here?"

"I didn't. Just guessed, and figured if Mercer's people held them off, we'd be safer with them than out on our own. How'd you get stuck here?"

Jed explained what had happened the day before, how Mercer roped them into working guard duty, and how they'd sheltered in his supply point after losing Parsons.

Jed let the silence hang between them for a bit. Radout broke it first.

"I knew Mercer. I should have told you, but I honestly figured you'd be in and out of this place and heading our way. We never spotted that car again. That was another reason I wanted to come here. In case Mercer was sheltering the driver. Wouldn't surprise me if he was. The dude was a whole week's worth of bad news."

"Had the same thought about him when I got here," Jed said. "Was hoping I'd be proven wrong, but… I found this in his office."

Jed held out the papers.

"That motherfucker," Radout said. "Who's Kipler? Anybody on Galveston have that name?"

"One of our squad leaders. Him and his people went AWOL a while back."

"And you didn't have any indication he might be dirty?"

"Nothing, man. I only met the dude a week before he took off, and hardly saw him more than twice."

Radout stewed on that for a bit, spit at the ground, then looked Jed in the eye.

"We've got a truck full of supplies. Stuffed pretty good," Radout said, aiming a thumb at the half-ton. "Let's load up what we can from that garage, then we'll hit the road."

"Where to?"

"Baytown. They have fortifications there. More than just chain link and razor wire."

"You know anybody there?"

"Got a few contacts. They value hard work up there, and security is always a good thing," he said, motioning to Jed's M4. "But you need to prove you're worth keeping around."

"How do we do that?"

"Bring them something they can use. The stuff in the supply here might do it. If not, then maybe Kipler's head on a plate. I'll get my truck in here. You can all climb on and help us load it."

Jed called for Mehta and Keoh to mount up on the half ton. Radout's guys wheeled the beast around the pick up and SUV, and headed down the street to the supply.

Before Jed moved out to follow the truck, he had Garza and McKitrick check Mercer's garage.

"See if there's a car out there for these keys."

He handed them to Garza and they moved out. McKitrick stuck her head out Mercer's front door a moment later.

"SUV in there, Sergeant," she said. "Bigger than the one we came in. It's in good shape."

"Bring it out by the gate, then join us at the supply."

Jed jogged to catch up to Radout at the head of the column.

"If that garage is stocked up like you say, it should help us get into Baytown. Sorry about what I said earlier, about Kipler's head. Baytown isn't really bloodthirsty, not like some of the wing nut groups out there. They just want you to come in with enough material to make it worth their while to share their food and water with you."

"So you gotta buy a seat if you want to sit. I get it."

"Pretty much. I just hope there's enough gear to get us all in."

They'd reached the supply house. Jed helped Radout's crew load up as much as they could. They grabbed the MREs and water first, then the wet weather gear, some tools, and a dozen bags of concrete. That left nearly a full pallet worth stacked around the garage doors.

Jed had Mehta carry the corpsman's bag, and as a last effort, they took some shovels and dug a grave for Parsons. Radout and his team helped dig, too. Jed and Mehta brought Parsons outside and laid him in the grave with his weapon. It took a good hour for them to finish, even with Radout's people helping.

"What about all the weapons around here?" Jed asked as they were getting back into the truck. "And the ammo?"

"They're pretty well armed up there. But we should take it anyway, at least whatever we can carry. We don't want the wing nuts finding all of this. We have some det cord we can use to torch anything we have to leave behind."

Jed and his squad walked in front of the half ton, leading it around the neighborhood. Whenever they found weapons or dead sailors, they'd stop and load up the gear. Radout walked with Jed, filling him in on the

Baytown people and how they ran things.

"They'll want to vet you guys good. So think about anything you can do to prove you're not going to be a problem. Last thing you want is for them to think you're a wing nut trying to infiltrate."

"You keep saying 'wing nuts'. Who's that?"

"I like to think of them as the locals, but who knows where they're all from originally. A few bands of them got together around Houston, out in the back country. They've mostly taken over rural suburbs, and some of them are pretty nasty about how they do things. I've never met them, just heard stories."

"Like what?"

"You don't want to know. Suffice to say they're the people you don't want surviving the apocalypse, except they did. So you're stuck either killing them first or staying the hell out of their way."

"Is everyone out here a wing nut?" Jed asked, leaning down to collect a battered M16 from a dead sailor.

"No, they're a minority really. The Lone Star Militia runs the show in Houston proper, and they're good people. Mostly. They didn't like it when the Army rolled in trying to establish martial law, but who can blame 'em? You have smaller groups, like at Baytown. Also good folks. They're on their own, separate from Lone Star; they follow their own rules and have their own command structure."

Jed had more questions, but he let it go.

It took them an hour or so to police the neighborhood for stray weapons and ammunition. They went by the crackhead's house, and Jed expected to find the man's body ripped up on the lawn, but he wasn't there, and wasn't in the house either.

"Somebody you wanted to find?" Radout asked as Jed came out.

"Just a druggie who was giving us shit last night. Saw him right when the things attacked. He was standing here smoking a cigarette in the middle of it all."

"Guess we know what happened to him then," Radout said.

Jed nodded, but he wasn't so sure. Something nagged at him about the crackhead's attitude, how he was so relaxed. Jed kept thinking about the guy and his dog while he helped Radout empty the guard towers of weapons. When they were done, they'd collected an arms room worth of gear from around the neighborhood, sliding the weapons into any gaps they could find in the back of the five-ton.

They only had to leave behind a few M16A2s. Jed rigged up a coil of det cord to destroy the weapons. They set the package up in Mercer's garage after McKitrick wheeled the commander's SUV out. She drove while Garza, Keoh, and Mehta shared the rear seat. Jed rode TC and they followed Radout's convoy through the front gate.

The sound of their demo charge echoed into the air behind them as they drove through the refinery field.

There was a radio in the vehicle, and Radout got them linked up to the blue net that Six Team used. It crackled as they got back on the highway.

"Hey, with that news about Kipler I almost forgot," Radout said. "I found out who it was that you fished out of the water."

"Yeah?" Jed asked.

"Guy named Palver. He'd joined us a few months ago. Used to be a Marine Raider. He was good with demo."

Jed let that sit in his mind. He was about to lift the mic to ask Radout for more about Palver when the radio crackled again and a strained voice broke through the static.

"Anyone receiving…this is Hometown Actual. Request nine—"

Jed snatched up the mic and replied, "Hometown, this is Shorewatch 1 prepared to copy." He dug into his cargo pocket for his notepad. It was a moment of tense silence in the truck while they waited for the LT's reply. When it came, his voice broke with pain.

"Line one…tip of Tiki Island. No map. Line two, this channel, Hometown Actual."

Jed scribbled the LT's location down and waited for the report of his condition.

"Line tree, alpha…one. Line four, alpha. Line five—"

The radio went silent. Jed waited before trying to raise the LT again.

"Hometown, Shorewatch, how copy?"

No reply came.

"LT's hurt bad," Keoh said.

He hailed Radout and told him they'd meet up at Baytown.

"Gotta go back for our man first."

"Okay, but make sure you have a white flag flying when you get to Baytown. They'll shoot first otherwise."

"Had enough of that with Mercer's crew. Thanks for the heads up."

"Hooah. Good luck," Radout said.

As Keoh took them back down the road toward the

causeway, Jed tried to reach the LT again.

"Hometown, this is Shorewatch 1. How copy?"

He kept trying as the scenery shifted from the refinery districts to the barren marshy wastes they'd come through the day before.

"Hometown, Shorewatch 1. We are en route. ETA ten minutes."

— 17 —

Emily woke up in a rush of panic. The men had dropped sacks over her and Danitha's heads and taken them in the van. They'd driven for a while, then stopped. Emily fell asleep at one point, and only woke briefly to feel someone stabbing a needle into her arm. Danitha was still with her, as far as she knew, but where was she?

She tried moving her left arm. It hurt like hell, and was still in the sling, but she couldn't move it at all. She couldn't move her head either. Emily felt with her other hand and found a velcro strap. It connected to an actual sling that wrapped her wrist and held it against her chest. A plastic collar ringed her neck and held her head fixed in place.

She put her hand out and felt beneath her. She was lying on a bed or a couch of some kind. It felt like a leather cushioned. The air was humid around her, thick and heavy on her face. She blinked her eyes and wiped at them with her good hand. Slowly her surroundings came into focus. Gauzy curtains wrapped around the space and blocked her view of anything else, but she could make out figures moving in the room beyond. Their voices were hushed and soft, and would have been pleasant if Emily didn't feel like she'd been taken prisoner.

Before she could decide whether or not to call for help, the curtain swished aside and a blond woman wearing green hospital scrubs came in.

"Well look who's awake," she said.

"Where am I?"

"Aid station, honey. My name's Jennifer. You can call me Jenny if you want."

"Where is Dani? What happened?"

"You're gonna be fine. Those boys that roughed you and your friend up feel real bad about it. I don't blame you if you're thinking you'd like to give them a piece of your mind. But they thought you was somebody else. You rest up now. There'll be time for reckoning later."

"Why can't I move my head?"

"Those boys hit you from behind pretty hard. Doctor's worried about your neck. We don't have X-rays here, so she put you in a brace for now. Just in case."

Aid station? Where? Which militia had captured them? Was Danitha alive or dead?

Another woman came in. She was dark skinned and wore a white doctor's coat.

"Hi Jenny," she said to the nurse. Then, to Emily, "Hello there. I'm Doctor Allison DuBois. How are you feeling?"

"I'm scared," Emily said. "Where is Danitha? What happened?"

Jennifer stepped out and Doctor DuBois came closer. She put a hand on Emily's shoulder. "You were captured by a few of our more impulsive border agents. They thought you were someone else. You were driving a truck that had been seen before, where people were killed. Brutally. Our people were on the hunt, but I guess you took out the bad guys for us."

"No, that was Angela. She—" Emily's voice caught in her throat as she recalled the girl's final moments.

"Your friend told us what happened, and about the girl who helped you. I'm sorry she died. The good news is you're here now, and we're going to take care of you."

"Is this Baytown?"

"Yes, it is," Doctor DuBois said.

"You had a bounty on Angela. She said you wanted her for killing a man who attacked her."

"That was her story. I remember her. I also remember the man she killed. I tried to save him."

"Did he tell you a different story?"

"No. He wasn't able to speak, because she destroyed his larynx when she stabbed him."

Emily thought about Angela, her temper and her attitude of always needing the upper hand, and how underneath she had simply been a young woman stuck in a world without rules or boundaries except those she made for herself.

"I believed Angie's story," Emily said. "When she told us, I believed her. I still do."

"Just between you and me, I believed her, too. But I'm only one member of the council. There are six others, and five of them thought she'd gone too far."

"So you put a price on her head?"

"That's how the Aftermath works. Everything has a cost now. The air we breathe, the water we drink, what little food we have left to eat. It all comes with a cost. That we can even be standing here having this conversation comes with a price paid by the people who are out there right now making sure this community is kept safe."

Emily stared at the doctor, thinking about what she and Danitha had left behind, and knowing they'd made the right choice to flee. But where they'd landed wasn't sounding very much better.

"What did you do with Dani? Where is she?"

"I'm right here, Professor," Danitha said from the other side of the curtain. Doctor DuBois drew it aside and Danitha stepped in. The nurse was with her and said something quietly to the doctor before leaving again. A bandage covered Danitha's left cheek, and she had cuts on her arms.

"What happened to you, Dani?" Emily asked.

"Hit the window when they rammed us. Got cut up by all the glass. Not as bad as you, but—"

Emily lifted her good arm to her face and felt bandages on both sides of her head.

Doctor DuBois put a hand on her shoulder again. "Rest up. You're going to be fine. We set your arm and have you on a cycle of antibiotics. I have to check on my other patients now."

Before the doctor could leave, Emily grabbed at her coat. "Wait, please. Are you in touch with the Marines on Galveston? Can you reach them? Tell them I'm here."

Doctor DuBois's face fell. She looked Emily in the eyes and said, with a flat voice, "We had radio contact with them, but…"

"*What is it? Tell me!*"

"We lost contact with Galveston yesterday morning, right about when the bridges were blown."

"What bridges? What do you—My brother was on Galveston. He is a Marine. Salvador Garza."

Doctor DuBois paused. "We have some survivors from Galveston at our larger clinic. I don't know if your brother is one of them."

"The clinic? How were they hurt? Was it the dogs or the bats? They could be—"

"Dogs and bats? No, the men were all pulled from the water and had nearly drowned. They're all in comas. Only one of them was conscious when we found them. The bay is full of pathogens; disease could spread quickly if we don't keep it contained. We're monitoring them, and I need—"

"I need to know if Salvador is here!" Emily screamed.

Doctor DuBois gently tugged her coat from Emily's grip. "I'll check with the nurses."

Emily fought to keep her voice down and said, "Thank you." After a breath, she described her brother, hoping it would help. "If he is here, please let me see him."

"I can't do that. Not until we're sure they aren't carriers of any contagion."

Doctor DuBois held up a hand to stop Emily's question.

"I will ask a nurse to find out if your brother is here. If he is, I will let you know. Now I have to go back to the clinic, so please…"

She motioned for Emily to lie down and then left.

Danitha stood nearby, shifting on her feet. "Don't feel right being here. Without Angie."

"They would have killed her," Emily said. "The doctor told me. They have a council of seven people. Five of them voted that Angie was in the wrong for what she did."

"And what did she do but teach a man to keep his hands to hisself? Even if it was permanent. Don't make it wrong in my book."

Emily wondered if Danitha had something in her recent past that would make her guilty in the council's eyes. She thought about her own past, the things she had done to survive since the virus. Had she been lucky, never having to make the choice between hurting or killing another in order to protect herself?

What choices would they have to make now that they had found this place of safety? How safe were they if their fate could be decided by seven people they had never even met?

— 18 —

The road back to Tiki Island was the same as it had been on their drive up the previous day. Empty of anything Jed cared about, except for the occasional wrecked vehicle that drew his attention as they passed by. He expected Variants to spring from every shadow and land on the truck. But nothing came flying at them, spitting and shrieking for his blood. Nothing but his memories anyway.

McKitrick took them down the highway as fast as she could, her determination reminding Jed of Sergeant Gallegos. But as she swerved them around another overturned car, Jed worried they'd spin out or flip.

"Keep it easy, McKitrick," he said.

"We gotta get there, Sergeant. LT's hurt. He could be bleeding out right now."

"Won't do him any good if we're all in the same shape because you rolled the truck. Keep it easy. Drive on, but watch the speed."

She backed off a bit, taking a longer arc around the next wreck they passed.

They were near the area where they'd seen the hunter and his dog on their way inland. Jed scanned the terrain, looking for any sign of movement. The more he thought about the hunter, the more he was reminded of the crackhead. Jed couldn't let go of his suspicions about the two men, but he kept his worries to himself. Some of the civilians on Galveston had adopted pets. He didn't need Keoh going rogue and shooting at every stray person who had found an animal to help them survive the apocalypse.

The causeway came into view on the horizon. Concrete chunks and burned up vehicles marked the gaps left by the bombs. The rooftops and fences of Tiki Island soon appeared off to their right. McKitrick angled them to the offramp.

Tiki was just a single street running down a strip of dirt sticking into the water. Storm-battered houses lined it on one side. The other side of the street was nothing but empty lots and the scattered remains of houses that once stood there.

Jed checked his notebook. "LT said tip of the island. Eyes out, and watch the roofs. We don't know shit about what's here."

As McKitrick slowed their progress, Jed scanned their path ahead, always swiveling his view left to right. Now that the monsters were a reality again, anything could be a threat. Jed focused carefully on every mound of debris or shredded remains of a house, watching for movement and fearing that each inch the truck rolled might be the last.

The island was quiet, though, at least for now. Soon, the tip was in sight, jutting into the water like a sidewalk somebody forgot to finish. The last house on the street was only inches from the shoreline. A smashed up fishing boat sat halfway in the water there, like it had been run aground on purpose. A radio sat in the mud beside it. Jed had McKitrick pull them up a few yards from the house. He got out and stepped to where he could see the front door. It was open a few inches.

"Garza, Keoh; dismount and stack on me."

They exited fast and lined up behind him. The trio moved forward, rushing to the door. Jed put his foot into it and it flew inward. He raced in, feeling Garza and Keoh right on his six.

LT Staples was lying on a couch in the next room. He stirred as Jed approached him.

"That you, Welch?"

"Oorah, sir. What the hell happened?"

"Broke my leg jumping out a window. Had to—"

He grimaced and reached a hand down to his right leg. Smears of blood stained his hands and the left side of his face was an angry mess of blood and blisters.

Jed turned to Keoh. "Get the med bag. Tell McKitrick to back the truck up the drive."

She moved out, and Garza came into the room with Jed and the LT.

"The fuck happened, sir?" Garza asked.

"Got caught in a fire. Had to jump. Secondary charges…outside the TOC. Somebody wanted me dead."

Jed waited for the LT to spill it, but the silence dragged out too long for his patience.

"Who, sir?"

"Ewell did it. Had to be Ewell."

"Gunny? No way," Garza said. "Maybe Kip, but—"

"You sure about that, sir?" Jed said, cutting Garza off with a look. He wasn't convinced Kip acted alone. LT knew something about the body they'd found that morning, and he hadn't said anything yet. If he was injured in the blast, it might have been because he was careless with his act of sabotage.

"Couldn't it have been someone else, sir? Or an accident?" Jed asked.

"*No*, Sergeant. It couldn't. Why the fuck would there *accidentally* be demo charges anywhere near the building? It was all stored in lockers at the ammo point."

"I mean, how do you know it was demo? The TOC wasn't that far from the Galveston end of the bridge—"

Keoh was back with the corpsman's bag. She got out a SAM splint and set to work getting LT's leg ready for them to move him.

"Sergeant, I'm telling you what I know," Staples said. He curled forward, resting on one elbow to stab a finger at Jed. Gritting his teeth, he said, "I was in the TOC when the blasts started. I had enough time to stand up, look out the window, and see the explosions getting closer. I saw a duffle bag standing against the wall, right by the door. It wasn't there when I entered, and it wasn't there when Ewell came in. It was put there sometime between when he left and when the bridges went up."

"Where'd he go? We figured—"

Staples laid down again, resting one arm across his chest. The other hand kept reaching toward his broken leg, like he could hold it together or squeeze it to stop the pain. Keoh was done with the splint and had saline ready, with burn ointment and bandages. Staples took the saline and sprayed it over his left cheek and around his hairline where the burns weren't as bad. He let Keoh swab at the rest and apply the ointment.

Jed and Garza helped the LT up and got him into the

back of the SUV. Jed told Mehta to move up front with McKitrick's 203 while he wedged into the back seat with Keoh in the middle and Garza on the other side.

"Let's get gone, McKitrick," he said as he tried to raise Radout. He got nothing back and figured they were out of range. The bigger radio Staples brought with him could have reached, but it had a dead battery.

Staples filled them in as they drove, telling them how the TOC caught fire after the demo went up, forcing him to jump from the second floor.

"I grabbed the radio and went out the window. I yelled for Ewell, but couldn't see him anywhere. Couldn't see anyone. Too much smoke and dust from the bridges going up."

"We lost Skip in that, sir," McKitrick said.

"Sorry to hear that. So Ewell's guilty of manslaughter at least."

"And you're sure it was him?" Jed asked again.

"Can't think of who else it could be. The duffle bag was there by the front door. I'm only alive because I stood up to see what was going on with the bridges. I saw the bag, my brain said IED. I ran up the stairs just in time. Ewell's the only one who could have put the bag there. He'd been giving me shit all morning and walked out right before I sent you to deliver that body to the engineers. First time I can honestly say I was happy to see his ass."

"What did Gunny go after you for?" Jed asked.

"I have no idea. He was just hollering about everything. First he said he was tired of doing nothing but sitting and shitting, then he bitched about Kipler, saying how he never hauled enough bodies out of the water, so it wasn't like we really lost anything when he went AWOL. I thought about ordering Ewell to stay put, but I couldn't fault him. We had a fuck ton of nothing to do on Galveston. The refugee ship was overdue and nobody could tell me when it might show up."

"Didn't you have a line back to Plum?" Jed asked, wondering if Mercer's story was about to proven.

McKitrick turned them off Tiki Island and they rode in silence for a while before Jed asked his question again.

Staples put a fist against his mouth, then said, "Only commo I've had was with Six Team, some of the civilians inland, and the refugee ship. They're somewhere around Florida last I heard from them."

"What about Plum Island?"

"Whoever was there is either dead or offline. I've been trying to reach them since we got here, but nobody's home."

"And you didn't think that might have been something we should know?" Garza demanded.

"Easy, Garza," Jed said.

"No, fuck that. We're out here on nobody's orders doing nobody's bidding, and this mother—"

"I said stand the *fuck* down!"

Jed stared Garza in the eyes, daring him to open his mouth again. The Lance Corporal was still fuming, but he backed down, then swiveled his head to look out the window.

"You're a good Marine, Garza," Staples said. "Hot tempered and trigger happy, but you're right. I should have told you. Should have told all of you."

Jed spoke up before Garza could get any more shots in. "Won't lie to you, sir. I was worried you had a hand in at first. When you sent us over the water with that body, I thought you were hiding something from us."

"Like what?"

"I didn't know really, still don't. Just had an itch about it."

"Still feel like scratching, Sergeant, or are we good?"

"We're good, sir. We—Shit, this is just adding insult to injury. We found these papers at a compound up the road. I wasn't sure what to think when I saw them. It looks like Kipler was the one who did it. Or he knows who did."

Jed handed the pages over the seat and waited while Staples read them.

"Looks like a bomber's diagram, but it also looks like bullshit. Who the fuck signs his name to something like this? Don't tell me you really thought Kip was responsible."

"I hope not, sir. But I can't figure it any other way."

Jed was quiet for a moment, holding in his anger as best he could. After everything Gunny Ewell had been through in Iraq, for him to use the very tactics that had taken so many American lives…

"You think Gunny's still alive, sir?"

"I don't know. If he is, and he's out here somewhere, I hope I see him before he sees us."

"What about the other squads, sir? Any word from them since we've been gone?" Keoh asked.

"Haven't had any contact since they left. I'd assumed they were dead, or adrift out here. But maybe Kip's alive and had a finger in this pie."

Staples asked for a report of their activities since they'd left, so Jed downloaded. He told the LT about linking up with Radout, then described Mercer's operation, how they were greeted and treated, and how the monsters came back and have evolved into canine forms.

"That's where we found the papers, sir. In Mercer's place."

"I knew Mercer. He was on the *Truxton* when the virus hit. Thought for sure he was dead, but I—Hey, where's your other man? Where's Parsons?" Staples asked.

"We lost him that night, sir," Jed said. He explained and Staples listened, nodding with his eyes closed.

"I'm sorry," he said.

"It's on me, sir," Jed said.

"Don't do that to yourself, Sergeant," Staples said.

They followed the highway in silence for a bit, until McKitrick aimed them at the fork going around Mercer's AO.

"So the plan is to link up with Radout?" Staples asked as they followed the highway around the refinery.

"Yes, sir. He said he was taking his people to Baytown. Said they got a barter system in place to gain entry. We helped him haul a lot out of Mercer's supply."

"That should do the trick. They're good people there as far as I know."

"How so?"

"I only talked to them a few times, and that was just to get with the Six Team crews in the area. But they sounded legit to me. When's the last time you talked to Radout?"

"Just before we left to get you. I should try him again here; we're probably in range."

Jed made two attempts to reach Radout, calling their location and ETA, but they still weren't close enough yet.

Either that, or Radout wasn't listening.

"Why would Gunny do it?" Mehta asked. "I don't get it."

"That's because you're a boot," Garza said.

Jed shot a look in the Lance Corporal's direction and Garza smirked. "Just fucking with him, Sergeant."

"Well stop it," Jed said. "No buddy fucking in my squad without consent."

Staples spoke up before Jed could answer Mehta's question.

"Ewell knew there was nobody up top anymore, so he went rogue and tried to lock down his own fiefdom. That's the only thing that makes sense to me. It's like that Mercer guy you ran into, setting up a little kingdom to rule over. That's my take anyway."

"That's pretty fucked up, sir," Mehta said.

"Exactly. But that's the reality we're faced with. World ended, Private Mehta. Out here, everybody is either a warlord, working for one, or they're prey."

"Can't be that way, sir," Keoh said. "We have to remember where we came from."

"Where we came from is how we got here."

"What do you mean?" Jed asked.

"None of you know this, and I'm technically not supposed to tell you, but—easy Garza—fuck the rules. Here's the truth about the monsters. The virus was a government project started during Vietnam. The mastermind was a man named Colonel Gibson who thought he knew how to make the world perfect. He lost his son to the war and wanted to develop a biological weapon that would end any war America got into, with our side coming out on top every time. That way, no other *American* parents would have to bury their children. In other words, he was fucking crazy and ended up doing the exact opposite of what he hoped. The country had a good run, but we're done. And all this rebuilding around here? All the clean up? Waste of fucking time. We're a long damn ways from being ready to rebuild as long as people like Mercer are out here playing boss man like they know what's best for everybody."

Jed said, "I saw some of that in New York, collaborators working with the Variants to protect their own and to hell with everyone else."

"Yep," Staples said. "That's the way of things now."

"Sounds like you're ready to call it quits, LT."

"Not even close. Only thing I'm ready for is the fight to make sure what we have left doesn't end up in the wrong hands. Let's get to Baytown. If they're good people, we'll help them fortify against whatever or whoever might bring the fight our way."

Jed's radio crackled.

"Hometown 1, this is Six Team actual."

"Hometown 1, over."

"You got your package?"

"Roger that. We're inbound, ETA twenty minutes."

"You're good to go. They were really happy with the gear we brought in. But be advised, this is a hot LZ. Bad company rolled up about five minutes ago. Just knocking on the door now, but they're strapped big."

"What are you looking at?"

"Those wing nuts I told you about. At least a company's worth. They're outside the gate and making a lot of noise. Nobody's shooting yet, but I don't know how long that'll last."

— 19 —

Emily watched the doctor leave and felt her lower lip trembling. Chava was either in a coma or dead. She was alone in the world. Her entire family was gone.

Danitha stepped closer to her and reached out a hand. "It'll be okay," she said. "We made it here, and we can make it to the next place. Wherever that is, we can—"

Shouting broke into the curtained space. Emily heard voices raised in anger, some in fear and shock.

The nurse, Jennifer, came back in and closed the curtains up tight around them. "Stay here, and don't move," she said. As she turned to leave, Emily noticed she had a pistol on her hip.

"What's going on?" Danitha asked, but Jennifer was already moving away. Danitha pulled the curtain aside and Emily got a view of the room beyond her confined area. She could just make out a restaurant equipment and a service counter.

"Dani? Where are we?"

"An old Dairy Queen. They got it set up like a clinic. Doctor said there's a bigger one with real beds over by the fire station."

Danitha poked her head out the curtains. She came

back to Emily's side. "I need to know what all these people are running around for and yelling about. You gon' be okay if I go out for a minute?"

"Don't leave me alone in here, please. I can't move my head, and—"

The nurse, Jennifer, came in again. She pushed by Danitha and handed Emily a bottle of water. "Doctor says you should drink, keep your fluid levels up." The shouting continued outside.

"What's happening out there?" Emily asked.

An amplified voice cut through the chaos, calling for everyone to stop moving. Jennifer snapped her attention to what was going on outside and quickly excused herself before either of them could ask her another question.

"Dani, please help me sit up. I need to see," Emily said.

Danitha scooted herself into the booth beside Emily's makeshift bed and helped her sit up, pushing the pillows together so she could rest against them. The neck brace meant she still only had a limited view of the world, but she could see a window now. Danitha moved the curtain aside further, letting in the weak rays of fading daylight, and a view of what was happening outside.

A heavy wrought iron gate separated two groups of people. On this side were men and women wearing construction hard hats and coveralls. Some of them wore military uniforms and carried guns. But most of the people had tools like axes or shovels. One person even had a sword.

She couldn't see beyond the fence.

"They can't be here just for us," Danitha said. "Ain't no way they brought all that here just to get us."

"What is it, Dani? What did they bring?"

"Got a hundred people outside that gate shouting to get in. All of them got guns."

"Do they have the dogs with them?"

"I don't see any."

Jennifer came back in and waved an angry hand at them both.

"Get yourselves down and out of sight. We don't need them knowing you're here."

Danitha moved to help Emily lie down again, but Jennifer was faster.

"Why do they want us so badly?" Emily asked. "We ran away from them, but that can't be enough to bring them all the way here."

"I don't have an answer for that," Jennifer said. "Just stay down and—"

The amplified voice outside drowned her out.

"Y'all have something of ours. We aim to get it. You can let us in or we can come in as we please. Up to you. I'm counting to ten."

Emily felt for Danitha's hand.

"Get me out of here, Dani. Help me stand up so I can run."

Jennifer put a hand up. "Y'all ain't running anywhere. No need to. We got people with weapons and the training to use 'em. They're gonna protect you and keep you safe. Just lie low, trust me."

Emily wanted to protest, but Jennifer's hand was resting on her gun now.

Footsteps raced into the room to Emily's left. She tried to turn her head, and the movement sent trails of pain into her left shoulder. Jennifer stepped out and drew her gun, but quickly relaxed and put it away again. Emily heard a man's voice and what sounded like a radio squawk, then Jennifer said, "Greg, I'm glad it's you. What's happening out there?"

"Wing nuts," the man said. "They're saying you've got prisoners of theirs. Two women."

"Prisoners? And what are they saying these women did to get themselves taken prisoner by a bunch of yahoos with more guns than sense?"

"Killed a man in his sleep and took his money," Greg said.

Jennifer barked out a laugh. "His *money*? Oh, that's good. I'm sure everyone's just raring to get them dangerous ladies back into custody. What do they think we are, idiots?"

The curtain moved aside and a man's face entered Emily's field of vision.

"This them?" he asked, turning over his shoulder to talk to Jennifer.

"Yes, and more hardened criminals I doubt you'll find anywhere."

"We didn't kill anyone," Emily said.

"Never said you did. What about your friend?"

Emily found Danitha's face and searched her eyes for an answer.

"Dani? What did you do?"

"Had to," she said. "Had no choice. He was trying to get on me, just like what that girl Angie had to deal with. It was time I was running out to meet you, so I stuck him with his own knife and left him there to bleed."

She stood between Jennifer and Greg, looking at their faces, then turning so she had her back to the curtain. "Guess I know how that council's gonna vote, so if you'll excuse me."

Danitha stepped back quickly, and neither Greg nor Jennifer moved to stop her. She hovered on the threshold of Emily's would-be hospital room. Emily tried to move her neck so she could see Danitha. She stood beyond the curtain, but hadn't left yet.

"Dani, please don't leave. Please," Emily said.

"Professor, you know well as I do how these folk gon' treat me. Same as they would've done to Angie. I'd rather take my chances out—"

The shouting started outside again, and was followed by a rattle of gunfire.

— 20 —

McKitrick floored it and they sped up Highway 146 past small neighborhoods and empty marshland. The whole time, Jed was on the radio with Radout, getting updates about the situation in Baytown.

"It's the militia from up north," Radout said. "The ones around Mont Belvieu. They say we've got two prisoners of theirs and they want them back. I mean, obvious bullshit is obvious, but when you're staring down a company strong force, you ask yourself things you never thought you would."

"What's their story about the prisoners?"

"One of them killed a guy in his sleep and took his money. The other one helped her escape."

"Her?"

"Yeah, it's two women they're after. They're playing the frontier law card, but I know a song and dance when I see it. We'll keep the parlay going."

"How's their trigger discipline?" Jed asked, dreading the answer.

"Good one. They're actually not shooting. We sent a warning volley their way just now, keeping them off our fence. Something tells me we don't have much to worry about from this bunch, except their numbers. How long until you get here?"

"Maybe ten minutes now," Jed said. "Keep us in the loop."

"Hooah, and don't forget your flag. Six out."

Jed had Keoh dig up some gauze from the corpsman's bag. It wasn't very big, but it was white and could be flapped out the side window like a flag. She handed it to Mehta up front.

The road along the coast remained clear, except at a small neighborhood just outside of LaPorte. The houses there were all in good shape, and the streets looked pretty clean, despite everything around the place being covered in storm debris.

As they got deeper into LaPorte, the LT faded in and out of consciousness. Keoh turned around in her seat to treat Staples for shock. Jed was watching her when he noticed about a dozen people wandering around near a cluster of homes. They looked like scavengers, picking around the remains of what used to be a wealthy suburb on the Texas coast. Most of them wandered without any real purpose, but a couple near the front of the group had their heads up, like they were sentries for the others. Jed watched them until one turned his attention to the truck.

It was the crackhead from Mercer's AO, still wearing the same dirty white shirt and popping candy into his mouth.

That's impossible, Jed thought. *No way that's him.*

"Is that who I think it is?" Garza asked.

"Can't be," Jed said.

They passed the scavengers, and Jed tried to get a

better look at the guy, but Garza's head blocked his view.

"I swear that was him," Garza said. "Swear on my soul. How the fuck did he get this far on foot?"

"Couldn't," Jed said. "Not in just a few hours."

Jed turned to look over his shoulder. Keoh was still working on the LT, and blocked Jed's view out the back window. As they left the suburb behind, he was able to see the whole group of scavengers again. They wandered a bit, then stopped in their tracks and all lifted their gaze to stare after the SUV.

In a sudden movement, the people fell to the ground and vanished from sight.

Jed searched the long grass for any sign of movement until McKitrick pumped the brakes and slowed them down. Their path became choked with vehicles up ahead, funneling all traffic into a single lane in the middle of the road. The bridge to Baytown was beyond the choke point. McKitrick brought them to an idle just before the road narrowed.

"What do we do, Sergeant?"

Jed checked the LT. Keoh had him stable. He was breathing steady, but his eyes were closed.

"Take us up slowly. Get the flag out."

Mehta hung the roll of gauze out the window and let some hang loose as he waved it up and down. McKitrick rolled them forward at a slow pace.

Jed dug out a pair of binos and scanned the bridge ahead. Two trucks had been backed together blocking the road at the far end of the choke point. They had .50 cals mounted in their beds. A small dark ball flew out from behind the trucks, and Jed's ears caught the heavy *choomp* a second later.

A smoke round burst behind their SUV, then the .50s opened up.

"Dismount!" Jed yelled as he tried to fling his door open. It rebounded and slammed into his arm. Garza struggled with his door, too. They'd already entered the narrowest stretch of road, with overturned cars blocking them from getting out. The gunners on the .50s kept chopping at the air around them, but no rounds impacted on the truck.

"The fuck are they shooting at?" Garza yelled.

"McKitrick, back us up," Jed said.

"No!" Keoh shouted. "Contacts back here."

Jed spun in his seat. The smoke obscured most of his vision out the back window, but he could make out shapes darting around faster than any human could move. They would pop up, then drop down only to appear again somewhere else. The smoke seemed to confuse them. Their orientation would shift each time they dropped from sight and came back up.

Sometimes one would jerk with the impact of a .50 caliber round, but most of them avoided the incoming fire. And they were getting closer. Jed couldn't believe what he was seeing.

"What the fuck? Are those—"

"Yes, Sergeant," Keoh said. "Those are Variants."

McKitrick stomped on the gas and they flew down the chute between the hulks of smashed cars and trucks. Another grenade round flew overhead and filled their wake with thick covering smoke, and still the .50s laid down suppressive fire. Jed wanted to help, but he couldn't safely stick his hand out the window, much less his weapon.

Up ahead, the trucks with the .50s crept apart, until the widening gap was just big enough for McKitrick to fit them through. They raced between the trucks and onto the bridge where McKitrick slowed down at Jed's order.

"Keep us close in case they need support," he said.

Behind them, the trucks reversed to close the gap. The gunners maintained their fire the whole time. A third person on the ground held up an M203 and fired another round. This one detonated in a starburst of white hot flame. Another burst of fire from the .50s finished the matter.

Jed grabbed the radio and hailed Radout.

"We're on the bridge. Contact behind us and coming fast. It's Variants!"

"Copy, Shorewatch. Get over here fast. We've got our own problems."

The bridge guards hailed Jed next and said they would follow him over.

"We have wounded," Jed said.

"Good copy. We'll get you to the aid station."

As McKitrick took them over the bridge, Jed thought about what they'd just seen and what they'd survived. It was a Variant ambush, plain as day. But what about the scavengers he'd seen before they reached the bridge? They dropped out of sight as soon as they spotted the truck. But the crackhead being there made it even more likely that Jed's suspicions were correct. If the scavengers were still there when the Variants showed up, they'd have been taken apart.

Unless they weren't just scavengers…

— 21 —

Hands grabbed Emily's shoulders, then her ankles. She was lifted and brought through the curtains. They carried her into the kitchen area behind the counter, moving fast and arguing about which way to go. All Emily could see were their shoulders and the industrial ceiling overhead.

"*Where are you taking me?*" she screamed.

"Out the back door," the man said. Emily tried to remember his name, but her mind was full with the sounds of violence behind them. They reached a door. Emily heard it open, and weak light spilled into the space. Then they were outside and she felt the humid air on her skin, thick like a blanket she couldn't throw off.

The screaming out front was louder, too. People were fighting there, but the shooting had stopped.

"This way," the man said.

Greg. His name was Greg, Emily thought.

Should she call out, ask where they were going? Were they delivering her to the militia? What about Dani? Was she helping them? Were they going to sacrifice her because she was injured?

"I can walk," she said. "Let me *go! I can walk!*"

If they heard her over the shouting and screaming, they didn't respond. After a few more steps, the group slowed down, and Emily was lowered to her feet.

She spun away from them all and looked around as best she could. Her head was still immobilized, but she felt no pain in her neck.

"Take this thing off me. My neck is fine. Dani, please!"

Danitha moved like she would help, but Jennifer stepped in first. She still had a hand on her hip, just above her gun.

"I'll take it off, but don't go blaming me if your neck's broken."

Emily let Jennifer come forward and remove the neck brace. When it fell away, she carefully pivoted her head to take in their surroundings. Her shoulder was still sore, and the wound in her arm hurt like hell. But she could move her head fine. They'd come to a copse of trees behind the Dairy Queen. She could see the group of people inside the fence, holding their tools as weapons, and a few with guns aimed toward the gate. The shouting and screaming continued. Greg looked at her and nodded.

"You'll be okay here? I need to go check my people. Make sure they're good."

"What're you gonna do?" Jennifer asked. "They've got a hundred people out there at least. We have that many or more, but not in one place. Half the community is on a salvage run across town."

"Shouldn't be a problem," Greg said. "Something tells me these dogs are all bark and no bite."

He jogged across the dirt to the Dairy Queen and snuck around the building toward the stand off.

"Dani, we need to go," Emily said. "We need to leave these people be. Go somewhere else."

"Where you gonna go?" Jennifer asked. "You can't survive on your own. You're wounded and need care. Plus, out there you're fair game. You stay inside our gates and they need to come up with a better reason to hand you over than saying you killed a man for his money. What'd they do to you up there? Did they—"

"No," Emily said. "They took over, and they killed people who didn't agree with them. But that's all they did."

"Not all they wanted to do," Danitha said. "I told you he was trying it with me when I stabbed him. And you heard them talking about *plantation living* again. You and me both know what they had planned, Professor."

Emily searched Danitha's eyes again, and saw the truth in every word she'd said. The same truth she felt inside but hadn't wanted to accept.

Greg came running back from around the building. He wore a grin as he jogged toward them.

Emily stepped out from under the trees to meet him. "Do they have any dogs with them?" she asked.

"Dogs? No. Just a bunch of dudes and bros with too much testosterone."

"What are they doing?" Danitha asked.

"Pushing on the gate. Making noise really, and not much else. I wouldn't give 'em a second thought, except there's enough of 'em that they could probably rush us and get a few guys in."

"So why aren't they in then?" Jennifer asked.

Greg smirked and said, "I'm betting they don't have any ammo. We do, and they know it. They're trying to intimidate us with numbers, but it's not going to work. The firefight has been one-sided so far, with our guys doing the shooting."

"What for?" Jennifer asked.

"Just warnings when a couple of theirs tried to climb the gate. They're all packing weapons out there, but none of them have fired a shot. That's why I think they're empty. Honestly, if I didn't know better, I'd say they're the leftovers from a bad cosplay routine. They're about as dangerous as the guy in his mom's basement playing video games and surfing for porn."

Danitha coughed out a curse. "That sounds like the ones we ran from. Except they had bullets when they showed up and took over our little neighborhood."

"Probably the only ones they had left," Greg said.

"So they're just here making noise, but they won't leave?" Jennifer asked.

"Nope. Not until they get what they came for. That's their words, not mine," he said, looking at Emily and Danitha. "Y'all are safe here."

"Let's prove it, Greg," Jennifer said. "Let's take these ladies out there where they can see them and make it known they're with us now. They're part of the community."

Emily and Danitha stepped back together, putting distance between them and the nurse. Her hand hadn't left the pistol on her hip the whole time they'd been talking.

"Y'all want to give us up just like that," Danitha said.

"No," Jennifer answered. "We're not going to give you up. Not to them or anyone else. I think if we show them that you're here, and stand beside you, they'll get the message loud and clear."

An engine roared nearby, and three vehicles pulled into the space behind the crowd of people with tools. Two pick ups with machine guns in the back drove forward as the people moved aside. An SUV followed behind them.

Greg lifted his radio and called for someone named *Shorewatch*.

"That you in the SUV?" Greg asked.

The radio crackled and a man's voice said, "Roger, Six Actual. We're inside. Brought a lot of bad news with us."

"Your man gonna be okay?"

"He needs aid, now. And we need to blow the bridge."

"What the hell for?"

"I told you. The Variants are back. And they've adapted again. What's your location?"

Greg didn't reply at first. He traded looks with Jennifer, and both of them eyed Emily and Danitha briefly. Greg lifted his mic again and said, "We're in the tree line behind the Dairy Queen. What's this about Variants?"

"I'll fill you in after we get LT taken care of. Heads up, the guys outside your gate here are losing their nerve. Guess a couple of .50s spooked them. Looks like they're wandering off."

"Good copy. I'll be there in a second."

Greg jogged away, heading for the SUV.

Emily wanted to follow him, to get closer so she could see what was happening. The constant hiding and waiting ate at her insides, and the news that Variants had returned sent fear racing through her. Danitha shifted her weight from one foot to the other, like she felt the same way.

"We should go," Danitha said. "Get out of here."

Jennifer waved a hand in their direction. "I wouldn't just go racing away in your condition. Only got three arms between you and a whole lot of nothing to help you make it outside the wire. And if the monsters are back, how do you think you'll survive?"

"Did fine coming here. Think we'll do fine leaving, too," Danitha said.

"What about our stuff?" Emily asked. "What did you do with our bags?"

"Wasn't much in 'em," Jennifer said. "But it's all part of the common supply now anyway. You want to take anything out with you, you'll have to ask permission. And with what just happened here at the gate, I wouldn't expect the answer to come back as *yes*."

"So we're prisoners again?" Danitha asked. "Just like Angie said, y'all ain't any better than the ones we running from."

"We're a damn sight better than those animals," Jennifer said.

"Yeah? And you want me to believe y'all would have let Angie live if she'd made it here with us? Y'all would have killed her and you know it. Y'all probably fixin' to kill me, too. They're the animals, out there? Really?"

Jennifer glared at Danitha, then stepped up close to her.

"I knew that girl and I know why she did what she did. I'm not saying we're perfect here. Hell, I don't think you can find anything like perfect in this world anymore, and you probably never could. But we're safe, and that's because we have rules we all agreed to follow. The Aftermath has plenty of places without rules, and you're welcome to try your luck with them if you want. But if you stay here, and I think you should, you'll have to accept how we do things in this community."

"And how's that? You let a woman take a beating and then wag your finger at her husband? Fuck all the way off if that's how y'all *'do things'*. I seen enough of that before the world ended."

"We can't have people deciding to take the law into their own hands the way Angie did. That's not how we keep people safe."

"How the fuck you expect people to feel safe when you tell them they can't defend themselves? What are we supposed to do, just let bad shit happen and then hope we get some justice? And don't think I'm stupid enough to believe it would be the same if it was you holding the knife instead of me. I know what justice looks like. Y'all can keep your *just us* bullshit."

Jennifer crossed her arms and stared at Danitha.

"You're part of the community for now. Nobody's opening that gate to let you out until those idiots leave. And I don't think you really want to be out there on your own." Jennifer's voice softened as she continued. "That means you contribute to the community's survival. By staying here, helping out, and providing whatever supplies or skills you can. Anything you do while you're here will be addressed by the community, and ultimately the council, if it comes to that. Anything you did before you got here isn't part of the equation. You'll be safe here."

Turning to look at Emily, she said, "You'll both be safe here."

Emily met Jennifer's gaze and nodded.

"I want to stay."

Danitha sniffed and shook her head, but said, "Guess I'm here too then."

"Then let's go to the gate and show them how standing together works."

"What if they shoot me?" Danitha asked. "You can think they out of ammo, but it ain't your body they want to put holes in."

"I'll go," Emily said. "Stay here, Dani. I'll go with Jennifer."

Danitha's eyes were wet with anger or maybe fear, but she nodded and said she'd wait. She wrapped her arms around herself and tucked back into the trees where she could stay hidden.

Emily and Jennifer walked slowly across the dirt and around the Dairy Queen building. Baytown residents were there in groups of three or four, some with weapons still aimed at the gate.

The militia had mostly left, with only a few stragglers still chucking rocks behind them as they walked away. The few still by the gate didn't even seem to recognize Emily. If they did, none of them said a word about it. Even the ones with guns in their hands didn't lift them or hold them like they would shoot. Emily watched one man throw a pistol into the dirt beside the road as he turned to walk away. Another man ran to grab it, and they argued. But none of them turned around to shoot.

From Emily's position behind the gate, it was easier to accept that Greg had been right. The militia she had been so afraid of were really just scared and hungry scavengers who happened to have weapons they couldn't use.

"We're a good community," Jennifer said to her as the last of the militia vanished from sight. "Trust me. Trust us, and tell your friend she's got nothing to be afraid of."

"I will," Emily said.

"It looks like everything's calmed down now, so I'm going to see what all this talk is about Variants and blowing up bridges."

She left Emily standing there and went to where Greg was, by the SUV that had driven up with the two pickups. Emily turned so she could see Danitha in the treeline. She was still half hidden, but lifted a hand to wave Emily over. The people with tools and weapons nearby went back to whatever they'd been doing when the militia showed up. Some stayed by the gate to confirm it wasn't damaged.

Emily went to join Danitha, but paused when she heard a familiar laugh. She turned to see Greg and Jennifer at the SUV. They were talking to whoever was inside. The doors opened and people in uniforms climbed out. Emily felt her heartbeat race as a familiar figure stepped out of the vehicle and hefted a weapon across his chest.

She was running straight for him and waving a second later, screaming her brother's name.

"*Salvador!*"

— 22 —

Jed stood by while Garza reunited with his sister. Keoh and the others got back into the SUV because Greg had recommended they take the LT over to a clinic by their fire station.

"We should take Emily, too, Sergeant," Garza said. "She's banged up bad. Got shot by one of those fuckers."

"How do you know it was them?" Jed asked.

Garza looked to his sister. She paused, then explained about how she and her friend had run through refinery towns east of Houston.

"We don't know if they were the same ones. The ones who shot us were—they had yellow eyes, and... They were still men, but they had teeth like the Variants, only—"

"*Variants?* Where did you seen them?" Jed asked.

"In the towns we went through. They were hunting something. They had a dog Variant with them."

"I thought you said the men were Variants."

"They were, but... It was like they hadn't changed fully. They were dressed... They had the same uniform as you. I only saw the ones Angie killed. But if they were the same as the ones with the dog, they had a Humvee, and we heard them say they wanted to collect bats for someone."

"Bats? What the hell for?"

"I don't know. They only said *'He wants bats'*. But the virus has affected bats, too. We saw them first, right after we escaped from the militia. They attacked alligators and took fish from the water, like raptors."

"Jesus, that's just what we need. And you're sure the people you saw were with the Variant dogs? Like they were *working* with them?"

"Yes, with the dog one. I thought they were the militia tracking us, but they had a dog monster with them, and they whistled for it and called it. Like it was their trained pet."

Jed added it up in his head and hated the answer that came to him. The person they'd seen on their march up the road wasn't a hunter out with his retriever. The crackhead in Ewell's neighborhood wasn't a druggie, and that wasn't a dog by his legs the night the place was attacked.

Greg was on his radio a few feet away. He came over as his conversation wrapped up.

"Yeah, I'll have 'em do that. We'll get whatever we can."

"What's up?" Jed asked.

"Mission brief. That was the Baytown council. They want us to hit the Home Depot and Lowe's up the street. Get as much as we can and bring it back to fortify the walls, help build up our defenses in case the wing nuts show up again."

"What about the Variants? This is bigger than making sure a bunch of whack-a-doos don't break into your little fort here."

Greg met Jed's stare, and waited a beat before replying. "The council isn't convinced they're really back."

"They're back," Jed said. "We saw them, and some of these people did, too, at the bridge and on their way here. Garza's sister here had eyes on them. You saw the dogs last night. What the—"

"I hear you, and I believe you. But the people in the trucks are saying it was scavengers they shot at out there. It's not the first time they've had to scare off gangs of hungry people who would rather steal than work for their survival."

"We saw the fucking things," Jed said.

"And the council's reluctant to buy your story without proof."

"Should we go out and get one? Bring it in so they can introduce themselves?"

Greg passed a hand over his head and sighed. "How certain are you that what you saw were Variants? Did you collect any bodies? Did they leave any marks on your vehicles?"

"Yes!" Garza's sister shouted. "We did see them, and shot them. They killed Angie—"

"That's great," Greg said. "But none of that happened here, so none of the people who make decisions here saw it happen."

"I know what I saw in Mercer's compound," Jed said. "And you know what happened at your camp."

"Yeah, I do. And as far as the council is concerned, we were attacked by wolves and wild dogs. They've seen packs of the things all over the place, and none of them have attacked Baytown. This place isn't ready for a Variant attack. None of the people here have seen one in over a year or more, and if we start making noise like that, the whole town could fall apart in chaos. People will freak the fuck out. We don't have any immediate threats inbound, at least not yet. Scouts and watchtowers are out there keeping an eye on the perimeter. The minute they see something, they'll call a *Red Event* and everyone will know about it. But until then, the council wants us to keep cool. Once we've hardened this place we can start talking to people, let them know what we *think* is happening out there."

"So we're going shopping at Home Depot while the Variants assess our strengths and find the weak spot. Or that company of morons finds some ammo and come back to put a hurt on us. Sounds brilliant."

"It's not my call, man. It's the council. Right now, they're the closest thing to CENTCOM that you'll find for a thousand miles in any direction. If you want a home inside their wire, then you and your people are on security for the materials run. That's the deal they're making."

"Another security detail. Just like Mercer. Fuck—"

Jed kicked at the ground and scanned around the area. The people holding axes and shovels had mostly dispersed. A group of six men worked on repairing the gate with an arc welder hooked up to a portable generator.

Baytown had built up defenses with trunk lids and hoods from cars welded onto lengths of train track and

173

set into concrete. It was impressive, and it would work wonders to stop any human attackers who didn't have an armored vehicle.

But Variants were a different threat. Walls were just vertical floors for those things. The dog Variants could climb as easily as the human versions, and if Garza's sister was telling the truth, the virus now affected a species that could fly.

"When do we leave?" Jed asked, looking at Greg again.

"Now. We'll stop at the clinic up the road and drop off your wounded." Greg motioned at Garza's sister.

She didn't look pleased to hear that she'd be left behind.

Greg motioned for Jed to follow him to a truck nearby. Jed waved for McKitrick to follow in the SUV.

They drove up the street a ways, passing gray corrugated buildings and fields of wrecked vehicles. A team of people worked to remove more hoods and trunk lids to pile onto a waiting flatbed trailer.

Greg turned them into the lot beside the clinic, and McKitrick pulled in behind them. A man in hospital scrubs came out with a stretcher. He helped Keoh get LT Staples onto the stretcher and then wheeled him into the clinic. Garza's sister and her friend went inside behind the nurse.

Garza got out of the SUV and stepped over to Greg's truck.

"I'll stay here, Sergeant," Garza said. "They need security."

Jed checked him with a look, but nodded and gave his Lance Corporal the okay. "Keep Mehta with you," Jed said, waving for the private to go inside.

"That puts us down two men," Greg said. "You sure that's a good idea?"

"Good as I got right now," Jed said. "I'm not leaving one man on his own here."

Greg put the truck back in gear and was about to roll out when Garza came rushing out of the clinic with Mehta following him.

"Sergeant, you gotta come in," Garza said. "Kip's squad is upstairs."

Jed was out of the truck in a flash and running for the door. Garza and Mehta were at his six. They got inside and nearly ran into a doctor and nurse who stood in the middle of a hallway leading to a set of patient rooms. A set of stairs led up to a landing in front of them.

"You got Marines up there?" Jed asked the doctor.

She stared him down and said, "We have six men who were pulled from the water yesterday. One of them—"

"Only six? Kip had eight men in his squad. Where are the others?"

"I don't know about any others. We found six men in the water. As I was saying, *one* has just regained consciousness, but the others remain in a comatose state."

Jed started to walk down the hall, but the doctor stepped in his path. "We can't allow visitors due to the possibility of contagion."

"That's great doc. I need to go see my brothers."

"I don't think you heard me—"

"Heard you just fine. Where are they?"

She held his gaze for a few breaths, then said, "The ones still in comas are on the second floor. The one who just woke up, the man named Kipler, is down the hall."

She pointed behind her. Before Jed could step around her, she was up close and in his face.

"If you want to risk exposing the entire community to Cholera or Hepatitis, by all means please disobey my orders to refrain from interacting with the patients. If you would like to visually confirm their safety, you may follow me and inspect them through the doors to their rooms."

Jed searched the doctor's eyes and found what he was looking for. She meant business, plain and simple. He may have been armed and furious, but he knew better than to start wagging his weapon around as a way of getting things done.

"Lead the way, ma'am," he said.

"Thank you," she answered before turning on her heel and marching down the hall. The nurse followed close by, putting himself between the doctor and Jed. He followed with Garza and Mehta, keeping back a few steps from the nurse.

"Emily's in there," Garza said as they passed a room on their right. "Her friend's in the next one. LT's at the end."

At the end of the hall, they turned a corner to the right, coming to a dead end with a door in each wall.

The doctor pointed to the nearest door. "Your lieutenant is in that room. Mr. Kipler is here," she said, approaching the door opposite the LT's room. She stopped in her tracks and looked through the narrow window, then slammed the door open and went inside. Jed pushed past the nurse and followed her in.

The bed was empty, but held a body until recently. The sheets were tossed like someone had flung them off. Blood spots marked the edges of the bed near a dangling

IV line. A trail of them led to the door and into the hall.

Jed spun around and followed the blood trail, kicking himself mentally. He'd been so focused on seeing one of his platoon mates, he hadn't paid attention to his surroundings.

Garza asked, "What's up, Sergeant?"

"Kipler's gone."

The doctor came out and spoke to the nurse, who rushed around the corner and back down the hall. His footsteps echoed on the tile floor.

"How about we go upstairs and check the others?" Jed suggested. "I'm guessing that's where Kip went. First thing I'd do is check my people."

"And I can appreciate that," the doctor said. "For now, I have to ask you to leave while I establish what happened with Mr. Kipler. I'm sure one of my nurses can explain."

"You want us to leave after we've been inside a building that might be contaminated because you lost a patient?" Jed asked, knowing his words would hit a nerve. He wasn't wrong.

"I have patients relying on me and my staff for their safety and well-being. Stay out of our way, and you can do whatever the hell you think you need to do."

She stormed away from him, through the door at the end of the hall.

"What now, Sergeant?" Garza asked as they turned around and headed to the stairs.

"Now we have a problem," Jed said.

Garza's sister poked her head out of her room. Jed motioned to Garza and Mehta that they should keep moving, but Emily had the same look of disappointment on her face from before.

"I'll follow you if you leave. What is the problem we have?"

Garza gave his sister a thumbs up. "She's good to go, Sergeant. Anything you need to say, she'll hear it from me later anyway. Not like there's any national security to worry about these days, right?"

"Okay," Jed said, leading them into Emily's room. "I want the whole squad to hear it, but—If I'm wrong, and if this gets around too much, we'll just be starting a panic for nothing."

"So what's up? You seem shook," Garza said.

"I'm worried about Kip. He was in a coma when they got here. He was supposed to be in that room, and the doctor seems to think he was taken somewhere. But I'm thinking it's something else."

Garza's sister perked up. She'd sat on her bed, but stood quickly and joined them by the door.

"You think the virus is active again," she said.

"Pretty much. You said you saw bats and dogs. We've seen the dogs, too. And we were attacked by the human variety on our way to the bridge. I'm thinking the virus changed, like it's been asleep or hiding the past two years and now it's starting to wake up."

"Can viruses do that?" Garza asked. "I thought they die without a host."

"*Sí*, that is one way they can die," his sister said. "But some can go into a latent state, waiting for a host to arrive."

"For two years?" Jed asked.

"If the virus is robust, it can survive outside an ideal host given the right conditions. Humidity helps, so it would make sense that the Variant virus would survive here."

Jed thought about the people they'd seen with the dogs. The hunter and the crackhead. If they were infected, they would show symptoms, wouldn't they? And their men who came in comatose. What if that was just the virus working on them?

"What about inside a host?" he asked. "Is it possible that a virus would live in an ideal host, but they wouldn't show symptoms yet? Like, could the virus decide to turn itself off or on?"

Garza's sister shook her head, but paused before replying.

"I thought about that when I saw the men Angie killed. Their eyes were just like a Variant's. The same color, I mean. But still human. And their teeth—it was like they had half developed, like the virus wasn't fully expressing in them."

"Or maybe it was waiting for the right moment?" Jed asked.

She paused and shook her head, with a sad look pulling her mouth into a frown.

"The bats," she said. "They—they hibernate. The rabies virus can hibernate inside them. If the Variant virus evolved to become like rabies, it could survive the same way."

"So it just lives in them until the bats wake up?" Jed asked.

"Rabies does not always express in bats. Even if they are carriers, they may never show symptoms. Some viruses can lie dormant within a host. Like herpes. It can be controlled, but is sometimes reactivated by environmental conditions."

"Like what?"

"Usually some kind of stress on the body, so the immune system becomes compromised and cannot effectively control the virus."

Jed saw a reality forming in his mind's eye, and it wasn't one he wanted to consider. He just had one more question that needed answering. Garza caught his eye and asked, "You got something you need to tell us, Sergeant? I ain't down with being left in the dark like what the LT did. You got something, you gotta let us know."

"I know, Garza, but I want the whole squad to hear it. Let's get with our people outside."

— 23 —

Emily followed her brother and the young Marine, Mehta. Chava's sergeant was outside already. He called to the other Marines, and they grouped up around him. Greg was in his truck on the radio, casting looks in their direction as he nodded along to his conversation. He opened his door as they passed his truck.

"Hey, Sergeant Welch! We don't leave soon, the sun's gonna set before we even get there. We need light to work."

Chava's sergeant yelled back. "We got bigger problems, Radout! We'll go when we're ready."

Emily felt the argument building, but both men seemed to prefer silence to more yelling. Greg closed his door and talked into his radio again. Emily followed her brother to where his fellow Marines stood beside the SUV they'd come in.

"What's the deal, Sergeant?" he asked.

"Deal is we have people upstairs in this building. One of them is unaccounted for. Only—Shit, there's no easy way to say this. I don't think he's one of ours anymore."

All of the Marines took this news differently. The woman named McKitrick was the first to say anything.

"You saying Sergeant Kip is infected?" she asked.

"I'm saying we need to police him up. If he is infected, then the best thing we can do is get him far away from this place before he does something that spreads the disease."

"But how is that possible?" the other woman asked. "Wouldn't he be showing signs? He'd have a sucker face, right?"

Emily felt the words on her tongue before she knew she was saying them.

"The virus could be latent inside him."

Everyone looked at her, and she continued. "If it is dormant, or prone to going dormant, then it could be that he's just a carrier. Like bats and rabies, or with herpes. You don't know a person has it just by looking at them, unless the virus is expressing at the time."

"And you said that stress could trigger it, right?" Chava's sergeant asked her.

"*Sí.* Yes, that can be true. But we don't know—"

The creak of a car door stopped her. Greg had left his truck and was walking toward them. All of the Marines tensed and held their guns a little tighter.

Greg said, "Sergeant, I'm out of time. My people are at the north gate already. We're moving out in fifteen minutes, with or without you. But if you don't come along, the council's going to be less happy with the idea of keeping you around. The gear we brought got us inside, but you gotta pull your weight to earn a place to lay your head at night. I'll wait for you at the gate just before the drainage canal. It's up the street. You can't miss it."

When Greg had gone back to his truck, Chava's

sergeant picked up Emily's explanation.

"I think the virus is living inside people around here. Not everyone, but enough to make me think we've got an enemy hiding in plain sight."

"How do you know this?" Emily asked him.

"You said you've seen people with symptoms. Yellow eyes, and the beginnings of those needle teeth. And we've seen people acting like they've got something wrong with them, or doing things that don't make sense. That hunter we saw on the way up here," he said to his people. "Who the hell wanders around the wilderness like that? Even before we confirmed the monsters were back, can you see anyone doing that these days?"

The Marines all nodded and mumbled their replies.

"So if the virus is working on people, making them act weird, but keeping them human, it has to be for a reason. Why does an enemy hide?"

"It's not ready to attack. Like it's waiting for the advantage," Mehta said.

"That's what I'm thinking," the sergeant replied. "That's what I'm thinking and it's what I'm worried about. We need to go inside, see which of our guys are in there and make sure they're all good to go. Especially Kip. If he's good, we take him with us on this mission. If he's not, we take him anyway and make sure we get him far away from these people before the virus decides to come out and play."

The group turned to go back inside, and Emily had to step backwards quickly to avoid being run down by one of the women Marines, the one named Keoh. She looked to Chava, but he waved for her to stay put.

"You're safer out here," he said, sending a wink in her direction.

Emily thought she should get into the SUV, so she wouldn't be out in the open. The door to the clinic swung out and the doctor and her nurse stood there scanning the parking area. The nurse's eyes landed on her and he called out.

"What are you doing out here? We need you inside under observation."

He waved for them to come back in. Emily looked to her brother again. His sergeant was motioning for her to do as the nurse asked. She stepped forward, but Chava spoke up before they got any closer to the building.

"I want to stay with them," he said.

"Okay, Garza. Stand post outside their rooms. We'll head upstairs and look for Kip. See who else is up there."

The doctor came over to them as they turned to go inside.

"You find Kip?" the sergeant asked.

"No, and we've looked everywhere, so I have to assume he left the building somehow. I'm on my way to inform the fire chief and advise the community to be on the watch for him."

"What about the other guys?"

"Their status has not changed. Still comatose."

"We're going up there to check. I need to know who you have inside."

"I'm fine with you checking on your people, but the same rule still applies. Their doors are locked. You can confirm their identity through the windows. I'm sorry if that's not good enough for you, but it's what I'm willing to offer. If you jeopardize the safety of this community by breaking into the rooms, you will be judged by the council and very likely cast out."

The sergeant stared at her, then quickly walked away with his other people, leaving Emily and Chava with the nurse. The doctor said something about going to the fire station, then marched away. Emily followed the nurse inside with her brother walking close behind her. He kept looking over his shoulder as they passed the empty rooms. When they reached Emily's room, he came to stand next to the door like a guard. Emily looked through the narrow window at the dark and empty space of her room.

"Can I be with Danitha?" she asked.

"Why?" the nurse demanded.

"Because if either of us is infected with something, the other one probably is, too. We have been through everything together the last two days."

The made some notes on charts hanging by their doors, gave a shrug, and left them outside the room. Emily walked down the hall to Danitha's room and found her rifling through drawers and cabinets around a sink in the corner.

"Ain't nothing in here," she said. "Not even the damn tongue sticks they use to make you say *Aaaah*. How we supposed to defend ourselves without a weapon?"

"You'll be okay," her brother said. "Both of you. Just stay put, and don't freak out if you start hearing things. I'll be right here."

Danitha stopped digging through the cabinets and looked at Emily. "You should tell him you're not a little girl, Professor. You shot one of them things with that pistol, remember? And we made it all this way without him."

"She's right," Emily said to her brother. "But I'm glad you're here just the same. If something happens, we'll be a team, all three of us."

"Oorah, Emi," Chava said, gripping her good shoulder. "Guess you're still my big sister after all."

He stepped into the hall, letting the door close part way. He looked over his shoulder at Emily, and she saw her fear reflected in his eyes.

"Stay put, okay," he said. "I'ma check up and down the hall quick."

He let the door close and moved out of Emily's line of sight. Danitha went back to digging through the drawers and cabinets, cursing quietly to herself. Raised voices vibrated through the space. It sounded like they were coming from upstairs. Rushing feet and shouting followed, and then a sound Emily was dreading to hear.

A shriek, like the monsters would make when they saw prey.

Danitha stopped searching and froze in the corner by the sink. Emily went to the door, but did not open it. Chava was nowhere in sight. Emily stepped away from the small window and felt the walls tighten around her. The room was cramped with a bed in the middle and two chairs against the wall by the door. If a single Variant got inside, it would kill her and Danitha before either of them could reach safety.

— 24 —

Jed took his people up the stairs in teams. McKitrick and Mehta had their six while he and Keoh took point, climbing the flight two steps at a time until they came to a set of doors at the landing. Jed went through first, checked his near corner and ran the left wall, leading to the patient rooms. His squad filed in behind him. Jed signaled his zone was clear and turned to see McKitrick echo it.

Jed relaxed his posture a little. Straight ahead from the doors was a check-in counter with a nurse's station behind it. Three African-American women and one Asian man in scrubs stepped into view behind the counter. When they spotted Jed and his people, they went stiff and quiet.

"You got Marines up here, right?" Jed asked them.

"Yeah," said one of the women. "Who are you?"

"Sergeant Welch, USMC. Which rooms?"

The nurses traded looks and mumbled until one of the women said, "All the rooms. They down the hall there, but you can't—"

"On me," Jed said. He motioned for his squad to follow and moved out, doing his best to ignore the burning fear in his gut. Something was off about the whole situation, and none of the people here seemed to notice it. They probably assumed the men were in comas because they'd nearly drowned. Jed felt certain it was a lot worse than that.

With Mehta and McKitrick in the lead, they moved down the hall in teams again. Doors lined the left side of the hall up here. Jed paused to check through the narrow window in the doors. Every room had a Marine in it, lying in a bed and hooked up to an IV.

"This ain't good, Sergeant," Keoh said as they passed the third set of rooms. "Sergeant Kipler's squad looks real sick. And I bet I know with what."

Jed had an answer on his tongue when Kipler stepped around the corner up ahead. He had on his pants and boots, but no jacket. His wrists and upper arms were bandaged. Streaks of dry blood lined one arm where he'd torn the IV out. He froze in his tracks and stared at them like he'd never seen them before. Jed's people had their weapons at the ready, but everyone's muzzle was still aimed at the floor. Kipler stood in place, shifting his weight side to side.

"Yo, Kip," Jed called to him. "Glad you made it."

He didn't respond, just kept staring. A trickle of blood, like a tear, spilled down Kip's cheek, and his mouth twitched into a sneer. His eyes clouded with a yellow haze and he twisted away, running around the corner he'd just turned. Jed raced forward, calling his team to stack behind him. One of the nurses yelled after them.

"What's going on? What's wrong?"

"Get everyone outside!" Jed shouted over his shoulder.

He rounded the corner into an empty hall with two doors at the end. His people came around with him.

"Mehta, McKitrick; keep an eye on our six. Keoh, on me. First door."

They were at the door when a shriek burst from deeper in the building. It was a sound that only a Variant could make, and it was followed by frightened voices and shouts.

Jed breached the first door and pushed into an empty office with Keoh close behind him.

"McKitrick; second door. We're on your six."

He heard the door open and his people rush inside. He and Keoh stacked and followed the others in.

They'd come into the area behind the reception desk. An office to their left had been converted to a makeshift surgery. Two closets faced them from the opposite wall. An x-ray room and offices were down a hall to their right. The light was dim, with fewer windows letting in what was left of the sun.

Another scream split through the building, and this time it was a human scream of agony. Shouts of fear and horror followed.

Jed led his people toward the sound, down the hall. He swiveled to check the x-ray as they passed it. The room was empty. The second was the same.

The third room was a waiting area that extended off the back of the nurse's station. Kipler was on the ground, hunched over a body in scrubs. And he was feeding.

Jed and Keoh lit him up, sending him spiraling away trailing blood and viscera from the nurse he had killed. It was one of the women. Jed stalked forward, maintaining aim at Kipler's still twitching body. He double-tapped him as he got closer. Kip's clawed hands curled up over his chest, like he was a dead spider. His legs continued to spasm, clicking as they jerked in and out for a moment before his body relaxed and went still.

"Shit," Keoh said. "Oh shit, oh shit, oh shit. I fucking knew it."

"They're back," McKitrick said. "But how did he—He fucking turned at will. He—"

"The virus is adaptive," Jed said. "The scientists I talked to on Plum were always saying that. It changes to survive, and it's made a big change now. It can hide until it's ready to strike."

The other nurses poked their heads out from an office further along the hall.

"Told y'all to get outside," Jed said.

None of the nurses said a word. They just stared at the dead Variant.

"You need to quarantine this building now," Jed said. "This floor is off limits."

"You can't make that call," one of the nurses said.

"No? Then who can?"

"Doctor DuBois. Her or another member of the council."

"She the lady from downstairs? Where is she now?"

"I don't know. I'll call her," the nurse said and grabbed for an intercom on the wall.

"Doctor DuBois!" she yelled into the mic.

"What is it? What's happening up there? Are those men shooting people?"

The nurse looked at Jed. Her finger was frozen above the intercom button.

"She's inside, in her office?"

The nurses all nodded. "Probably, yeah," the Asian man said.

"Go downstairs, all of you," Jed said. "Let her know what happened and get outside. We'll be right behind you."

The nurses scrambled to be the first through the doors and down the stairs. Jed grabbed the mic from Mehta's radio and hailed Greg.

"Six Actual, Shorewatch 1, over."

"You finally ready to go?"

"No, we lost another man. But I got your proof. Call the council and tell them we're doing a partial evac and lock down here."

"What? Why—and why partial?"

"Because our people they fished out of the bay may be carrying a new form of the original virus."

The radio was silent for a few beats. Then Greg came on.

"Okay, Sergeant. You got your wish. But the council wants to verify your proof. Can you bring it out?"

"Negative. We're not touching it. Doctor DuBois will verify it for them. After that, this second floor gets locked down and nobody comes in without PPE."

"Good luck with that. Nobody has that kind of gear around here, and they're not going to like taking orders from a military man. These people are mostly civilians who survived on their own. If we're being honest, they don't trust you any farther than they can throw you. Most of them blame the military for what happened."

"Well they can un-blame us because we just saved them a whole lot of hurt. Be sure you tell them to watch their own people. Anybody acting weird, standoffish, hanging around the fringes. They're probably carriers and need to be quarantined. Yellow eyes is a dead give away, but don't freak them out. Stress could trigger them to change."

"Okay, I'll relay the message."

Jed motioned for his people to follow as he went back the way they'd come. They stopped in front of every room in the ward, checking the comatose Marines for any indication they were about to wake up as Variants. Each man slept like the dead as far as Jed could tell.

Keoh was nearby, looking in the window beside him while the others maintained security.

"Should we kill them, Sergeant? For mercy?"

Jed thought about it for a second, then tried the door. It was locked, just like the doctor said.

"Guess that's our answer. For now anyway."

Jed wanted to give Kip's squad the mercy they deserved. Providing they didn't wake up, it would just mean a quick double tap to save those men from the hell of being consumed by the Hemorrhage Virus. The remaining biohazard would be a threat though, and he couldn't see any way to address that without burning the place to the ground.

He signaled the team to head for the stairs. They needed to get Garza and the others out of this building.

— 25 —

The shooting upstairs stopped almost as soon as it started. Emily's brother had come running into the room to stand watch. He was by the door, looking out the slim window.

"What was that, Chava?" she asked. "Why were they shooting?"

"Only one reason, and it ain't a good one. *Shit!* I knew we should have stayed together. Bunch of bullshit letting that nurse stick us in here."

He backed away from the door and turned to face her and Danitha. "You need to be ready to move, and grab a weapon. Anything you can use. Fire extinguisher, scalpel, whatever."

"Already looked all over this room," Danitha said. "Ain't nothing worth taking that won't slow us down except maybe the IV stand."

She grabbed it and flipped it over. The base was bolted onto the stem, making it hard to balance as a spear. But she could use it to push a monster away. Emily knew it was foolish to think they'd survive with that as their only weapon, but it was what they had for now.

Her brother was about to open the door when it was flung open, pushing him backward. He brought his gun up and aimed at a cluster of people charging into the room.

"Chava, *no!*" Emily yelled.

It was Doctor DuBois and two nurses. They stumbled into the room, nearly knocking Danitha over as they bustled into the farthest corner from the door.

"What are they shooting at?" Doctor DuBois asked, looking at the ceiling.

"My guess is a Variant," Chava said.

They stayed in the room like that, clustered in corners and staring at the ceiling and door. Emily feared any second that it would burst open, spilling a mob of snarling monsters into the confines of their shelter.

When footsteps sounded in the corridor outside, Emily's heart jumped. Her brother waved everyone to stay behind him and took a stance opposite the door with his weapon raised.

Emily could hear doors opening and closing in the hall. Someone knocked on the door, but she couldn't see anyone through the little window.

"Variants don't knock," Danitha said. "Guessing that's your friends from upstairs, right?"

Chava took a step toward the door. "Who is it?" he called out.

"It's us, Garza. We're good," a man's voice said. Her brother went to the door and opened it with one hand, then quickly stepped back with his gun aimed at the door. It swung inward gently and his sergeant looked into the room.

"Good to see you, too, Garza," he said, motioning for

Chava to lower his gun. The sergeant came in, with his people at the door behind him. The two women stayed outside with Mehta.

Doctor DuBois asked what happened upstairs. The sergeant told them they had found one of their people. Only he had been infected by the virus, and it reactivated when they approached him.

"He changed and killed a nurse before we could stop him. We had our weapons on him. That could have spooked him, stressed him out enough that the virus took over and forced him to change."

"True," Doctor DuBois said. "The virus might be triggered by stress indicating a threat to the host organism. But it could also be that he was always going to change, no matter what. We don't know for sure if it's simply latency we're dealing with. And we don't have the facilities to test the virus to determine what it is or how it operates. The best I can do is test for its presence."

"So what do we do?" Emily asked. "We can't stay here. What if the virus is airborne?"

"Then we're all infected anyway and should just kill ourselves," one of the nurses said.

"The hell we do," Chava said. "What's the plan, Sergeant?"

"We lock down the second floor. Nobody goes in without security and PPE, and only if it's essential to the community's survival. We have to write off the sick people upstairs."

"You got *more* people inside this building with the *virus* in 'em?" Danitha demanded "Good*bye*, y'all. I'm out. The hell with this."

She moved to leave, but Chava put an arm out to bar

her exit. She tried to push past, until the other Marines blocked her as well.

"Fine," Danitha said. "Y'all motherfuckers keep us here like prisoners. I hope I change first so I can fuck you up."

Emily went to her and put her good arm around her shoulders. "We are with the right people, Dani. They're not like the militia."

"Sure look and act like it," she said.

Chava and his sergeant started talking in quiet voices. Mehta went back outside, then Chava followed him. He looked back at Emily and motioned for her to stay put. When she frowned at him, he relaxed his face and said, "We're just keeping watch in the hall. Y'all are safer inside than out here."

Chava's sergeant asked Doctor DuBois, "When did Kip wake up? What time? And how long was he out?"

"He—it must have been an hour ago. He was semi-conscious when we found them yesterday, but slipped into a coma overnight. I'd say he was unconscious for at least sixteen hours. Maybe a little less."

"And the other guys have been out cold since they got here?"

"Yes, but they had all nearly drowned. Their boat was overturned just off shore. Mr. Kipler had pulled two of them from the water himself. He was going back for a third when our people arrived to help."

"So you don't know how long any of them have been unconscious. Which means they could change at any minute," the sergeant said.

"Or they could just be carriers of the virus."

"Keep talking like that, doc, and you'll get a chance to

know for sure. Only it won't matter because we'll all be dead. The men upstairs are infected, just like Kip was, with the original virus. Only it's evolved so that it can hide until it wants to attack."

"The *original* virus?" Doctor DuBois asked. "If that's true—"

"*How do we fight against it?*" one of the nurses demanded. "If the virus hides now, how do we know who is a carrier and who isn't? We could all be carriers, right?" The nurse grew more frantic with each word that passed his lips.

Doctor DuBois looked the man in the eye. She crossed the room to stand in front of him and slapped him.

"Go on," she encouraged him. "Your turn." When he didn't move to strike her she went to Danitha and smacked her across the face. Danitha had a hand raised in a flash, but held back.

"Go ahead, but remember I might be saving your life someday," Doctor DuBois said.

Danitha struck her with enough force to make a sound and turn the woman's head to the side. After a few seconds, Doctor DuBois regarded the room.

"I think it's safe to say that neither Nurse Ray, this young lady, nor myself are infected. If stress or threat to the host is the trigger that activates the virus, we should all be growing claws and tearing the rest of you to pieces."

"What if you'd been wrong?" Emily asked.

"Then I'd have been very foolish, and also very dead. I'm not suggesting we all take the same test, but I do think we have a good indication of how to assess a person's susceptibility." She looked from the nurse to Danitha as she spoke. "Anyone displaying signs of emotional distress and anger is probably just frightened, and who wouldn't be? But people acting like they're under threat of harm at inappropriate times or under illogical conditions—those are people we'll want to be careful around. I don't see anyone here acting strangely, so I'm going to assume we're all clean."

"Sounds like a good way to get people killed," Danitha said.

"Yes, it does. That's why I'm going to insist on blood tests for everyone in this building. My office is down the hall. We'll compare the samples to those already taken from the persons on the second floor."

"What about the body up there, Doctor?" one of the nurses asked.

"We'll block off the stairwell as best we can. Sergeant, I assume you and your people won't continue to take orders from me, being only a civilian, but I was at one time a Lieutenant Commander in the Navy. If that suffices, I'll ask that you proceed to complete the supply run the council asked of you when you arrived, providing you leave two people here to assist with security in the building. Alternately, you can all go, and I'll inform the council that you cannot be relied upon to help protect the community."

Emily waited as Chava's sergeant faced off with Doctor DuBois. Finally, he said, "I'm not sure whose orders I should be following, ma'am. At some point, I'll probably just go with feels right to me, but I'll do what you ask. *After* we've dealt with our brothers upstairs."

Emily released a breath she hadn't realized she was

holding. Danitha slumped against the bed. "We gon' die in here," she said, crossing her arms over her chest.

"You're welcome to stay here," Doctor DuBois said to her. "But I'm moving all non-essential personnel to the fire station next door. There's a day room with beds and a kitchen there. You both look like you could use some—"

A scream cut her off. Everyone in the room tensed, and the Marines spilled into the hallway with their weapons up. Emily stayed with the doctor and the others inside the room.

"It came from down the hall," McKitrick said.

Chava's sergeant called for them to follow, but he left Keoh and Mehta behind. They stayed inside the room, on either side of the door, watching the hallway.

Gunfire erupted, echoing through the building and Emily slapped her hands over her ears, praying for her brother's safety and for all of their lives.

— 26 —

The screams came from the end of the hall, around the corner where the LT was supposed to be. Jed ran forward with his M4 up and ready. He felt McKitrick and Garza behind him. The screaming cut short with a gurgling sound and a shriek. Banging followed, like doors being slammed open and closed. At the corner, Jed spun right and darted to the opposite wall. A sucker face crouched on all fours with its back to him, half in and half out of the door at the end of the hallway. Jed fired a burst at it as he ran forward. He missed and the monster raced away, disappearing deeper into the clinic. Jed pulled up short a few steps from the LT's room.

The door to the room was open, and blood splatter stained the walls and floor of the hall. The door at the end of the hall was still open, and trails of gore showed the path the monster had taken. Without PPE, Jed wasn't going anywhere near the mess. He backed up a step, but kept his weapon trained on the door straight ahead as it slowly swung closed with a heavy click.

"Somebody upstairs woke up."

"So they're all infected," McKitrick said. "We have to—"

"We don't know that," Garza said.

Jed wanted to believe they could save some of Kip's squad. Having more Marines around him meant more security. More safety.

"Let's get back to the others," he said. "Maintain three-sixty security. Move out."

They shuffled back down the hall with McKitrick leading the way and Jed covering their six. Garza stayed in the middle, rotating his view front to back. When they reached the room with the others, Jed called for them all to exit.

"We're going outside. Everyone stay close and tight. Mehta, Keoh; take point. McKitrick, back here with me."

"We're saying LT's gone?" Garza asked. "Do we confirm?"

"Negative. Nobody goes near that room. Nobody stays in this building. We torch it. Everyone out."

The doctor had something to say about that. "You're going to burn my clinic down? Do you have any idea how long it took to rebuild this place and get it even halfway functional as a sterile facility? You can't—"

"Were you a doctor when the virus broke the first time?" Jed asked.

"Yes, I was. In Houston. I saw—"

"Then you know how fast one of those things can tear through a building. You had five of them sleeping upstairs. That number is now down to four, and there's no telling when the others are going to wake up. They might be awake and busting out of their rooms right now just like the first one did."

Jed paused. He hated the words that found their way to his tongue, but he knew he had no choice.

"We need to put them down before any more of them come back as sucker faces, and then we need to burn this building to the ground. You have biohazards on both floors now, and no way of dealing with them. More importantly, you have a sucker face loose down here. The longer we wait, the more likely it finds a way outside. We need to kill it while it's contained, and the best way to do that is to torch this building."

"You're willing to burn those men alive without knowing for certain that they're infected?" Doctor DuBois asked.

"You have samples of their blood, right?"

"Yes. We collected blood, skin, and saliva samples from all of them."

"Then test it. Do you have a lab here? Anything you can use?"

"I don't have much, but I should be able to confirm if the virus is present. If it is, what then? You're still talking about setting fire to the only hospital we have and with your own people still alive inside it."

It cut deep to think about killing his own brothers while they were in comas, even though it meant saving them from a worse fate. But he hated waiting on the doctor for approval. As much as he understood her wish to keep the clinic intact, they had a live Variant inside and two kill sites covered in hazardous material. The CDC was a long way from here, if it even existed anymore. Nobody was going to clean that place up, not without risk of spreading the virus even farther.

Sergeant Kipler and one of his Marines had proven Jed's fears were well founded. They'd seen enough to know what they were dealing with.

The Hemorrhage Virus was alive and well, and it had evolved to be more deadly than before.

"If they have the virus in them, they're not really alive. You know that as well as I do. Give me proof that they're infected. We'll go in and put them down. Then we burn the place."

— 27 —

Jed's squad, minus Garza, provided security for Doctor DuBois while she gathered lab materials from her office, including blood sample vials, syringes, and cheek swabs. They maintained watch up and down the halls, and moved quickly to rejoin the others, making the whole trip without sighting the Variant once. They heard it though, clicking and scrabbling around the second floor.

After the doctor collected samples from everyone, she and her nurses went to the fire station where they would determine if anyone was infected. Jed and McKitrick followed her over as security while Keoh and Mehta kept watch on the clinic doors. Garza escorted his sister and her friend over, then went to monitor the clinic.

Jed made sure the doctor was good to go, and he gave her one of the radios they got from Mercer.

McKitrick tested it with her and confirmed good commo. That done, the doctor went to work examining the blood samples. McKitrick joined the rest of the squad outside, but Jed hung back for a moment. He needed to ask the doctor for a favor.

"Let me know first if you find anything, okay? If any

of my people are compromised, I mean. I want—I'll deal with it."

"That's fine by me," Doctor DuBois said. "I'll let you know as soon as I get any results. Fingers crossed they'll all be good."

"*Errah.* We'll be outside, watching the place in case any of Kip's people wake up and get loose."

Kipler's squad was still comatose as far as they knew. No new shrieks or screeches had been heard since they evacuated the building. But they still had one Variant loose inside.

Jed joined the squad set in a perimeter around the clinic. It wasn't much, with only five of them on the ground, but they at least had full visual coverage of the building. They would see any Variants that managed to escape. The building was a wide squat box with a second floor set back on the side nearest the fire station to make room for a helipad.

The bird was gone, and probably smashed in a bayou somewhere.

Jed called to rotate positions every fifteen minutes. Standing in one place, staring at the same stupid wall was a good way to let boredom sink in, and that would just make room for complacency to follow along for the ride. Even with rotations, Jed couldn't stop himself from dreaming that they'd find a helicopter that would get them back to Galveston. Just as fast, his thoughts turned to the futility of doing that.

Why the hell should we go back there? LT's dead, Gunny's a traitor, and the civilians are all beach bums.

McKitrick's radio crackled. "Sergeant Welch," Doctor DuBois said.

He walked over and took the mic from McKitrick. "I'm here. What do you have?"

"All clear, Sergeant. Your people, that is. I'm afraid the men we have upstairs…"

"I need confirmation, Doctor," Jed said.

"They're infected. All of them. I'm showing signs of viral infection in all six men. But, of course, we already know two of them were infected, so it's not surprising they all are. I'm sorry, Sergeant. I know they were your… I know they're like your family."

"Roger," Jed said.

"We have some sedatives and morphine that may help. It would amount to a lethal injection, but in their comatose state, assuming they are all still unconscious, I doubt they'd experience any discomfort. You could administer the doses yourself."

"Thanks, Doctor."

Jed rounded up his squad and filled them in. "Think of it as a mercy mission. We're doing this for our brothers."

"What about the one that's already changed?" Keoh asked.

"We see him, we put him down. Don't hesitate. He's not our brother anymore. That man is already dead and gone. You'll just be killing a monster."

A nurse exited the fire station, carrying a small bundle. He held it out to Jed along with a set of keys and said, "There's five syringes in there, loaded with the sedative-morphine mixture. It should stop their hearts. But you guys have guns if you need to make sure. Those are Doctor DuBois's keys. She'll need them back when you're done."

Jed took the bundle and gave it to Mehta to carry. He

pocketed the keys, then led the squad back to the clinic.

They entered in teams, with him and Keoh on point, Garza and McKitrick at their six, and Mehta in the middle carrying the bundle of syringes.

The bottom floor was quiet. No scrabbling sounds echoed from anywhere. No doors banged open. No shrieks pierced the stillness.

Walking heel-toe, and checking every room they passed, Jed took them down the hall to the corner at the end.

"I want to confirm the LT's gone for good. Watch your feet and don't get any of the blood on you. McKitrick and Garza, stay at our six, watching the hall. Keoh, cover the door at the end, where the Variant went through. We've got one in here with us; remember that. Eyes and ears open and we all come out of this. *Errah?*"

They all replied with a grunted *Errr* and followed him around the corner. The blood had begun to dry and separate in areas. Spatters colored the tile floor in a trail, like the blood itself wanted to escape the LT's room. Jed shook the horror movie ideas from his head and stepped carefully around the pools and streaks until he could see inside.

LT Staples, or what was left of him, was lying in the bed. He'd been shredded by the sucker face and would not be getting back up, even if the virus did incubate inside him somehow.

"LT is confirmed dead," he said as he lifted his rifle and aimed. He had to be sure. Jed fired a single shot into the LT's body, right in the heart. It helped that his target was visible.

The team moved back down the hall and upstairs,

maintaining formation around Mehta. At the top, Jed and Keoh breached and the others filed in behind them. McKitrick posted by the doors, watching the stairs for contact. Keoh and Garza kept security of the upper floor and hallway.

Jed and Mehta went to the first room. One of Kip's guys was in there, hooked up to the IV and lying silently on the bed. Jed unlocked the door and opened it a crack. He blocked it with his foot while he took the syringes from Mehta.

They moved in with weapons up. He had Mehta take position in the doorway, covering the man in the bed.

Without thinking about what he was actually doing, Jed readied a syringe and inserted the needle into a node in the IV line, whispering an apology as he pushed the plunger all the way down.

"I'm sorry, brother. Semper Fi."

Seconds ticked by and the body slowly relaxed. Jed felt for a pulse and waited until he confirmed the man's heart wasn't beating.

They proceeded down the hall in the same way, working as quickly as they could and always against the fear that one of the remaining men would wake up before they got to him, or that the one who had already awakened would burst out of a hiding place. But they went through four rooms and four syringes with the only difficulty being the pain Jed felt at what he had to do.

"What do we do with the last syringe?" Mehta asked.

Jed held it in his hand, weighing its value. If one of them became infected… He stuck the syringe in an empty ammo pouch.

"Let's get out of here, and—"

A Variant's shriek cut him off. It sounded like it came from the first floor.

"Downstairs! Rally outside! If you see it, kill it!"

Keoh joined Jed and Mehta as they retreated down the hall, pivoting as they moved and covering every access point they could see. The telltale clicking of a Variant's joints came to Jed's ears, then the scraping of its claws.

"It's up here, Sergeant," Keoh said as she moved down the hall ahead of him.

"I hear it. Sounds like it's back where Kip was at. Keep moving."

Mehta was at their six. Jed tapped him on the shoulder and swapped positions. He wasn't going to lose anyone this time.

They reached the last room before the stairs. Garza and McKitrick were there, holding positions to cover the reception area and the landing. McKitrick aimed the 203 toward the door to the stairs. She only had smoke rounds left, but that might be just what they needed. If it confused the Variant enough, they could probably kill it before it could strike.

"Garza, Keoh; watch our six. We follow McKitrick down the stairs. Move out." Jed slapped Mehta on the shoulder, urging him forward. He turned back to check the hall behind him when a dark shape flew from behind the reception counter.

Garza opened up with the M27 and Keoh added a burst, but they missed. The thing was too damn fast. It slammed through the doors and skittered down the stairs before they could correct their aim.

McKitrick and Garza pushed after it, firing as they moved through the doors. Keoh waited for Mehta and

Jed. They raced down the stairs after the others and grouped up by the door.

"Anyone see it?" Jed asked.

A chorus of *No* answered him.

"It's gone," Garza said. "Motherfucker got out."

Jed checked the door. It didn't show signs of a Variant passing through it. No scratches or claw marks showed on the surface. He checked the floor and ceiling tiles leading into the hall. A trail of blood led down to a door near the end. It was cracked a few inches and slowly closed as he watched it.

"That room. Stack on me."

The squad filed down the hall with their weapons up and ready. They pivoted to each room they passed and confirmed it was empty. Jed's finger itched to squeeze the trigger each time he rotated his aim into a room, but he forced himself to keep it extended along the receiver. He'd fire when it was time. When he could see his enemy.

The door up ahead opened and a foot appeared. Jed focused his aim and almost squeezed the trigger. The foot was wearing a shredded boot below digi-cam pants that were just as torn up. The leg was human. It was one of Kip's men, but…

"Who is that? Are you hurt?" Jed called out.

"N—no. It's me, Sergeant. PFC Alford. Why're y'all shooting at me?"

"Ain't shooting at you, Alfie. There's a Variant in here. It was upstairs and now it's down here. What the fuck are you doing down here? How'd you get out of your room?"

"Doctor let me out," Alford said. "She said I was good to go. Can I come out?"

Jed waited before answering. He checked his people.

They were all focused on their zones, and each of them was on full alert, adrenaline pushing them just like it was pushing him.

"Okay," Jed called. "C'mon out, Alfie. We'll get you out of here."

The Marine stepped into the hall. He was one of the men from Kip's squad all right. Jed recognized him even though he'd only seen him a few times before Kip bailed from Galveston.

Alford moved with a limp as he walked down the hall. His other leg was bleeding from a gunshot wound in his thigh, and a trail of blood marked where an IV had been ripped from his arm.

"Thought you said you weren't hurt, Alfie. And why'd you rip out the IV if Doc said you were good to go?"

Alford stopped and lowered his head. He looked up again and his eyes had turned a sickly yellow, lined with bloody veins. His mouth changed as Jed stared, unable to believe what he was seeing. Before Alford could fully turn, McKitrick opened up on him, sending the infected Marine tumbling to the floor with holes in his belly. He crashed down and scrabbled around, bleeding from the wounds. Jed double-tapped him and he went still.

"Oh fuck, *fuck!*" Mehta said. "They can change back. They—Shit, how do we know, Sergeant? If one of us—"

"We're clean!" Jed said, eyeing every member of his squad in turn. "Doc said we're all clean. She confirmed Kip's squad wasn't."

"Time to GTFO, right Sergeant?" Garza said.

"Lead the way, Garza. You and Keoh."

They moved as a unit, with Mehta in the middle and Jed and McKitrick stepping backwards. His gaze went from the dead Variant on the floor to the doors they passed on the way to the exit. At the bottom of the stairwell, Garza and Keoh breached the door leading outside, and the squad filed out in a column, exiting the building for what Jed hoped would be the final time.

— 28 —

The squad rallied at the fire station. Doctor DuBois came out from the engineer's office, where she'd set up her makeshift lab. The fire chief was with her, and didn't look too happy to see Jed and his people anywhere near Baytown.

"We need to blow that place," Jed said to the chief.

The man shrugged and looked at Doctor DuBois. "You tell him how things work here?"

"Briefly," she said, then, to Jed, "Sergeant, the council will need to accept your proposal before we can do anything. I'm inclined to agree with your assessment that we cannot properly address the biohazards inside the clinic. But I'm not sure such a drastic move as demolishing the building is necessary."

Before Jed could reply, his radio crackled. Greg came on.

"We're heading back now, but we're doing another run in the morning. You need to be on this one if you want to make things good with the council."

"Copy, Six. Wait one."

Jed let the mic hang and looked at the doctor and fire chief. "Y'all are on the council, right?"

They both nodded.

"So approve the demo. We need to make sure the virus is dead and gone."

The fire chief spoke up first. "How about you make sure we're supplied. That seems like a fair trade to me."

"Fair trade? You're talking about the most deadly biohazard on earth being inside that building right there, and you won't burn it down or blow it up until I come back with a hammer and nails and some wood? Y'all are fucking crazy."

"Sergeant, please," Doctor DuBois said. "I'm sure the council will see the wisdom of your suggestion, even though it means destroying our only functional clinic. The safety of the community is paramount. We'll address the issue in the morning, you have my word."

"Why not now?"

"Because I am exhausted, and the threat is neutralized. Nobody needs to go inside that building tonight, and you killed all of the infected persons, right?"

"Yeah, but there's no way to know for sure if the virus won't spread. We don't have PPE. The place has to burn."

"It will. I promise."

"You got demo somewhere?"

"Yes, the council maintains a—"

The fire chief put a hand up to cut her off. Jed sniffed at that and said, "Great. Get it, and some kerosene or propane tanks. We need fuel. We're blowing the place."

"I'll take care of it in the morning," the fire chief said. "We'll run a controlled burn exercise. Can't risk it tonight though. Too much chance something goes bad, and in the dark, when we're all tired, that means people die."

Jed had run out of argument. And he couldn't disagree with the chief's point. Just like a firefight at night was far worse than one by day, he could imagine how fighting an actual fire would be far more dangerous when visibility was limited to only what the flames revealed.

"Where can we sleep?" he asked.

"Day room's good to go," the chief said. "Plenty of bunks in there for y'all to rack out and catch some shuteye. Shower works, sort of. There's a bucket in there, and a case of baby wipes. Don't use 'em all, okay?"

Jed smirked at the guy, then turned to his squad. They'd been going almost twelve hours straight, and with not much to call rest or relaxation.

"Okay, y'all. We're bunking down. Clean your weapons, grab some chow. We'll shower in the morning, and let's not use all the nice man's baby wipes."

Doctor DuBois stepped aside to let them into the building. The fire chief showed them to the day room and left them alone there.

The *Hellhounds* circled up and went through the ritual of unwinding. Garza dropped his body armor first and stripped off his jacket. The rest of the squad followed suit and soon they were all either scraping carbon residue from their upper receivers or ripping into one of the MREs they'd pulled from Mercer's supply.

As Jed ate, he thought about the virus, imagined it as a living thing, with its own mind and desires. Its own needs for safety and security, for food and a way to maintain its presence in the world.

Those thoughts followed him into his dreams, where he was a monster hiding inside a house he couldn't escape.

— 29 —

Jed woke up to someone shaking his shoulder. It was Keoh. They'd bunked in the day room and Jed had given them all the night off from pulling any watch duty. The fire chief said they'd have someone monitoring the area and the radios. It wasn't too different from being at a rear base, only nobody was hollering at Jed to get his squad up for PT in the middle of a war.

"What time is it, Keoh?"

"About 0600. Doctor DuBois is outside. She's with the fire chief and some guys with fifty-five gallon drums and demo gear."

"About fucking time," Jed said as he rolled up and dropped his feet onto the cold floor. He grabbed his boots, laced them up, got to his feet, and rolled the kinks out where he could. "Get everyone else up, rah? Have chow, hit the head, whatever else feels good. I'll be back."

He took his weapon, but left his gear behind. The doctor, fire chief, and a few other men were by the clinic doors. They had three barrels with them, a roll of det cord and some bricks of C4. Jed took his time walking over to them.

"Good morning, Sergeant," Doctor DuBois said. "I hope you had a good night's rest."

"Sure," Jed said, wanting to get this over with. He knew what was coming, and the doctor didn't disappoint.

"You can see we're prepared to carry out the destruction of the clinic. I hope you and your people will now fulfill your part of the bargain. You'll leave two of them here to assist with security."

Jed agreed with a nod. "Anything else y'all gonna need us to do? Or do we just come back and each pick out a house to live in?"

"The council will select a building for you and your squad. With five of you, they'll ask that you occupy only one. Any role you have here will be determined by your choice and the community's need. We're hoping you'll choose to remain, but nothing will be required of you."

"Just this shopping trip. All right," he said. "When do we leave?"

"Greg said he'll be at the gate around 0830," the fire chief said.

Jed gave them a limp salute and went back to his people. They were all up and either pulling their boots on or digging into an MRE. They took turns using the shower, which amounted to filling a bucket and having someone else dump it over their head. They scrubbed down with some soap and a rag, and then had a buddy dump another bucket over them to rinse off. Jed went last, and ate last. His radio crackled as he was finishing his breakfast.

"Shorewatch, Six. Over."

"Go ahead, Six."

"You about ready? We're at the gate."

"Roger. Moving out here in about ten minutes."

"Okay. We're going to Lowe's first. It's about two klicks up the main road and then make a left. Can't miss it. We'll meet you there."

"Yut!" Jed said into the mic before tossing it aside.

"Feels like bullshit, eh, Sergeant?" Garza asked.

"Yeah, smells like it, too."

They were in the SUV a few minutes later with McKitrick driving. Keoh was in the back with the M27. Jed left Garza and Mehta behind, as Doctor DuBois requested. It didn't sit right with Jed to divide the squad, but he'd been given no choice. He could either take all his people and risk being stuck outside the wire indefinitely, or he could leave two of them to help secure the community.

With any luck, this would be a quick run for supplies and they'd be inside the wire before lunchtime. It would take them easily two hours to load up enough to make the trip worth it. Greg's people had two flat beds and the now empty five ton truck. The goal was concrete, rebar, and as much plywood as they could possible carry. Houses would be double walled on the lower stories. Windows would be fitted with barricades that could be quickly put in place from the inside. Doors would get a second layer and additional barricades that could be emplaced with minimal effort.

Greg also wanted to grab every air compressor and portable generator they could find, along with all the nail guns and cartridges.

"Nothing shoots better at close range," he'd said. "For people who don't know firearms, it's a good weapon for home defense."

They got to the Lowe's and pulled into the lot. Jed could tell before going in that the place was already cleaned out. Scattered bits of building lumber and pallet wrap filled the parking area. Jed lifted the mic.

"Six, Shorewatch. We're out front, over."

"Loading dock behind the store, over."

Jed confirmed and McKitrick drove them around back. Soon they were all standing in the open bay of what used to be a home repair center. The place was trashed now.

"Should we waste our time?" Jed asked as Greg surveyed the scattered remains.

"There's gotta be something in there we can use. Quick run, get whatever you can grab. We'll drive a flatbed in. One team on the truck to keep the haul organized, the rest of us making a hole, grabbing what we can, and tossing it on board."

Jed told McKitrick and Keoh to stay at their six.

"Stay frosty and keep your eyes open, in case anyone's watching and decides to roll up on us."

They both muttered an *Err* his way before stepping to the rear of the flatbed. Greg's driver wheeled it into the store and Jed joined the other Six Team people pushing display stands and debris out of the way of the truck.

It took over an hour to empty the place of as much useful wood and tools as they could find. Most of it was picked over pretty well, but they got two pallets of concrete thanks to a functioning forklift they found in a corner of the store.

The sun had nearly crested in the sky when they got out, sending blazing light straight down on them and turning the empty parking lot into a sticky field of tar.

Their next stop was across the street and down a bit. Jed's vehicle ended up in the point position because McKitrick was anxious to get back to Baytown.

"We shouldn't be out here, Sergeant. This far from our people. I don't like it."

"I don't like it either, McKitrick. It's bullshit served on a silver platter. Still stinks and tastes bad no matter what you put on it."

She turned them onto the main road dividing the Lowe's lot from the rest of the commercial district. Up and down the street, parking lots were ringed with cars and trucks on their sides or piled on top of one another.

Jed watched the area for movement, in case the automobile barricades hid more danger than they kept out.

McKitrick maneuvered their SUV across a median strip and toward the Home Depot. The lot there was wide open and empty. Just a stretch of ugly pavement with weeds growing out of the cracks. She was turning into the lot when a car raced out from one of the fortified lots a few blocks ahead. It sped in their direction, then veered off down a side street with a squeal of rubber and a cloud of smoke. Jed lifted his weapon to get a better view through his ACOG. He couldn't see the driver, but he could see the car just fine. It was a dark colored Subaru wagon with a surfboard rack on the top.

Jed picked up his mic and called to Greg.

"Six Actual, Shorewatch. You see that?"

"I did. Probably another scavenger. We'll make this as quick as we can and get back inside."

"Negative, Six. That was our bomber. Same car from that morning."

"Shit, you kidding me?"

"I say again. Same vehicle. Didn't see the driver, but I'd bet he has hair to his ass and his breath smells like patchouli."

"What's your thinking? We good to Charlie-Mike? Council isn't going to like it if we're back too late. They're expecting this load by midday, and it's already close to noon."

"He might have been collecting materials or he might have been laying in IEDs. But he'd have to know we were coming. You sure Baytown is good people? Nobody has a grudge against us, do they?"

"I'd be surprised as hell if that were the case. But we can just ask 'em. They're on a different channel. Wait one."

McKitrick steered them into the lot and stopped in the first aisle. Greg came back a moment later.

"Council and watchtowers confirm Baytown is buttoned up tight. Nobody outside the wire but us. They're breathing down my neck to get this stuff back. Somebody's taking your word about the Variants seriously, at least. How you wanna handle the Depot?"

Jed let scenarios play out in his thoughts. In one, they don't make it across the parking lot before taking fire from snipers hidden around the building. In another, they hit an IED before they get halfway to the building. And then the one he wanted more than anything: they go in, load up, and get gone.

"The fucking council's going to piss me off someday," he said.

Keoh said, "They've already pissed me off, and it's not even lunchtime."

AJ Sikes

The radio crackled. "Shorewatch, this is Six. We good to go? How copy? Council's waiting."

Jed looked at his people before replying. If McKitrick or Keoh's eyes rolled any farther, they'd be looking out the back window.

"Good copy, Six. Let us scout it first, just in case."

"Okay. We'll take it slow and careful."

"Shorewatch out."

McKitrick took them across the lot and circled toward the front entrance. The pavement was torn up around each of the lamps they passed. Exposed piping showed where vandals had ripped the wiring out of electrical conduits.

Chunks of pavement spilled across their path as they got closer to the store, trailing bits of pulverized concrete. Jed had McKitrick stop just outside the damaged area. hailed Greg before going any farther.

"Signs of explosives here. Tell your people to hang back and wait for our word."

"Roger, Shorewatch."

"Get us around this and over by the front of the store," Jed said. "And stop before you get under the breezeway."

McKitrick muttered *Errr*, and took them around the damaged section of the lot. She pulled up beside the scattered remains of a barbecue display on the sidewalk in front of the store. Gas grills and smaller Webers were strewn across the pavement like broken black shells. Up ahead, beneath the breezeway, the roll up doors were closed and mounds of trash and concrete debris blocked them from the outside. Jed eyed the mess, looking for any wires or other telltale signs of an IED. The problem was, everything looked like it could be a bomb. If they went forward, they'd could be going right into a trap that would turn them all into a memory.

— 30 —

"Try the loading dock, Sergeant?" Keoh asked.

Jed nodded and motioned for McKitrick to get them behind the store. His guts twisted with worry that they would be blown up any second. He'd only done a handful of patrols in Iraq before he was chaptered out, but it was enough to make him look twice at anything they passed by.

They got to the back of the building and found the loading dock door in the same condition as the ones out front. Sealed up with shattered concrete and pavement that had been torn up from around the perimeter.

Jed shook his head and said, "Let's get with Greg. Let him know whoever was using this place, they didn't want anyone going in. I'm betting it's either mined or already emptied out."

They met Greg at the edge of the parking lot. The five-ton and one flatbed trailer had already gone back with their loads. Jed wanted that to be enough, but he had to confirm it with Greg first.

"Somebody doesn't want us going in there," he said. "Looks like the main doors and loading dock were sealed up a long time ago, but—"

"What about the garden?" Greg asked. "They usually have a side door. Truck won't fit, but we could walk stuff back to the flatbed. Check it out, okay?"

"You really want this, don't you?"

"Not me, man. It's the council. They're the only reason we have a place to call home right now. They can shitcan us just as quick as they let us in."

Jed put a hand on his M4, thinking about how easy it would be to use a weapon to dictate his terms.

"You sure that's how you want to play this?" Greg asked, eyeing Jed's rifle. "I know plenty of places you can try that and have a good chance it'll work. Baytown's not one of them. Let's get in there, grab what we can. If it's a waste of time, I'll call it in and we can bail. But we have to at least give it a look."

"Right," Jed said. "Sure thing, boss."

They drove to the garden side of the store. It looked jammed up like everything else.

"Think somebody's still in there?" McKitrick asked.

Jed shrugged and said, "Maybe, or maybe it was that hippie dude's hideout and he bailed when he saw us coming. Still no way to get in though."

He was ready to call it quits when he spotted an open door between shelves of broken pottery and display stands full of dead and rotting plants.

"Hold up," Jed said.

He got out and had Keoh follow. They moved in a low crouch, keeping covered behind the fence around the garden entrance. Jed told McKitrick to keep the engine running.

"We'll be quick. Just need to confirm it's worth the trouble," he said.

"*Errr,* Sergeant."

Jed let Keoh take point and they made their way into the garden area. With a little effort, the nursery tables and tool racks could be pushed aside to make room for the other flatbed to back in. They'd be stuck carrying things through the store unless they could find a larger access point. At the door, Jed scanned for any movement inside. The place felt dead and empty, but that didn't mean it wasn't hiding any number of scavengers, each of which could turn out to be an enemy if they were infected, or just plain hostile and wanted to be left alone.

He and Keoh moved inside. The acrid stink of fertilizer hit Jed's nose as he stepped into the store itself. Spilled bags of the stuff lay everywhere, along with mounds of potting soil and who knew what else. He and Keoh stayed low and took cover behind an overturned shelf just inside the door.

"Doesn't feel occupied," Keoh said. "Feels fucking dead."

Jed had to agree. For being sealed up on the outside, the building didn't have much to offer. Maybe the doors outside were closed up to protect people from the Variants, and the place had been abandoned after the monsters vanished.

He stood and walked a little further into the place. Light was limited to what came down from skylights and the few windows on the front wall. But it was enough to show Jed row after row of empty shelves. The place was entirely cleaned out as far as he could tell. Keoh wandered over to a display of pool toys. They were the only things remotely serviceable that Jed could see.

"Fuck it," he said. "Let's go tell Greg and get the fuck

back to Baytown."

He turned to leave and stepped into a pile of fertilizer pellets that rolled under his boot. He stooped down to inspect the mess on the ground. It was mostly clumps of dark, dry soil, but here and there were little white pellets scattered around the area. At first, he thought they were just part of the fertilizer mix, but they had a familiar quality to them.

The blast knocked Jed off his feet. He went down hard on his side onto a pile of earth that he tumbled over. He ended up on his back, and had to draw his legs down to curl up behind the dirt pile. He tried to roll to a kneeling position, but blasts kept rocking the building, sending debris flying around the space and rattling off the walls. It was all he could do to keep his head down and stay covered by the mound of dirt he'd fallen over.

When the explosions stopped, Jed shakily got to his knees. His ears rang with a steady pulse and his guts felt like they might turn over any second. Jed held a hand over his nose as he breathed, fighting the urge to retch. The air stank of ammonia.

He breathed into his hand until his vision and hearing stabilized, and he was finally able to stand up.

Smoke and dust filled the space in a hazy cloud. Pieces of metal fell somewhere in the building, clanging and echoing around the high ceilinged space.

Keoh was lying on her stomach near the doors they'd come in. Her body armor was split down the middle and a dark stain spread across her uniform underneath. Something jagged and metallic jutted from her back. Jed stumbled across the dirty floor and reached her just as McKitrick got there.

"That fucker," McKitrick said. *"The motherfucker!"*

She collapsed to her knees next to Keoh. Jed knelt down and put one hand on her shoulder. He put the other on Keoh's outstretched hand.

Greg's pickup screeched to a halt beyond the fence outside. He came running in and drew up short just outside the doors.

"Ah shit. Shit, I'm—"

Jed stared at him, daring him to say another word. Greg backed up, and climbed into his truck.

"We have to get him, Sergeant," McKitrick said. "We saw which way he went. We go after him, we get him, and we fuck. Him. *Up.*"

Jed felt the same way, and he knew their mission in Texas would not be complete without retribution. But he also knew they were two people on their own, and with next to nothing for support behind them. They needed to get the team together in one place, regroup and stock up, and then they could move to contact.

"C'mon," he said to McKitrick, forcing himself to his feet. "Get her shoulders. I'll get her legs. Gotta take her home before we do anything else."

McKitrick moved like a machine, with silent anger written across her face. She hoisted Keoh under her arms. Jed grabbed her weapon and laid it across her body, then picked up her legs. They carried her to the SUV and put her in the back.

Greg was out of his truck, by the driver's door.

"My guys saw which way they went. If you want to go after them, I can't stop you, but—"

"No, you can't," Jed said as he and McKitrick climbed into their vehicle.

"They've got two Humvees, with turrets. You'll want more than small arms if you plan on coming back alive."

Jed stared at him, half hearing Greg's words repeated in his mind.

"What do you mean *they*? We saw the guy. Same guy was at the bridge two days ago."

"Maybe he's involved. Maybe he's the boss and the guys we just saw are the muscle. I don't know. But as soon as this place started banging, two trucks scooted out from behind the diner across the street. Their gunners sprayed us and nearly took out the flatbed."

Jed stared at Greg for a second, then motioned for McKitrick to get them out of there. She reversed them away from the garden space. Tears streamed down her face as she looked in the rear view mirror. Jed checked over his shoulder.

Keoh's head was just visible over the back seat.

They drove to Baytown in silence. Greg hailed him once, but Jed didn't respond. He had plenty he wanted to say to the man, but it wasn't Greg's fault they'd been blown up. It wasn't Greg's fault that Keoh was killed.

I shouldn't have taken us outside the wire, he thought. *Should have hung back and made sure my people were okay instead of this shopping trip bullshit.*

They got back to the fire station, and the still standing clinic. Doctor DuBois came out to meet them as McKitrick pulled in beside the fire station doors.

"I'm sorry," she said. "Greg told me—"

"Good," Jed shot back as he jumped out of the vehicle. "So now you know what happens when I take orders from you. That ends now. You're going to give us whatever we need, food, water, and ammunition. We are moving out on a payback mission. And we can talk about why that clinic is still standing when I get back."

Doctor DuBois met his gaze and crossed her arms.

"Sergeant, the council—"

"Can eat a dick. We aren't having this conversation, Doc."

He stormed off, calling for Garza and Mehta. They came out the fire station's side door.

"It's Keoh," Jed told them.

Mehta ran to the SUV and looked inside. He stumbled back, puked on his boots, and fell to his hands and knees sobbing. Jed walked over to him. He paused when Greg shouted for his attention.

"*Hey!* Sergeant Welch! North gate says your hippie pal just rolled up. He says he has intel we want."

"That's fucking great," Jed said. "We've got something for him, too."

Jed grabbed Mehta by his armor and hauled him to his feet, then called for his squad.

"Mount up, Hellhounds!"

McKitrick took the wheel. She had to weave them around a group of people running from the direction of the gate. Doctor DuBois went to greet them. Jed watched them in the car's mirrors. The doctor darted away from the group and ran after Jed's squad, waving and hollering for them to stop.

"Hold up," Jed said. He let DuBois catch up instead of reversing to meet her halfway. She was half out of breath but Jed caught the important words.

"*Variants…* In the housing tract."

— 31 —

Emily and Danitha huddled together in the dining nook of their cottage. The council offered it to them in exchange for help with planting the spring crops. Every backyard in the housing area had been converted to farmland, and they'd spent the morning putting plants in the ground, sowing seeds, and digging irrigation trenches.

Now they hid, their safety ripped from them in a flash of claws and blood and screaming. All around the area, she heard echoes of people shouting *Red Event*, the community's code for a Variant attack. The monsters lurked outside, in little clusters on the fence. They clung to the metal barrier and rotated their heads back and forth, like devilish birds of prey. The dogs stayed on the ground, and moved their heads the same way.

"We can't stay here," Emily said. "They will find a way in."

"Only if you keep giving them something to look at," Danitha said. "Get away from the damn window."

Emily had been watching a Variant crawl along the fence line. It would skitter around, then twitch its head back and forth, slowly stalking along the edge of the farmland. A trio of the dog monsters followed it through

231

the gardens, all the time rotating their heads as they moved.

The hunting packs had leaped the fence and torn through the people working in the gardens. Their bodies were still out there, torn and bloody in the mud. Emily and Danitha were lucky that they'd worked the earliest shift. They were inside on a break when the monsters came.

Now they were stuck here, trapped in a two-room house with an attic they could hide in, but couldn't reach. The only furniture in the house was a fold out couch and an end table, and neither would get them high enough to unlatch the attic trapdoor.

"Dani, we need to leave. I only see one now. We have to run back to Chava and his people."

"We go outside and we are *dead*."

"And if we stay in here, then what? When the monsters start looking in every window, sniffing every door. Then what do we do?"

"Where are they now? What're they doing?"

Emily peeked around the edge of the window again. A dog monster relieved itself on a patch of concrete that used to be the cottage's back patio. It ambled off to join two others still following the larger Variant through the gardens. The smaller monsters moved just like dogs, trotting and stalking. But their heads stayed up, instead of lowered to the ground like a dog's would.

The larger Variant kept swiveling its head as it moved, reminding Emily of something. She heard a clicking sound from nearby and shrank away from the window.

"What's that noise? One of them in the attic?" Danitha asked.

"I don't know. It came from outside."

The clicking came again. It wasn't the harsh ratcheting of the Variant's joints, but a softer, more rapid sound, almost staccato like—

"They are echolocating," Emily said.

"They what?"

"Like a bat. The monster makes noise to locate prey. This means I was right about the virus. It hibernated in bats, just like rabies does. And now it has changed what it can do to people it infects."

Danitha gave Emily a deadpan stare. "And how is this supposed to help me feel better? What the fu—"

"We can distract them. Like the bats we ran from in the woods. Enough noise will interfere with their ability to find us."

"Won't they just see us?"

"I don't think so."

"You don't *think* so."

"Look out the window. They don't use their eyes. They make the clicking noise and move their heads to hear where the echo comes from."

Danitha leaned up to see outside then jerked back down and hid.

Claws scraped somewhere nearby, then raced up the outside of the house and onto the roof. Another, smaller set of claws followed the first, and then another. After that, the only sounds Emily heard beneath her and Danitha's frightened breathing were scrabbling and clicking as the monsters ripped at the roof tiles.

When they shattered the attic window and raced into the upper story, Emily spun from the window and into the kitchen. She flung open a cabinet with her good hand, calling for Danitha to help. The monsters were in the attic, scraping around and snarling.

Emily yanked out the sauce pan and cast iron skillet the council had given them.

"You really think we can kill these things with a couple of pans?" Danitha asked.

"These will help. Trust me. We will run to where my brother is. If we see the monsters, we bang the pans together and keep doing it. That should be enough noise to distract them from fixing on us."

Danitha grabbed the skillet and spun to face the attic trapdoor. It had begun rattling as the monsters clawed at it and tried to force it open. The latch held for now, but it wouldn't last. It gave a jump and almost opened.

Emily took the saucepan and went to the front of the house. She looked out the window at the empty street.

"I don't see them. I'm going out."

Danitha helped her unlock the deadbolt. They opened the door and stumbled onto the front walk as the attic trapdoor began to crack open. A snarling muzzle shot out. Another followed.

Emily and Danitha ran for the street. A truck turned a corner up ahead. It had a machine gun mounted in the back. Before Emily or Danitha could get the driver's attention, the truck sped forward, across the street and into the area behind the houses. Heavy chopping gunfire echoed around the neighborhood, mixed with the screeching and howling of the dog Variants.

The women continued to run, and Emily listened for the clicking sound she'd heard earlier. Danitha veered away from her, and she yelled for her to stay close.

A dog Variant climbed up a house and perched on a

roof behind them, making a clicking sound and howling. The screeches and whines of other dogs echoed around the houses. Then they came, in groups of two or three, until a cluster of at least a dozen formed in the street and raced for them.

Emily got close enough to Danitha and swung the saucepan at the skillet. "Hold it still!" she shouted. Danitha stopped running and turned to face the onrushing swarm of dog Variants.

"We're gonna die banging a couple of fucking pots together!"

The dogs were a few houses back still, but they would reach them soon enough.

"We are not going to die, Dani! The monsters evolved to hunt and kill better than any other animal, but they are still animals themselves. The virus changed them again, and this time, they have a weakness we can exploit."

Emily held the saucepan against her hip. "Strike it!"

Danitha brought the skillet down with a clang. The dogs kept running, but a few of them staggered off from the main pack for a few steps. They quickly rejoined the group though.

"Again!" Emily screamed.

Danitha hit the pan again. The dogs staggered. She grabbed the pan from Emily and hit them both together in front of her. The pack split up as pairs and single dogs peeled off to the side. One of them went headfirst into a tree stump and wheeled around only to be hit by another dog as it ran from the pack.

Emily and Danitha jogged backwards, casting looks over their shoulders as they moved. And Danitha kept banging the pots together, until Emily's ears rang with the echo. But the dogs did not follow them. Some wandered in the street, and some got into fights, snarling at each other and rolling around biting and barking.

The truck with the machine gun came around a house farther back on the street. It roared forward and Emily urged Danitha out of the line of fire as the gunner shot at the monsters, scattering them and killing several.

"The cottage!" Danitha yelled. "There's a big one in the cottage!"

Emily felt her stomach turn as the monster flew out of their front door and across the street. It leaped onto the tailgate before the gunner could spin around.

Danitha slammed the pans together, but the Variant had already attacked. The gunner's screams drowned out the sound of clanging metal.

The driver got out with a gun and shot the monster, then climbed in and drove to where Emily and Danitha stood in the street.

Two dog Variants stalked out from behind the truck as it pulled to a stop. Danitha banged the pans together and the handle of the saucepan broke off.

The dogs recovered their direction and stepped forward, snarling and dripping spittle from their muzzles.

Emily waved for the driver to get out. "Two dogs! There's two dogs here!" she yelled.

The driver got out, and was jumped from behind by another dog that had climbed into the truck bed. The two in front of Emily and Danitha leaped for them.

— 32 —

"My sister's there!" Garza yelled as McKitrick sped them away from the doctor.

"Hold up!" Jed shouted. "Make a call, Garza. Where you want to be?"

Garza was out the door and running back to Doctor DuBois. McKitrick stomped on the gas as soon as the door was closed.

"You want to settle yourself, McKitrick," Jed said. "I know you're burning. Same with me and Mehta."

Jed held his weapon out the window, ready to fire on the hippie as soon as they spotted his vehicle. The road to the North gate had a few cars on it now as people from the junkyard dropped their work to respond to the Variant threat.

"What about the Variants, Sergeant?" Mehta asked from the back seat.

"We'll join the fight as soon as we finish things with this hippie ass bomb maker."

As they neared the gate, Jed saw it wouldn't be long before they were turned around and heading toward the Variants. A Subaru wagon sat just inside the North gate, with two guards holding weapons on the driver from either side. The driver side door was open.

McKitrick sped them forward and braked a few feet from the Subaru's grill. Jed was out before they'd fully stopped and put two rounds into the passenger side of the windshield. The hippie tumbled out of the car, flopping to the ground. He got to his knees with his hands out, shaking like he'd piss himself.

The gate guards yelled at Jed to stand down, but he kept his weapon up and fired two more into the dirt next to the hippie's knees.

"I didn't do it!" the guy screamed through tears. He fell forward and coughed up a mouthful of blood.

A car door slammed behind Jed and more rounds cracked out of McKitrick's rifle, striking the hippie in the arm and chest. He fell onto his side, still alive, and clutching at his wounds. Jed stalked forward. He put a hand up to hold McKitrick back, maintaining his aim on the bomber.

The gate guards had stepped away, but one of them hollered at Jed. "He said he had information. But I guess you're one of those shoot first, ask later types. Fucking asshole."

Jed had to fight the urge to swivel his aim and put the guard down. The hippie had blown up their only road home, and he'd killed Keoh. Or he worked with the people who did. Either way, Jed was writing the ROE for this one. He'd reached the end of his patience. Or maybe his sanity. Staring at the dying man on the ground, Jed wondered how much either of those things mattered anymore.

"Why'd you blow us up?" he asked, staring into the hippie's eyes.

The man's face shook and wobbled with fear. He sobbed around his words, making it hard to understand him. Jed only caught a few words.

"I didn't... Pills. I need..."

A plastic prescription bottle rolled in the dirt next to the car's front tire.

Jed put the muzzle of his weapon against the bomber's forehead and leaned down to pick up the pills.

It was some kind of anti-viral drug.

Jed looked at his enemy's face, stared into his eyes. A yellowish haze began filling them in, but receded to the edges.

"He's infected!" Jed shouted, stepping back with his weapon up.

The bomber shouted, "No! It was Ewell!"

Jed double tapped the man, ending it. McKitrick came forward, but Jed put an arm up to bar her from going closer. She spit at the ground, turned and got back into the vehicle. Mehta had come out and stood off to Jed's right. He'd circled to flank the hippie and was looking into the car.

"Sergeant, he had a radio."

"A what?"

Jed darted around the passenger side of the car and ripped open the door. A radio was piled on the front with camera bags and two notebooks. The backseat was a mess of clothing and sleeping bags. Jed went around back and opened the hatch. He grabbed clothing and blankets and tossed them to the ground, looking for ANFO, C4, anything that could be used to make a bomb. He stopped when he saw boxes full of pills.

They were all sealed, and most of them were the same

drug as what had been in the little bottle on the ground.

"Sergeant Welch!" Mehta yelled.

Jed went around the car with his weapon up, but Mehta was fine. He held the mic from the radio in the front seat.

"Traffic just came from Radout. He's talking to someone on the council."

"How the hell does that radio—ah, *shit!* He's been listening in the whole time. That's how he knew our AO."

Jed took the mic from Mehta and hailed Radout.

"Six, Shorewatch. Over."

"We're handling the Variants. Your man Garza's okay. He helped put three of them down, but reports are at least two more got inside the wire. I think we're good to go. Could use your help making sure."

"Roger. We're inbound. Shorewatch out."

Jed tossed the mic on the front seat next to the radio and notebooks. Mehta had opened the camera bag. He had the guy's fancy rig out and was flipping through pictures on the viewscreen. "Sergeant, this is fucked up," he said.

"What is?"

"It's Gunny—Oh fuck, look at this!"

Jed grabbed the camera. The picture was taken at night. Gunny Ewell stood outside the TOC with his head turned to the side, like he didn't know he was being photographed. A dog Variant sat by his feet. In another picture, Gunny and Sergeant Jordan led a Marine from Jordan's squad into a covered patio between two houses. It was a building Jed recognized from Galveston.

The next photo sealed Gunny's fate. He and Jordan held the young Marine to the ground while Gunny's *pet* bit the man on the arm.

"He turned them, but he controlled it," Mehta said.

Jed thought about the drugs in the hippie's wagon, and the bottle that fell out with him.

"Mount up," he said. "Grab the radio and the notebooks, too."

The gate guards milled around the base of their watchtowers. One of them came over as Jed made to leave.

"Hey, you just gonna leave this shit here?"

"The car has medicine in it. Keep it secure."

"What about the body, asshole?"

Jed stared at the guy. He was dressed like most of the Baytown security people in some combination of military costume under a Carhartt jacket.

"Okay, Operator," Jed said. "The body is a biohazard; don't touch it," he said, and left the guard standing there with his mouth open. Jed climbed into the SUV with Mehta and the gear they took from the hippie's car.

"Get us back to the fire station," he said, then lifted the mic. "Six, Shorewatch."

"Go ahead, Shorewatch."

"Bomber wasn't working alone. We'll help mop things up here. Then we gotta hit the road."

"Where to?"

"Gotta see an old friend. I'll tell you when we get back."

— 33 —

Emily retreated from the dog, holding the broken saucepan handle out like a knife. The monster landed in front of her and stalked forward, slavering and growling. Danitha had swung the skillet, striking the dog that leaped at her. But it only knocked the animal to the side. Now it was stalking toward her, and had her pinned against the truck. She tried to slide to her left, but the animal darted forward and barked, showing its maw of needle teeth. All the time, both dogs made a slight clicking noise from deep in their throats.

Emily wanted them to attack, so she could at least have a chance of defending herself. Danitha tried to move again, but the dog leaped to cut her off. In the corner of Emily's vision, the driver struggled with the dog that had jumped from the truck bed. They rolled side to side on the ground. Snarling and growling mixed with grunts from the driver. The dogs in front of Emily and Danitha snarled and kept pressing forward, holding both women from moving.

Why don't they attack? Emily wondered.

The telltale clicking of a Variant's joints sounded behind her. She ran to her left, toward the nearest house, but the dog was faster and penned her again. The Variant was getting closer. Its clicking joints mixed with the snarls of the dogs, and Emily felt every bit of hope drain from her chest.

A gun shot cracked, then a grunt followed by two more shots. Both dogs backed up a pace before charging forward to bite at Emily and Danitha's legs.

Emily stabbed with the pan handle, jabbing the dog in the head. It skittered to the side and moved for another attack. A heavy *clang* sounded, then another gun shot. The dog in front of Emily spun away with a hole in its side.

Emily looked up. Danitha held the skillet over a dead dog Variant in front of her. Its head was a mess of ragged skin and blood. Emily spun around, expecting a Variant to leap at her.

It was lying in the middle of the street, just a few feet away, with blood leaking from wounds in its head.

The driver came over and held a gun on them. Emily couldn't tell if it was a man or woman. The person wore heavy coveralls and their face was covered in a scarf and goggles. A pilot's cap covered their hair.

Blood stained the front of the driver's coverall, and a jagged bloody tear near the collar showed where the dog Variant got its teeth in.

The driver took off their goggles and tugged the scarf down. Her round face was pulled with grief and sorrow. She teetered and stumbled back a step, then fell forward, catching herself on the hood of the truck. The driver's eyes were rimmed with blood, and her mouth shook as she lifted the gun and asked, "Did they bite you, too?"

"*No!*" Emily and Danitha shouted together and put their hands out.

"Lucky," the driver said, then turned the gun on herself. Emily and Danitha looked away before the shot.

The street was still and quiet with only the echo of the driver's suicide ringing in Emily's ears. She and Danitha stepped around the body and got into the truck. Emily scooted across the bench seat so Danitha could take the wheel.

"Keys still in it at least."

She closed the door and reversed them a few feet so they could go around the driver's body.

They left the neighborhood and got onto the road to the fire station.

Danitha asked, "Why'd she do that? Why'd she kill herself? We could have helped her. Could have taken her to that doctor. Maybe she has some medicine or something that could help."

"There is no medicine for the virus, Dani. No cure exists."

They drove quietly the rest of the way. People gathered outside of larger buildings as they got deeper into town. Some of them wore coveralls and goggles, like the driver. Emily kept seeing the woman in each of them, kept hearing her last word.

Lucky.

— 34 —

Jed flipped open one of the hippie's notebooks as McKitrick took them back into town. A slip of paper fell out with two radio freqs on it. Jed recognized one of them as the blue net they used for commo with Greg Radout. He handed the paper to Mehta in the back seat.

"Try that other freq," he said.

Mehta dialed it in. The radio was silent and stayed that way as they pulled into the shadow of the fire station.

Doctor DuBois was outside ushering injured people into the building. Some of them had cuts and scrapes, one limped with a broken leg. Jed couldn't tell if any of them had been attacked by Variants, and he hoped the good doctor would have the sense to quarantine anyone who did.

He got out and walked up to her. Garza was nearby, talking with some of the Baytown militia, a mix of men and women. They all wore the same high speed costume as the gate guards. One of them, a tall woman with close cut blond hair, stood out as a leader. She directed three of the militia to support the demo effort at the clinic.

"The rest of you secure the neighborhood. House by

house. Take everything to the northern burn trench."

Jed approached and waved to the woman. She met him halfway.

"Sergeant Welch," she said. "I'm Councilwoman Day. My guardsmen tell me you executed a prisoner at the north gate."

"They spelled *infected terrorist* wrong, but otherwise that's correct, ma'am."

She blanched, and Jed explained what they'd found, how the hippie was infected and had a stash of anti-viral pills with him.

Doctor DuBois suggested he might have been using them to keep the infection from taking over.

"If that's possible, we may have a route to a cure," Day said.

"Doubtful, unless we also gain access to a secure and sterile lab facility," Doctor DuBois answered.

"I'll trust you to head up the effort to build one someday," Day said. "Meanwhile, I have biohazards to address."

She left to join her team of people outside the clinic. They were laying in charges around the building, and placing the fifty-five gallon drums of fuel inside the door and at the top of the staircase.

Both radios in Jed's vehicle crackled. He took the one they'd got from the hippie, ignoring the other. It was Greg talking about something outside the fence line.

The hippie's set had more important traffic on it. A man's voice came across, sounding haggard and weak. Even though Jed had only spoken to him a few times, he knew he was listening to Sergeant Jordan.

"Attempted infil. I think we softened them, but it cost

us. They took out all the dogs up here and put down three of my people. I'm injured. We need to regroup with the rest of the wolf pack if we're going to take this place."

Gunny Ewell replied.

"How bad are you hurt?"

"Leg wound. It'll heal."

"Any sign of Kip's people?"

"Negative."

"What about the snoop?"

"Almost had him at the Home Depot, but he slipped our net right before we took out Welch. At least there's one headache we don't have anymore."

Jed felt his blood turn to fire the longer he listened. The conversation was partly in code, with other names and locations Jed couldn't identify, but he'd heard enough to know his next steps. Parsons and Keoh would be avenged.

He threw the mic down when the conversation ended with Ewell closing the traffic. As he made his way to the fire station, two trucks pulled into the area. One held Greg and a few of his Six Team people. The other was one of the .50 call pickups from the bridge. It shuddered to a stop and Garza's sister nearly fell out the passenger door. He ran over to help her while her friend climbed out from behind the wheel.

"Garza, they okay?" Jed called over.

"Rah, Sergeant. Just shook."

Jed waved Garza off to the day room. McKitrick and Mehta had taken Keoh's body around to a trailer the Baytown folks used to move the dead. She'd be buried, unlike the people killed in the Variant attack.

Greg came over to Jed and extended a hand. "I'm

sorry about what happened. I know that doesn't help, but—"

"Forget it. You couldn't have known they were listening to our commo."

"*What the—?*"

"Hippie was on the blue net. He had another freq he used that put him in touch with Ewell, back on Galveston. Gunny's behind all this."

Greg chewed on the info, kicked at the dirt.

"That explains the Humvees then. Saw two of them racing off after the attack here, same ones from this morning. Sounds like some of your own people went rogue."

"They did, but they aren't our people anymore. Anybody working with Ewell is no better than bin Laden."

"You going back for him?"

"Don't see how I can avoid it. Soon as we're squared away, we're moving out."

Greg nodded and said, "You're gonna need watercraft. There's a launch by the Goose Creek Graveyard. Right at the south edge of the community. Should be a boat there you can take, but I'll talk to the council to make sure."

"Appreciate it. And make sure they know we aren't asking permission."

Greg gave Jed a look that said he understood, then walked over to the clinic where Councilwoman Day was standing with her demo crew.

Jed set up a rough operations order in his head as he went back to the fire station.

They knew their enemy, could estimate his strength, knew the terrain on Galveston. Jed was still puzzling over how they would conduct the mission when he got to the fire station and nearly ran into Garza coming out the door.

"Mehta's been reading that hippie's notebooks, Sergeant. Some wild shit in there."

"Like what?"

"Like a whole fucking diary of how Gunny did it. He blew the bridge, like LT said."

Garza filled him in as they went inside and joined the others in the day room.

"The hippie dude, his name was Lou. He was a pharmacist here. Had a stash of every drug you can think of. Used to trade them for sex and whatever he needed, until Gunny came to him with a bite. This was all before we got to Galveston, any of us. Kip, Jordan, even LT."

"So he was a drug dealer. I'm still not sad he's dead," Jed said.

"It's more than that, Sergeant," Mehta said. "Lou didn't know that Gunny was sick with the actual virus, but the pills he had helped him keep it down. Then Gunny started bringing other people in with bites. Kip's squad first, and then after they left, Jordan and his people. Lou figured it was rats biting everybody, or something like that, but then he saw a bat in Gunny's rack spot. That's when he started taking pictures. We looked at all of them. They're pretty fucked up, Sergeant. Gunny went nuts."

Jed lifted the camera and checked. The photos went back several months, and showed a progression of horror the Gunnery Sergeant had brought upon his own Marines, turning them into monsters that he could control. The earliest photos were of bats roosting in and around Ewell's rack. Then the dogs appeared. The most recent pictures of him were taken from high up, like Lou had been inside the TOC on the second floor looking down on Ewell's rack spot behind the building. One picture showed Ewell feeding the dogs and bats from a sack. In another, the sack went into a refrigerator next to the Gunnery Sergeant's rack. In another, he pet one of the dog Variants while it chewed on a human arm.

The Variants had vanished, and Ewell had brought them back as his children.

Jed picked up one of the notebooks and thumbed through it. Lou had taken detailed notes of everything Gunny was doing. Including setting up the bombs that would take out the bridge.

He said he was going to bulldoze the cars off the causeway, make a path for the refugees. He did, but he also planted bombs all along the route. He made me and one of the engineers help him. I didn't understand, but wasn't about to ask him why he did it. He told Jordan though, and I was in the room. They'd turned me the night before. I guess they thought I was really one of the pack.

They don't have enough dogs to take over the bigger settlements on the mainland. Ewell's afraid they'll be slaughtered if they try to attack Baytown now, but he wants to try for the garrison at Texas City. They were talking about putting one of the turned people from Galveston into the garrison community. Jordan took the guy with him when he left.

Jed kept flipping through the book, growing more furious with Gunny Ewell as he scanned Lou's notes.

They've killed most of the other survivors. Just a few of us are left, and I heard Ewell saying they'd be used to feed the pack. I'm getting out tonight or tomorrow morning. If anyone finds this, I'm already dead. The anti-virals don't kill the bug, but they slow it down enough that you can feel human. Mostly.

Sometimes I see the other Marines, the ones who aren't turned yet. Sometimes I want to—

Jed closed the notebook and tossed it with the rest of Lou's stuff.

McKitrick took out her cleaning kit and disassembled her weapon. She looked at Jed as she worked and asked when they were heading out.

"Tomorrow, first light. We put Keoh to rest, then hit the water. There's a boat launch by the graveyard."

— 35 —

The squad had loaded up as much as they could fit in the SUV, piling their packs in the back, along with tools to dig Keoh's grave. Councilwoman Day authorized two HE rounds for McKitrick's 203. Everyone carried a near max load of ammo for their rifles. Jed and Garza both received sidearms as well. Keoh's body was wrapped in a sheet and on a trailer hooked up to their vehicle. Councilwoman Day and Doctor DuBois stood by as the squad mounted up.

"We'll see what we can do with the antivirals," Doctor DuBois said.

Jed didn't respond. He knew this could be his final mission, and he wasn't about to distract himself by hoping about a cure for the virus.

"Good luck, Sergeant," Councilwoman Day said, coming around to the passenger door.

He nodded and lifted a hand, but kept his mind focused on the mission ahead. Day joined a group of her people outside the clinic. They were finally going to blow it this morning.

Garza lingered by the fire station, saying goodbye to his sister. She and her friend were safe now. They'd survived running through the wilderness, and they'd defended themselves in the recent attack. Garza took his time saying goodbye, though. When he got to the SUV, everyone else was inside and ready to roll.

"They'll be okay, Garza," Jed said. "Good people here. They'll watch out for your sister."

"Rah, Sergeant."

"And we'll watch out for you," McKitrick said, looking at Garza in the rear view mirror. "We all go out, we all come back."

She wheeled them onto the street and through the community. All along their route, Baytown residents held up hands and waved. Some people shouted good luck or God bless. Greg had spread the word about what they were doing. It was hardly the send off Jed had wanted. He'd have preferred empty streets and silence to let him focus. But he understood it. These people were only alive because their security teams fought off the Variant attack. They needed to see somebody playing the dragon slayer.

The road to the graveyard wound through the community and crossed a narrow stretch of Goose Creek near its headwaters. They veered under a highway and around the ruins of housing tracts yet to be reclaimed. Goose Creek widened after an oxbow, and the graveyard came into view at the water's edge with a narrow parking area to one side. A small pier sat at the far end of the lot, with a few fishing vessels moored.

Jed and the squad worked in silence, taking turns digging and providing security, with one person in the SUV to monitor the radios. After two hours of work, they lowered Keoh's body into the grave with her rifle, just as they'd done for Parsons. Everyone took turns tossing in a handful of earth before filling the hole.

They moved their gear to the biggest boat, a cabin cruiser like the one they'd ridden around the bay, with Skip at the helm. McKitrick got them moving at a slow clip. Mehta was their RTO now, with both radios at his feet.

"We're going into unknown territory," Jed said. He sat against the gunwale at the back of the boat. "We know Galveston, but we don't now what Ewell's done to it since we left. And we don't really know his strength either. Could be he's got the whole place crawling with Variants or he could be alone there."

"Sergeant Jordan can't get back in Humvees, right?" Mehta asked.

"Far as we know. But he might have a way across the water. We should assume his squad is there."

"So we recon from offshore," Garza said. "Where do we start?"

"I'm guessing he's still around the TOC. That's the safest place on the island right now. It's the most built up, easiest to harden. He'll be watching the water wherever he is, but we can approach from the east, give ourselves some distance to walk in and scout his AO. Assume IED threats, people. The only good news is he doesn't know we're coming. I heard him and Jordan on the radio and they think I'm dead. Probably think the same thing about y'all. Doesn't change our mission. This is straight movement to contact. We look for a fight until we find it and end it."

The squad gave back mumbled *Errrs*.

McKitrick put on a little speed and they rounded a second point extending off the Texas coast. The remains of Commander Mercer's domain were up ahead. Someone had already begun dismantling the fencing.

Scavengers probably, Jed thought. But he kept a corner of his mind open for the idea that Ewell had been here and taken what he could to help fortify himself on Galveston.

By the time they reached the island, Jed had come up with a dozen ways the mission could go wrong, and his doubts didn't let up after he stepped onto dry land again. They left the blue net radio behind, but Mehta carried the one tuned to Ewell's channel. Jed hoped the traitor didn't change his freq before they reached him.

The team moved through a shipyard and around the skeletons of industrial buildings, crossing a highway to the marshland on either side of railroad lines that extended down the length of the island. They moved fast over a narrow strip of swampy soil, with Jed in the lead. He knew the danger of an IED and an ambush, and also knew the longer they delayed, the more time their enemy would have to prepare for their arrival. If they'd been spotted, Ewell could be laying in defenses right now, setting up an ambush, or putting his Variant servants on the hunt.

Jed followed the railroad tracks, with Mehta behind him monitoring Ewell's commo. All they'd heard so far were short bursts of chatter between Jordan and Ewell, and none of it helpful at determining their enemy's strength or location.

Garza and McKitrick trailed a few yards back, watching the team's six.

They neared a cross street that marked the end of the marshland. The remains of Galveston's industrial centers sat on the other side with scrub brush and trees forming a boundary along the railroad. Tattered buildings hugged the ground in heaps and lumps. Their metal siding was splayed out and their roofs half gone from the storms. Jed was a few steps from the road when the first shots cracked across the sky and rounds zipped past his head. Sustained bursts from an M240 added to the incoming fire. The team took cover beside the road and Jed yelled for them to return fire. He lifted to shoot back and caught a spray of gravel and pavement chips as bullets spit against the road in front of him.

Jed tucked back behind the roadside berm with the others. The enemy had to be shooting from a distance, and he'd been lucky they didn't correct their aim before he dropped back down. But his people were pinned beside the road and the nearest cover was dead ahead, under enemy fire.

"They're in the first building, Sergeant!" McKitrick shouted to him. She was on the far end of their line.

Jed snapped up for a single shot toward the building, hoping to catch sight of movement or muzzle bursts. A flash showed him where the 240 gunner was positioned, just inside the building using a collapsed part of the roof for cover. Jed dropped down again as more bullets zipped by and picked at the road.

"Under the busted roof, McKitrick. Me and Garza will cover you."

Waiting for a burst to end, Jed slapped Garza's shoulder and they both raised up, sending rounds toward the enemy position. McKitrick lifted up and sent an HE grenade downrange. They all dropped behind cover as soon as she'd fired.

Bullets rained in, and they shrank down tight against

the berm. The HE impacted and Jed shouted for them to move across the road. They raced forward, with Garza firing bursts at the machine gun nest as they went. The 240 opened up and Jed felt a stinging tear across his leg; he kept rushing with his people, firing as they moved.

On the other side of the road, they grouped up behind mounds of scrap metal and rusting cars. Jed checked his leg. An angry furrow crossed his left thigh, welling with blood. He pulled a bandage out while the others maintained security. The machine gun was quiet for now, but that didn't mean the enemy wasn't moving on their position.

With his leg wrapped, Jed counted his people.

One, two—

"Where the fuck is Mehta?"

— 36 —

"Mehta!"

Jed yelled the private's name again, but got no response. He couldn't see a body behind them, but also couldn't see much more than the road and the swampy landscape they'd come through. If Mehta was cut down before he crossed, he would have fallen out of sight.

"We can't leave him behind," Jed said. "Y'all cover me."

He moved away from their cover and jerked backward as the 240 lit up the ground in front of him.

"Fuck! McKitrick, smoke."

She fit the round into her 203 and lifted it, ready to fire.

"On three," Jed said and counted with his fingers. He got to one when a grenade exploded nearby. A man screamed from the direction of the buildings. Single shots from an M4 followed and silenced him.

"What the fuck was that?" Garza asked.

Jed was about to tell McKitrick to fire the smoke when Mehta called out, "All clear! I got a prisoner here!"

The team rushed out from cover, weapons up, and stalked forward. Metha stood by the machine gun position, covered head to toe in mud. He held his rifle on a man lying beside the building. The man's leg was shredded, and his chest heaved as he struggled to sit up. Jed took his people over, monitoring the area around them. Garza had their six and McKitrick had the smoke round ready to provide cover.

"How'd you get here, Mehta?" Jed asked when they'd reached him.

"Split off when we crossed. I had to. This guy and his buddy were tracking fire toward me, so I went down on my face. Low crawled my ass this way. Gave 'em Parsons' grenade from their flank."

Garza clapped a hand on Metha's shoulder.

The man at their feet was one of Jordan's squad, a dude named Prager. He groaned and reached for the muzzle of Mehta's weapon. The young Marine pulled it back and Jed stepped around to cover their prisoner.

"You infected?" Jed asked him.

Prager's eyes weren't yellow, but they were lined with blood. He shook his head, and flicked his gaze to the side. Jed knew a tell when he saw one.

"Where's Ewell? Is he at the TOC? *Where?*"

Prager opened his mouth like he'd answer, but all that came out was a Variant's shriek. Jed double tapped him. Another shriek sounded from around the building and was joined by the snarling of dog Variants on the hunt. They were still some distance away from the sound of it, but would get here soon.

"Grab ammo, anything they had!" Jed yelled.

The team picked up what they could, snatching magazines from ammo pouches on Prager's chest and the gunner. Jed went for the machine gun, but the 240 was wrecked by Mehta's grenade. As they moved out, the first two monsters appeared around the far corner of the building. Garza lit them up with a burst, but they were replaced by five more scrabbling through the loose gravel and patches of mud. More of the monsters appeared on the beams and panels of the folded up metal roof.

Garza continued to fire. Mehta and McKitrick added to the counterattack, while Jed spun to find their safest path of escape. They had the road they'd crossed and the railroad tracks that passed through patchy scrub and bush cover, heading straight toward the old TOC.

The dog monsters fell to the squad's fire one by one, but a few got close enough to bite at Jed's feet. He put them down and regrouped, teaming up with McKitrick.

"Everyone fall back to the road."

The air around them buzzed now. Jed expected Variants to swarm them from the marshland or come racing down the railroad. They crossed the muddy gravel with Garza and Mehta at their six, watching for more dogs to come from the ruined buildings. They made the berm on the near side of the road, but that's as far as they got. Jed caught the scent of rotten fruit just as four human Variants stalked toward them from the marshland and spread out across the road. They closed in, but didn't attack. Jed sighted on one. It skittered left and right, dodging behind bushes and forcing Jed to jerk his aim to follow it.

"Why aren't they rushing us?" McKitrick asked.

"They're fucking with us. Trying to get us to waste ammo," Jed said.

"Sergeant, we got a clear path up the railroad," Garza said.

"Lead the way, Garza. It's a trap; has to be. So stay frosty."

"What about those fuckers?" McKitrick asked, lifting her weapon to track one of the monsters as it dodged side to side.

Jed watched them closely, keeping his weapon up and ready, but maintaining visual on all four monsters. Their joints clicked as they danced back and forth, flicking ropy tongues around their bulging lips. They each wore shreds of digi-cams and even under their transformed faces, Jed could still identify the men from Sergeant Jordan's squad.

He fired a warning shot at the Variants, purposefully aiming at the ground in front of them. They darted away, but came back to form a barrier along the road.

"Garza, Mehta; y'all move out. We'll be right behind you. Watch for IEDs and whatever the fuck else Ewell's got waiting for us. McKitrick, smoke 'em when we get some distance between us."

The team moved out, slowly pacing down the tracks. McKitrick fired the smoke round, sending up a plume beside the road. The Variants came flying out of it, charging straight for them. Jed and McKitrick opened up. The lead Variant went down with holes in its face. The others fanned out and disappeared into the scrub brush and trees beside the tracks.

Jed hollered for Garza and Mehta to double time. They sped down the tracks with Jed and McKitrick watching their six now. Clicking joints and snarls sounded from all sides as the team moved through the terrain. Two Variants leaped from the bushes to skitter down the railway. Jed fired, striking one monster in the arm, but it kept coming. Its partner bounded away from the tracks and disappeared in the foliage again.

McKitrick took out the one on the tracks as it jumped forward. She sent a three round burst at its chest. It tumbled onto the tracks, then reared up with its claws ready to slash at her. She put another burst into it, and the monster fell onto its back, twitching.

"Where are the others?" Jed yelled as he and McKitrick ran to keep up with Garza and Mehta. He scanned the tree line beside them. "Garza, you got 'em up there?"

"Negative. Nothing but bushes and mud, Sergeant."

More clicking sounded nearby, then a shriek. Jed fired into the brush to his left, taking random shots as the team fled down the tracks. Garza's weapon chattered behind him, and a Variant's dying screech pierced the air.

"One more down!" Garza yelled.

That left only one chasing them through the vegetation. He could hear its shrieks and clicking joints, but where the hell was it? Dogs howled in the distance, and the squad continued to run. Jed fired at the plants alongside the railroad, hoping to hit the Variant before it took one of his people down. The reek of rotting fruit filled the air, but Jed couldn't place the source. He only knew the monster was near them, and could attack at any moment.

"Keep going, y'all. Keep moving," Jed said as he sent another round into the bushes where he saw movement. If he hit the Variant, it gave no sign of being struck. The only sounds were the team's boots stomping across the railroad ties, the dogs' howling that was growing closer, and the clicking of a Variant's joints as it stalked them through the brush.

Up ahead muddy tracts separated the industrial area from paved streets winding around the TOC. If they could make it that far, they'd have a better chance against the Variant and any dogs that showed up. Here on the tracks, they had two routes of escape unless they wanted to slog through the mud. With Variants on their tail, movement through that terrain would be a fast trip to a faster end.

Mehta fired at something and Jed spun to see the Variant leaping from the bushes to tackle the young private to the ground, only to bound away and disappear into the bushes again.

Jed and McKitrick covered the bushes. The strip of scrub growth narrowed here to no more than five yards across, with a road on the other side. Wherever the monster was hiding, it wasn't making any sound or moving. Garza helped Mehta up, checking him for bites, and shook him by the shoulder.

"You good? Did it get you?" he demanded.

"No, man. Fuck! I'm fine!" Mehta reeled away, with a mad look in his eyes. Garza stepped back as if to lift his weapon, but Jed got between them.

"Garza, you're with McKitrick. Watch the bushes." He stared Mehta in the face, looking for any sign in his eyes that he'd been bitten. No yellow mist clouded them, no blood welled around his eyelids. His uniform was ripped along his arms where the monster's claws had grabbed him. Mehta shrugged off the injuries.

"Just scraped me up, Sergeant."

Jed kept watching his eyes, waiting for the telltale shift in color. It didn't come. Jed slapped a hand on Mehta's shoulder and told him he was good to go.

"What the fuck is it doing?" McKitrick asked as they moved out again. "Why'd it just leave like that? They don't do that."

"It's playing with us," Jed said. "Listen; the dogs are getting closer. McKitrick, get that last smoke round loaded."

She gave a quick *Rah* and readied her weapon.

The dogs' growls and snarls grew louder. McKitrick stood tensed and scanning the brush beside the tracks. Garza moved beside her doing the same. The first sign of the dogs was a sharp cry that was half bark, half shriek, coming from near the building where they'd taken out the machine gun nest. The animal cry was echoed by a similar sound from the bushes, maybe three yards ahead of their position.

The whole team moved as one now, continuing down the tracks with their attention on the foliage around them. Jed took point position and divided his focus between their path ahead and the bushes where the Variant hid. Garza was at their six. Mehta covered their left flank and McKitrick their right.

More dogs howled and snarled ahead of them, and the first few jumped into view at the edge of the muddy area. The animals formed a line there, almost as if they dared the squad to approach, just as the Variants had done before. Easily a dozen of the dogs blocked their path now, in a row of slavering, growling death. Behind them, the first row of rebuilt homes waited like a safe haven. The doors and windows were all intact and new, the siding was all flush and clean.

A shriek caught Jed's attention and he flashed a look over his shoulder. The Variant hadn't come out of its hiding place yet, but he knew it would at any minute. It had to. They were trapped now, with a line of the dogs in front of them, and a smaller pack charging down the railroad from behind.

Garza fired a burst at the ones racing their way, sending the first two to the ground. The others kept coming. Jed yelled for McKitrick to fire the smoke behind them as he charged forward with Mehta, firing into the line of dogs that blocked their path. The smoke grenade exploded. Blasts from Garza's and McKitrick's weapons mixed with the cries and snarls of the monsters.

Jed knew they hadn't escaped, even as the line of dogs in front him fell away. The survivors bounded off to vanish in the bushes where the Variant hid. Their snarls mixed with shrieks and growls and Jed worried again that he had led his people into disaster. He and Mehta reached solid soil beyond the mud and took up position, firing at any dogs they could see. They came from every direction, leaping out of the scrub brush and trees, racing through the mud.

McKitrick and Garza ran forward with stragglers from the pack almost close enough to bite at their heels.

The team fired round after round into the onrushing mass. One dog sailed past them to circle around and attack from behind. Jed pivoted and tracked it as it moved, firing before it got its feet stable enough to jump. Two more raced around the team, pinning them against each others' backs. Jed and his people fired and fired, dropping magazines and palming new ones in until they were nearly dry.

Finally, with short bursts from the M27, Garza put the last of the dogs down. A Variant's shriek split the air, angry and long, and then cut short. It was replaced with muffled groaning and grunting. Jed couldn't tell where the monster was. Sound echoed around his head, and his ears rang from all the gunfire. With his eyes still focused on the terrain around them, he waved his people forward.

"Y'all keep together. Three-sixty security. Move to the TOC."

"I'm down to one mag, Sergeant," McKitrick said as they moved.

"You got the HE still?"

"Last one. Only round left."

"Ammo count, everybody."

"I got two mags, Sergeant," Mehta said.

"Last one in the weapon," Garza said.

Jed checked his pouches. He had one mag left, and the syringe. He thought about tossing it, but let it fall back into his pouch. If one of them got infected and he was quick enough, he could save them the horror of being turned.

"Everybody top off. Do it as we move. Mehta, give your spare to Garza."

As they advanced down the road toward the TOC, a reek of decay and burned meat filled the air. Jed scanned the area, looking for any sign of where the smell came from. All he saw were the houses, the road, and the burned out shell of the TOC. The stink made it hard to stay focused, and he had no idea where the Variant was hiding.

"Where the fuck did it go?" Garza asked. "We'd hear it move, right?"

Jed motioned for silence. The houses beside them were empty, or at least appeared to be. He didn't notice any sign of Variants using them for shelter. Up ahead, the road led straight to the causeway, and the first break in the bridge was visible. Blast marks and craters showed where Ewell had laid in the bombs, and a bigger crater marked what had been the front step of the TOC off the road to the left. The two-story house was now just ash and coal at the backside of the crater. Ewell's rack spot was the first house beside it, and it was still standing.

The Variant's call came from the housing now, like it was leading them on a chase.

"It's trying to lure us in, Sergeant," Mehta said.

"Yeah, it is. Remember we're here for Ewell first. Forget the Variant unless it comes for us. We move in teams, around the TOC, and approach from that side. If Ewell's in his rack, we get him there."

"What if he's not there?" Garza asked.

"Then we find his ass, and kill him where he stands."

— 37 —

Jed stayed on point with Mehta. The radio had been silent since they arrived, but he wasn't ready to dump it, just in case Ewell had human allies on the island with him as well as his Variant army.

They circled the ashen remains of the old TOC. Jed eyeballed every mound of earth along their path, and every scrap of debris that littered the area. The terror of a firefight or a Variant attack almost paled against the constant fear that his next step might end in a flash of light and an explosion he would never hear.

The stink of death grew stronger as they rounded the TOC and approached the street that led behind the housing units. At first it looked like any old suburban street, with homes on either side and empty earth waiting for sod to be laid down out front. But after a few steps down that street, Jed found the source of the smell.

Bodies lay mounded in a heap against a garage door about twenty yards ahead.

"Eyes out, y'all. Stay frosty and watch the rooftops."

The radio crackled briefly, but no traffic followed. Jed signaled for the team to move forward to Ewell's rack spot. The single-story home had been the last one built, and still needed a coat of paint on its siding. Jed couldn't see through the windows because Ewell had covered them with blankets and whatever else he could find. The front door was cracked a few inches.

"He knows we'd breach and clear. Door might be rigged," Jed said. "Let's check the garage."

The team moved around the house and stacked behind Jed by the side garage door. It was wide open. On his signal, they rushed in, weapons up and light on. The team posted with Mehta behind him and the others along the adjacent wall. Jed ran his wall and confirmed the space was clear. He made quick eye contact with Garza on the other wall and flashed a thumbs up.

The garage was empty, and the door leading inside the house hung open over a single concrete step. Jed paused before moving ahead. This wasn't what he'd expected. Ewell was no idiot, but it wasn't like him to give up either. He wouldn't have bailed and left the Variants behind. But Jed couldn't deny his gut. The house was empty, and had been for a long time. Wherever Ewell was hiding, it wasn't here.

"He's not here," Jed said. "Garza, lead us out, and everybody watch high and low. Let's check those bodies."

Moving fast, and scanning in every direction, the team crossed the street and headed for the carnage filling a driveway up ahead, passing three houses along the way. Jed checked into the windows of each one and listened for the click of a Variant's joints. He tried to find the rotting fruit stink underneath the reek of the bodies. It was so strong they had to yank up their shirts to cover their noses, and still the rancid stench got through. Mehta doubled over and heaved onto the ground. Jed forced back the impulse to vomit and got close enough to identify a few of the corpses. They were civilians who had been on Galveston when he arrived.

A trail of blood, bone, and gore led around the house. Jed waved everyone to follow. At the back of the house, his questions were answered. Most of them anyway.

Ewell had been to Mercer's neighborhood since the night they were attacked. Fencing and razor wire were set up along the yards behind the houses, forming a long kennel. The team stood at one end, with an open gate in front of them. The kennel stretched at least four or five house-lengths, with bits of gore scattered around in the dirt. It was big enough to hold most of the dogs they'd seen, and maybe more.

A low growl came from behind them and Jed spun to see a pack of dogs stalking around the side of a house with a team of four Variants behind them. Even now, this close, their smell was covered by the rotting corpses.

Garza opened up with sustained bursts, and the dogs rushed forward into his fire. Some went down, others peeled off to circle for another attack. The rest of the team fired at the monsters, picking off a few more. The Variants leaped now, springing from the ground to the back wall of the nearest house and then jumping for the team.

Jed and Mehta tracked them, taking one down. But even as it fell face first into the mud, a second one tackled McKitrick, and a third grabbed Garza. The fourth skittered left and right, circling around them using Jed's teammates as cover against his fire.

The Variants hauled McKitrick toward the kennel, and Garza with her. Jed rushed for them, swinging a boot into the first one's face. When it reared back from the blow he doubled tapped it, freeing McKitrick. She scrambled backwards, away from the monsters, getting her feet under and firing at the remaining dogs that jumped forward with their jaws gnashing. They bit at the air and snarled, trying to force her back. The fourth Variant leaped forward, grappling Garza's legs, helping its partner drag him into the kennel.

Mehta blasted one with a headshot, then raced into the kennel after the other. He gave it a buttstroke across its mouth, and reversed to slam it in the side of the head. It spun away, released Garza, and scrambled around in the mud, flanking Mehta before he could line up a shot. The Variant got its claws around Mehta's leg, yanking him to the ground. Before it could leap, Jed put a shot into its gut, sending it sprawling to the side. It flipped over and crawled for Mehta. Garza fired a burst at its face, and it collapsed into the mud.

Jed checked himself, then his people.

"No bites? We all good?"

The team nodded and muttered *Rah*.

A groan came from one of the Variants outside the kennel, the first one they shot. Jed rushed over to it, and nearly tripped as he jerked his foot back a step. The Variant was shifting back to its human form. The skin softened, and the mouth shrank around a normal set of human teeth. The eyes were still ringed in blood, but the yellowy haze was diluted.

Jed stared at Sergeant Jordan, not wanting to believe his eyes, but having no choice but to accept what he had just seen.

"Jordy, what the fuck?"

"Welch. Pretty weird, isn't it?"

Jordan had three holes in his torso, two below the heart and one closer to his collar. He didn't have long, and he was infected, but…

Jed had only one question he cared about anymore. Knowing why Jordan had joined Ewell's sick plan didn't matter. But how was it possible that the man was lying there, human, when only seconds ago he had been a Variant?

"How, man? How the fuck—"

"Lou's drugs. Anti-virals…" Jordan said. "Helps keep the virus from taking over all the way. Let's you control it."

He coughed up a mouthful of blood and Jed stepped back even farther, afraid to get anything on him, afraid to even be breathing the same air as Jordan.

The rest of the team grouped around him, all of them monitoring the area in between staring at the dying man on the ground.

"You control it," Jed said. "And then what? You try to kill us? Fuck this—"

"Wait!" Jordan said. His voice softened. "It makes you stronger, Welch. Helps you see better. When you're in control…there's nothing else like it. Nothing."

"That's great, man. Where the fuck is Ewell?"

Jordan smiled, and his mouth began to stretch. His lips bulged and his tongue thickened, swirling around as his teeth pulled in to be replaced by the spines of a Variant's sucker mouth.

Jed put him down with a headshot before he could shriek. It didn't matter, though. The growls and snarls of dogs grew louder as a pack emerged from around the last house at the end of the row. And standing in the middle of the swarming dogs was an alpha, like the wolf they'd seen in Mercer's AO. Jed was so focused on it that he didn't see the two Variants slinking down the side of the nearest house until they were already leaping through the air, claws outstretched and mouths open with shrieks of hatred and hunger pouring out.

— 38 —

Jed was struck across the head by a Variant's foot as it leaped for Mehta. The other one tackled Garza. Jed swung around to line up a shot at the monster, but it had already taken Garza to the ground and was rolling with him in the mud. And the dogs were rushing the team in a wave. McKitrick let loose with their last HE round, sending a mass of the monsters spiraling away. Jed fired at the others, but his team was going to be overrun.

If this is it, then fuck it, this is it, Jed thought as he whirled around to help Mehta. A burst from the M27 told him Garza was still in the game, and McKitrick hadn't stopped firing. The Variant on Mehta had him face down in the mud and was dragging him around the side of the next house. Jed ran forward, following the monster. He reached the corner of the house and was yanked forward by a hand that grabbed him from above. He sprawled on his stomach in the dirt, landing hard on his weapon. Something heavy landed in the mud by Jed's feet. Mehta was being pulled away in front of him, struggling with the Variant that had its claws around his throat.

Jed reached for his sidearm and felt it batted out of his hand. He twisted, to roll over and face his attacker when a blow to his back knocked the wind out of him. As he fought for breath, he felt himself being hauled up and thrown across the space between the houses, where he crashed against the siding and fell to the ground. He reached a shaking hand to where his weapon should have been, but only felt the dangling end of the sling. His vision blurred as a foot swung toward him and connected with his gut, doubling him up.

A sharp crack in his side sent burning agony through his stomach and chest. Another kick connected with his groin, and he fought to get a hand up, to stop the attack. His hands felt like pillows. Still he tried to lift them as he sucked in a breath, forcing air into his battered lungs. The effort sent spikes of pain through his side where the ends of his broken rib ground against each other.

Jed rolled onto his front, using the balls of his hands and his knees to hold him off the ground. He fell back onto his heels, expecting a bullet to pierce his heart or head. His eyes swam with blurred scenes of carnage as the air filled with snarls and the shrieks of Variants. He couldn't hear his team firing anymore, couldn't hear their voices.

They'd lost. He should have stayed away from Galveston. Parsons and Keoh were already dead because he wasn't smart enough or quick enough to prevent it. Now he'd led the rest of his team into a hell of their own making. They could have stayed at Baytown, waited for Ewell to show up, if he ever did.

Jed's sidearm was in the mud just a few feet to his side. If he reached down for it—

A mud covered boot swung toward the weapon and sent it flying. Jed fought to focus his vision. He tracked the boot, followed it up the leg and body, and stared into Gunny Ewell's twisted face. The man laughed and threw a fist at Jed, smashing him in the mouth. Blood welled up, thick and coppery on his tongue.

"Nice of you to show up, Welch," Ewell said.

Another blow struck Jed from the other side, this one just a backhand. But it put his nose sideways and sent blood spraying. Jed slumped to the side, catching himself with his elbow. Fiery pain lanced into his side again. Every breath was agony.

Jed rolled forward onto his hands and knees, struggling to stand up. He put his hands over his rib, clutching his armor and ammo pouches like he would hold himself together. Ewell stood a few feet away, fists raised like a boxer.

"Gotta hand it to you, Welch," he said. "You made it past everything we threw your way. That means you've got the brains even if you're lacking in brawn."

Ewell stepped forward and threw a right cross. Jed staggered away just in time, but couldn't dodge the left hook that followed and sent stars into his eyes.

Jed opened his ammo pouch and staggered back, nearly tripping over his M4.

"You won't get it before I get you, son. Just call it a day and let me show you how good life can be when you're the alpha."

Through swollen lips and sputtering blood, Jed said, "Fuck you."

Ewell laughed. It was a sharp, barking sound, and was followed by the half-shrieks and snarls of the dog pack. They came in clusters from around the back of the houses, into the narrow space between the buildings. The dogs stood in ranks behind Ewell, some biting at the air, others sitting like sentinels, waiting for the command to rip Jed to pieces.

The alpha wolf appeared from around the corner, carrying Mehta by his armor. He was alive, as far as Jed could tell. His eyes were open, but at this distance Jed couldn't see if they were yellow or not. The monster dropped him, then vanished around the corner again. It came back with Garza in its jaws, dropped him, and went back for McKitrick. The three of them stayed down, huddled together in the swarm of monsters.

"You can join us, Welch," Ewell said. "Be part of the pack. And *you* might even be me, someday, if you live long enough. I thought Kipler would be my right hand, but he got scared and ran away. Jordan was good, almost too good. But he couldn't stop you, proving I was wrong to put my faith in him. So it's down to you... I could see you claiming alpha status, Welch. Maybe even take part of Texas for your own. When the refugees get here, we'll divide them up. Build an army."

Jed felt his breathing flag. The rib must have punctured a lung. He stumbled forward, still clutching his side. Ewell stepped up to meet him, putting his hands under Jed's armpits and holding him off the ground, so only his toes touched the earth. He stared straight into Ewell's yellow eyes. Veins of blood pulsed through them.

"You only get once chance, Welch. Tell me you want to live, and we'll call it a day. Otherwise, you're all dog food."

Jed nodded as he let his hands fall away from his side. One hand dropped the cap of the syringe and he jabbed with the other, sinking the needle deep into Ewell's stomach as he mashed down the plunger.

Ewell screamed in rage and flung him aside. Jed landed on his back and lost his breath again. His eyes were like lead, dragging his mind down to the darkness. He fought it, watching as Ewell's body shifted. His mouth opened wide, and then collapsed around his ropy tongue as he fell forward, landing face down in the mud at Jed's feet.

A howl and cry went up from the dogs and the alpha growled low and deep. Jed put up a hand and waved them back as his consciousness faded. The last thing he saw were the muzzles of the dog Variants surrounding him.

— 39 —

Weak sunlight filtered through a window above Jed's head. He was lying in a bed inside the day room at the Baytown fire station. A bandage covered his right eye, and his chest was taped tight. He moved his hands over his torso and arms, feeling for IV connections and other bandages. His tongue felt heavy. He swirled it around his mouth, checking his teeth and fearing he would feel a set of needles poking out from his gums. Everything was normal.

A radio crackled near his head, and Jed reached a hand to the table beside him. One of the radios they'd got from Mercer sat there. He lifted the mic and did his best to speak. He managed to get out something that sounded like *Thorwath* before the door to the room flew open and Garza led the team in.

"Sergeant Welch! You good?"

They gathered around his bed, Garza, Mehta, and McKitrick. Each of them had bandages covering parts of their faces and necks, and Mehta's right arm was in a sling. But they were all human, every last one of them. Their eyes were white and clear, except for a few tears that found their way out as they smiled at him.

"Thought you were done, man," Garza said. "Gunny went wall-to-wall with your ass."

McKitrick laughed and said, "I never thought I'd see that done literally."

Jed felt the instinct to laugh, but his chest hurt with even the slightest breath. He put a hand up and gently tapped over his ribs as he clamped his teeth together.

"Shit," Garza said. "You're still pretty fucked up, huh? Doc DuBois and the nurses worked on you for hours, man."

Jed opened his mouth, wondering if he should try to say anything. His tongue still felt like a foam plug in his mouth.

"*Wather*," he said.

McKitrick held up a canteen. "It's just water, Sergeant. No brake cleaner added."

"*Dang*," Jed said, half laughing, despite the pain. It was good to be with his people again. Good to be back. The team stayed with him for a while, until they were ushered out by Doctor DuBois. She told him to sleep some more, and he did.

It was morning when she came in again to check on him. Greg Radout was with her. She went through her ritual and left them.

Greg pulled up a chair to sit beside the bed. He said, "You look like shit, man."

"Nah, you're just looking in a mirror," Jed said. "Can you tell me what the fuck happened? How I got here? I figured we were dead."

"You almost were. Your people told me about it. After you got grabbed, they had the dogs and Variants on them, and figured they were done. Garza took out the one dragging him, and Mehta killed the other one when it tried to haul him back to the dogs. It lost its grip and he got off a shot, right up its ass. They were out of ammo pretty quick though, and got cornered by the dogs. Then you took out Ewell. The doggies all circled up on you and started sniffing. Even the big one. Garza said they growled like hell, but didn't attack them until they tried to help you. Soon as one of your people got close, the dogs rushed out and charged at them, like they were guarding you. So your people backed off. The dogs just hung tight around you."

"But how'd we get back?"

"The radio you had was strong enough to call. Just needed an antenna to get the signal to us here. Mehta handled it."

"Yeah, he's good with gear. He rigged up an antenna?"

"Nah, no MacGyver tricks with coat hangers. He found a long-whip in one of the houses. Ewell's guys had stashed all their gear in a garage there. They had weapons and ammo, too. Garza got up on a roof and put the dogs down one at a time. They never moved, just sat there and took it. He said it was like they were protecting you."

"Figured I was the alpha since I killed Ewell."

"Maybe."

"So now I get better, and we see what happens?"

"Pretty much. Hospital bill is gonna be through the roof. Hope you have insurance."

Greg said it with a straight face and Jed almost thought he was serious. Then Greg laughed out loud until his face went red.

"Okay, smart ass," Jed said, holding in his own laughter as Greg composed himself and sat up straight.

"Serious now, you've done a lot for Baytown, and they're not going to forget it. But they used a load of resources getting you and your people home, and putting you back together. What can you bring to the table? Like skills I mean. Baytown has a reputation of rewarding labor, but skilled labor gets you better treatment."

Jed had to think a bit before he answered. "I got a couple people with languages. Garza knows Spanish, like his sister. That'll help I guess if we get refugees from south of the border."

"There's plenty of Spanish speakers here already, and not all of them know English that well. Can't hurt to have another 'terp in the community."

"Mehta could do that, too, if we get people from Afghanistan. He speaks a little Pashto and wanted to be a 'terp before everything went ass up. And he knows computer shit."

"What about the girl?"

"Her name's McKitrick. And don't let her hear you calling her a *girl*. She's a Marine, *rah?*"

"Yeah, okay. Hooah, I guess. What's McKitrick do?"

"Grew up on a farm. She knows her way around a barnyard, can drive just about anything with an engine."

"That's good stuff. All of it. Baytown likes people who can do more than just dig in the dirt and eat what comes out of it. What about you?"

"Me? I'm just a grunt, man. Give me a Sharpie, I'll draw a dick on anything."

"You can lead, can't you?"

Jed waited a beat before answering. "We're already down two from the first time you and me met."

"You said 'already down' like you expect to lose more

people. Don't think like that, man. Whatever you might have done differently, whatever you didn't do but think you should have... Don't go there. Trust me. It... That's not how you get through this."

Jed nodded and told Greg he needed to sleep some more. He spent the rest of the day, and the next, sipping from a canteen, staring at the wall, and thinking about Keoh and Parsons.

— 40 —

Two months later...

Droplets of blood speckled the barren earth at Jed's feet. He gripped the chain link fence with one hand to steady himself, while keeping his M9 trained on the body snagged in the concertina wire above.

"Another one bites the dust," Garza said.

"We should get it down. Before any kids see it," McKitrick said.

Jed grunted his agreement and holstered his sidearm. So many words had been replaced with grunts over the past few months. After the team told him they would rather stay Marines than do anything else, Jed had taken up running security for Baytown under Councilwoman Day's leadership. He was the acting Gunny now for three squads. They stood post in towers, walked patrols around the perimeter, and trained the residents. They'd even recruited a few new faces from the population, people who showed the interest and ability.

"Y'all get the boots up here. They're on graves detail this morning," Jed said.

Mehta gave a muttered *Rah* as he moved out. McKitrick shifted next to Jed. He looked up and met her eyes. A tear streaked down her cheek.

"You still thinking about them?" Jed asked her.

"Yeah. Always do when I see one of these people. We lost Parsons and Keoh fighting these fuckers. They're still out there, and there's more of them than us."

Mehta came back with two young men in a combination of woodland camo and ACUs, and wearing respirators and heavy latex gloves. They pushed a bicycle cart like a wheelbarrow.

McKitrick and Garza went back to their patrol route while the newest members of Jed's platoon hauled the infected body off the fence. After some yanking, and more cursing than grunting, they got the corpse down. It landed on its back with a wet flop, arms and legs bent and folded like a paper doll's.

The holes Jed had put in the man's chest still leaked crimson. Jed watched the blood soak into the man's grimy shirt, mixing with the sand and dirt of however many months or years the guy had been surviving in the wilderness before the virus found him. Just like Emily had said, the Variant virus evolved to act like rabies. It would hide inside carriers, sometimes expressing, and sometimes just driving the carrier crazy. That was the only way to identify them now – just waiting until they revealed themselves.

"You good, Sergeant?" Mehta asked.

"Yeah. I'm fine. Let's get back to walking the line, Mehta."

They moved out along the fence. In the fields beside them, Baytown residents dug in the earth, planting the next round of crops, and harvesting from the previous planting. Garza's sister was out there, with her friend and most of the school-age children in the community. Between the two of them, Emily and Danitha were teaching the kids everything they could. Emily's arm was finally healed up, but she'd lost some mobility. That didn't stop her from sharing her expertise with the kids, though. And Danitha found a calling of her own, leading the children around the gardens hunting for insects that would improve the yield by controlling other pests.

Jed and Mehta continued on their route, heading down the line of houses. Greg and his people were up ahead laying in an irrigation line.

Even with the food they could grow and store, Jed knew that McKitrick was right. The virus was winning outside the fence, and all it took was one drop of bad blood to infect Baytown and bring everything to an end. Doctor DuBois was working with the drugs they'd collected from the hippie's car, but there wasn't much she could do without a full lab at her disposal.

"You think we'll survive, Sergeant?" Mehta asked.

"I like to believe so."

They came alongside Greg's crew and paused. Greg came over and shook Jed's hand.

"Sounds like the new north gate is ready," Greg said.

They'd built it a few blocks out from the old one, bringing more acreage into the reclaimed territory. Jed didn't like to think about it because the community voted to name it after Keoh.

"Keep naming 'em after dead people," Jed said. "Maybe someday we can name one for someone still alive."

"Maybe. Until then, just keep up the fire," Greg said, slapping a hand over his heart.

Jed nodded and marched forward on his patrol route.

END OF BOOK THREE
The final book in the trilogy.

Continue reading the main storyline with

EXTINCTION HORIZON

book 1 of the Extinction Cycle saga

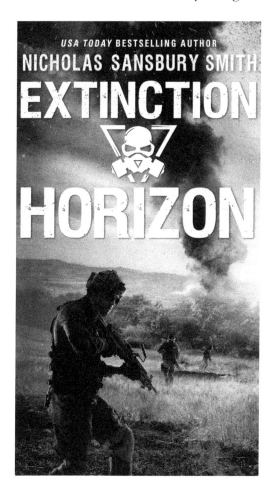

Available wherever books are sold.

About the Author, AJ Sikes

AJ Sikes is a freelance editor and author. His short stories have been published by Fox Spirit Books and Hamilton Springs Press. Sikes is a US Army veteran, father, and woodworker. If he's not at his desk, he's in his shop. Or possibly dealing with whatever the children or cats have gotten into.

Follow him on Twitter @AJSikes_Author
Join his spam free mailing list here: AJSikes.com

About the Author, Nicholas Sansbury Smith

Nicholas Sansbury Smith is the New York Times and USA Today bestselling author of the Hell Divers series. His other work includes the Extinction Cycle series, the Trackers series, and the Orbs series. He worked for Iowa Homeland Security and Emergency Management in disaster planning and mitigation before switching careers to focus on his one true passion—writing. When he isn't writing or daydreaming about the apocalypse, he enjoys running, biking, spending time with his family, and traveling the world. He is an Ironman triathlete and lives in Iowa with his wife, their dogs, and a house full of books.

Are you a Nicholas Sansbury Smith fan?
Join him on social media.
He would love to hear from you!

Facebook Fan Club: Join the NSS army!
Facebook Author Page: **Nicholas Sansbury Smith**
Twitter: @GreatWaveInk
Website: NicholasSansburySmith.com
Instagram: instagram.com/author_sansbury
Email: Greatwaveink@gmail.com

CPSIA information can be obtained
at www.ICGtesting.com
Printed in the USA
LVHW082318030419
612910LV00036B/902/P

9 781793 853950